GRIT

MARGARET MCHEYZER

GRIT

©2014 Margaret McHeyzer

All rights reserved. This book is copyright. Apart from the fair purpose of private study, research or review as permitted by the Copyright Act, no part may be reproduced without written permission.
This is a work of fiction. Names, characters, places and incidents are the product of the author's imagination or are used fictitiously. Any resemblance to actual events, locales or persons, living or dead, is entirely coincidental.

Cover created by Kellie Dennis of Book Cover By Design
Formatted by Max Henry of Max Effect

PB ISBN: 978-0-9925621-3-7

FIGHT
FOR WHAT YOU
BELIEVE IN

PROLOGUE
back when it all started

"GET THE FUCK OUT, YOU USELESS PIECE OF SHIT!" HE SCREAMS AT ME, rousing me from slumber.

"What?" I ask, completely disoriented as I try to blink sleep away.

"I said get the fuck out of here. Move your skinny, worthless ass out and stay out," Dad spits, as he drags the dirty blanket off my body, shocking me awake.

"What did I do, Dad?" I stand from the sunken mattress on its noisy box springs and look for a hoodie to pull on.

"No way do you take anything with you. I fucking warned you. Now get out," he yells, face red as he stands face-to-face with me.

I can smell the smokiness of the cheap whiskey he drinks. It mingles with his usual bad breath. He chest-bumps me back so I can't get past him and stands with his hands on his hips.

"What did I do?" I ask again.

"I told you; you need to bring in one thousand a week. You only gave me nine hundred this week. I'm sick and tired of carrying your useless ass."

"Dad, the kids at school aren't buying. The last lot of E you gave me to sell was shit. No one wants to buy from me." I manage to pull a hoodie on and zip the front up.

"That's your problem, not mine. It costs me money to feed you, to clothe you, and to keep you alive. Seeing as you're not making me any money, you're better off dead as far as I'm concerned. Your cunt of a mother begged me not to kill you, so you're lucky I'm letting you live. But let me tell you, Jaeger, I'll be happy to make you my first victim," Dad says as he sways slightly from the alcohol and whatever else is in his system.

"I tried hard, Dad. Please don't kick me out."

"You got five minutes to pack your shit and get the fuck out." He turns and walks out the bedroom door.

What the hell am I supposed to do now?

I'm barely sixteen years old, with not a single dollar to my name.

Every cent I earned went to Dad. He supplied the drugs and made me sell them for him.

Where the hell am I supposed to go?

I grab my ratty backpack, and shove every broken possession I have into it. I've got a pair of ripped jeans, a couple of t-shirts and a couple of hoodies. Not much, but it's all I've got.

I quickly fasten my backpack and frantically look around the room for something of value that I can pawn.

Can't take the springy, noisy bed–it's too big to carry and filthy.

Can't take the old color TV–it doesn't work.

Can't take the wardrobe–it's too heavy.

"You better be getting your scrawny ass out of here," I hear my father's voice from the family room, slurring loudly.

I put my hand on the doorknob of my bedroom door, open it and walk through it, knowing that this is it for me.

I now have nowhere to live, nowhere to stay, and no one I can trust.

As I take my last trip down the hallway from my bedroom to the front door, I hear my drunken father yelling at my mother. When I look into the family room, Mom's slumped on the old, worn, discolored sofa, probably passed out from some ill-fated hit she's taken.

Dad's yelling and spittle is flying out of his mouth. Mom is completely oblivious to him. Maybe she took this hit to escape him; maybe she took it because she doesn't want to see me go. Either way, she can't help me now.

"Bye," I say in a small voice to no one.

"Don't ever come back," Dad says over his shoulder, completely disregarding me, like I'm nothing to him.

I turn the handle on the front door and look back down the hallway toward my bedroom.

This really is it.

As I walk out into the blackness of the night without one gleam of light, a sense of desperate bleakness overcomes me.

I look down at the old, shabby Timex watch that I got for my tenth birthday, and see it's just before 3 a.m. It's damned cold outside. The fall winds are picking up and there's dew on the sparse lawns in the ghetto I'm being chucked out of.

I need to find somewhere I can rest, even if it's just for the night. There's a bridge at the other end of town where I know the homeless sleep. It's not usually patrolled by police, and it's definitely not safe. But for the rest of tonight, I'll have to call it home.

- four years later -

I CAN HEAR THEM.

Chanting.

They're calling for me.

"Jaeger, Jaeger, Jaeger."

Hundreds, maybe even a thousand voices. All blending together, shouting in a chorus, singing the hypnotic sound of my name.

"Jaeger, Jaeger, Jaeger."

"You ready?" Aaron asks, coming through the door.

"Yeah. Sounds like a hungry crowd out there tonight."

GRIT

Aaron looks at me with a sinister glint in his eyes. "You win, it's worth just over thirty grand to you. You lose, you're leaving in a bag." Aaron's been setting up these fights since he watched me take down someone twice my size in a back alley one night.

He approached me after the fight was over, as I was counting my roll of twenties. He told me he could make me ten times the amount I held in my hand, if I just paid attention and kept my head on straight.

At the time we met, I was fighting to eat and to pay for a place to lay my head each night. Now I do it strictly for the money. Fights like tonight's are fights to the death. They don't happen often, but when they do, they're worth big cash. But the price is bigger for the loser.

Rolling my shoulders as I walk around the room, the chanting grows louder.

I straighten my back, throw a few air punches and get my mind right.

Aaron knows the drill.

Leave me the fuck alone.

I close my eyes for a moment and crack my neck to the right, then to the left. The blood in my veins pumps loud and strong through my entire body. The vibration of excitement is so forceful I can feel it pulsating in my eardrums. It's almost like the heavy beat of bass when you walk into a nightclub.

"Jaeger, Jaeger, Jaeger."

My heart hammers in my chest.

"Jaeger, Jaeger, Jaeger."

My anxiety reaches a fever pitch.

"Jaeger, Jaeger, Jaeger."

My nerves are completely exposed, raw.

"Jaeger, Jaeger, Jaeger."

Anger rips through me.

"I'm gonna kill that motherfucker," I say, my tone deadly. I mean every fucking word. My opponent will die tonight.

Kill or be killed.

For thirty grand, it's kill.

"I'm ready."

Aaron walks ahead of me to open the door and steps aside for me to go first.

In tonight's fight, there will be no taped hands, no gloves, and no protection of any kind.

Kill or be killed. A fight to the death.

I start walking and Aaron moves swiftly to walk in front of me. The stretch down the cold, dim corridor that leads to the underground space where the fight is being held is short and sterile.

Kill him.

I can't hear the crowd anymore. In this room, on this stage, there are only two people. Me and him. I don't know who he is; I've never fought him before. And after tonight, I won't fight him again.

I hone in on him, and immediately I see it in his eyes. Death. My death.

But just behind him, I see her. And instantly her flaming, wild, red hair is everywhere. She's clinging to a man who looks like he's old enough to be her father. She's cowering back from the ring and appears fearful and frightened. She doesn't belong in a place like this. What the hell is she doing here? Who the fuck is she? One look, though, and I know I can make her moan while I taste her pussy, licking her, enjoying her. I want her.

Smash.

A fist connects with my jaw and my body gets slammed back.

I stumble back a few steps, and in those few seconds she's wiped from my mind. Now my focus is on the fight. I need to win.

I regain my footing, and bring my hands up to cover my face. I take an agitated, menacing step forward. My left uppercut connects with his chin, and I follow with a right into his stomach. He steps back, obviously winded.

I pounce while he leans forward to get his breath. I hold him down with my right arm and keep my left arm pounding into his face and his chest. He moves back a step, breaks my hold, and aims a roundhouse kick at my head. My body snaps to the left as I bring my arm up to block what's coming at me.

But he manages to sidestep and come around behind me, landing blow upon blow to my ribs. I feel one snap, but I manage to hold in the excruciating pain. I need to get him off me.

I turn and jab him with a right. He comes in close and grabs my left leg, smashing it with his shin, then turns and takes me down. He's on top of me now and really starts laying into me. My eyebrow splits and blood spills out everywhere.

Now I've got him in my guard. My legs lock around him. With a burst of effort, I force his arm inside, across his chest and down between my knees. I bring my leg up higher and lift my hips clear off the ground. Locking my ankles behind his head, I bite down heavy with my left leg, pull on my right shin and incapacitate his arm. I pull down on his head and apply pressure on his neck. Slowly the flailing eases. He can't escape a triangle choke hold.

I administer more tension to his neck by lifting my hips further and flexing into his side. He can't get out. I've got him down. The blood flow to his head is restricted; he'll pass out in seconds.

His eyes drift closed and his body becomes lax against my legs. I tighten the triangle until I know for sure he's out.

I relax the hold and get up.

"Jaeger, Jaeger, Jaeger."

I hear them again. I look up to see where she is, but she's gone.

I kneel down next to the limp body lying on the floor.

I take his head between my hands and look into the broken face of the fool who chose to fight me.

With a turn and lift of the head, his neck cracks and all the life in him is gone.

"Jaeger, Jaeger, Jaeger."

Standing up, I swipe my hand across my face and flick the blood off me. Without any remorse, I leave the corpse and turn to walk away.

Aaron's by my side the moment I step off the small stage.

"There's a guy that wants to meet you."

"This isn't a meet and greet. Tell him to fuck off." I wipe some more blood away.

"It's worth six figures, Jaeger."

I stop walking before I reach the door that leads into the cold corridor.

"Okay. Show the fucker in. And find me the redhead that was standing over near the exit. I need a slut to open her legs."

"What redhead?"

I look back at where she was standing, but she's nowhere to be seen. I'm glad she's gone. I shouldn't want her. She's probably too good for this shit, for a place where the stench of death hangs so strong in the air. "Doesn't matter, just find me a slut."

ONE

five years later

"**Y**OU DON'T NEED A CONDOM, BABY. YOU CAN TRUST ME," THE SLUT says in her husky voice, looking up at me.

"Just for that, I'm not screwing you. Keep your lips around my cock and shut the fuck up, or leave." I look down at Julie, or Jennifer, or whatever the hell her name is.

"You're an asshole," she mumbles around my hard-on.

I pull my cock out of her mouth and sit down on one of the small sofas in my office. "I'm an asshole, am I?"

"Well, yeah, Jaeger let's face it. You pretty much are." She sits back on her haunches and gives me a 'what are you going to do about it' look. Well, screw this bitch.

"Don't fucking move," I say to her as I stand up, tuck my cock into my jeans and walk to the door.

I can hear music coming from the bar area and Aaron, my VP, is sitting on a stool with another one of the club wenches kneeling between his legs giving him a blow job.

Cindy–I think that's her name–sees me and her eyes light up like a damned Christmas tree.

"Hi, Jaeger." She giggles and hops up from the sofa she was sitting on, comes over and wraps her arms around me.

"My dick needs sucking."

"Oh, I'd love to do that for you, Mr. Prez." She fucking giggles again.

I take her by the hand and lead her into my roomy office, where Julie, or whoever she is, is still kneeling on the floor. I close the door and point to the floor between my feet. Without a moment's hesitation, Cindy gracefully slides to her knees, opens my fly and wraps her plump lips around me.

She's doing a decent job, nothing overly fancy, just the normal bobbing of her head up and down the length of me. She adds in a bit of tongue swirling, some sucking and kissing my knob. She's not the best I've ever had, but I suppose she'll do.

Julie moves to get up off the floor, but I stop her with just a look. "You wanted to spout off, so you miss out. Instead, you can sit there and watch Cindy fuck me with her mouth." I grab Cindy's head, weave my fingers into her hair, and really start going to town. I move her head the way I want it, until I'm thrusting hard into her mouth.

"Let me join in," Julie says in a hungry, husky voice.

Ordinarily, screwing a few skanks together would be fine with me, but this bitch talked back and called me an asshole. So I'm showing her just how much of an asshole I can be.

"No," I manage to get out between moans.

This Cindy chick is alright, she's coping what I give her and she's letting me fuck her mouth as hard as I want.

My balls swell, my heart races and I shoot my load down Cindy's throat. She swallows everything I give her, and when I pull out of her mouth and tuck myself away, she looks up at me with those big brown eyes, like she's asking me for some sort of approval.

"You can go, Cindy." I turn around and walk toward my desk.

"It's Sandy, Jaeger," she says as she gets up off the floor.

"Sorry. You can go, Sandy." Sandy turns around and walks through the door, closing it behind her.

"Now, Julie," I begin saying.

"It's Jennifer," she corrects.

Eh, fifty-fifty chance I'd get it wrong.

"Okay, Jennifer. Get out. And by out, I mean get the fuck out of the clubhouse and don't come back. You're no longer welcome." I sit in my comfortable leather office chair and light a cigarette.

"What? Why? This isn't fair. I promise I'll do better next time. I'm so sorry." She starts walking toward me, but I put my hand up to stop her.

"Because you're no longer of use around here. Now fucking leave," I say, finality in my voice. Julie turns and walks out the door, crying and sobbing as she leaves.

I give her a minute to get out, then go to the bar area. Aaron no longer has a chick attached to his dick; he's sitting on his stool nursing the bourbon in his glass. I pour one for myself.

"Make sure she doesn't come back. Tell the prospects to kick her out."

"Yep," he answers casually.

"We need to talk," I say as I walk back to my office.

Carrying his drink, Aaron follows me in, then closes and locks the door behind him.

"What's happening, brother?" He sits in the chair opposite me and brings one leg up so his ankle's propped on the other knee.

"Old man Ward's skipped or something. He's a week behind, so I'm gonna take a ride out there and kill him."

"When are you going?"

"Leaving in the morning, taking Sarge with me. You got it here?" I lean onto the desk with my elbows, as I steeple my fingers together.

"Yeah, you're covered." Aaron sits further back into his chair, relaxing.

"I'm gonna take a couple of the prospects, too." I sit back in my chair and bring my hands up behind my head and lean back in the chair. I look to Aaron, whose brows are furrowed together, deep in thought. "What are you thinking, VP?"

"How much does Ward owe the club again?" he asks as he unfolds his legs and sits forward.

"Just over two hundred."

"What's the farm worth?"

"Not sure. It's just over ten thousand acres with around five thousand head of cattle. I'd say it's worth six, maybe seven hundred."

"What are you going to do with it?"

"I don't know what condition it's in. I haven't been out there for a couple of months. Ward was paying on time so I didn't need to go check things out."

"Might be a good place to store the guns."

"Yeah, definitely," I say as I consider Aaron's words. "When I get back I'll set up a meeting with Cain about it. But I need to go see what's happening first, and get rid of Ward."

"Doesn't the old man have a son? Will he be a problem?"

"Yeah, name's Dillon. Never met him though. Ward just mentioned the kid once. But if he becomes a problem, I'll bury him beside his old man."

Aaron chuckles and shakes his head at me. "You sure you need to take anyone with you?" He stands from his chair. "I mean, you'd kill 'em just as soon as look at 'em." He chuckles again and walks to the door.

"Fuck off. Go get another blow job."

"I think I will." He leaves and closes the door behind him.

I rise from my chair and walk out of my office, down the hall through my bedroom and into the bathroom. I turn the shower on to scalding hot as the steam begins to fill the bathroom, fogging the mirror over the vanity. I strip off my clothes, already having deposited my cut on the bed as I walked through.

I don't bother testing the intensity of the hot water. I want it to burn, to hurt.

I want to rinse away the horror that drips from my every pore. Evil is so deeply embedded in me that I can't stop it from coming to the surface. The hate I carry for nearly every fucker in this dreary, dark world. I want it all gone; I want to be washed clean.

Standing under the pelting stream, I allow the water's touch to caress my body. I let the contact lull me into believing I'm not an arrogant asshole.

But nothing changes.

This MC is my home, my family, and sometimes I hate it. Sometimes I wish I could go back to *that* night and change what made me so damned spiteful.

Cain.

And her.

I'd give anything if I could only go back to that night and change everything about it.

I close my eyes and lean my forehead against the tiled shower wall.

Her flaming red hair.

If it were possible to do one thing over again, I'd go back to that night, skip the fight and take *her* away.

Never let her go. Never let her slip away. Always have her close to me.

Instead I'm left with the memory of her wild red hair and the look of absolute terror on her pretty face as she gripped the formless man standing next to her.

Fuck, I need to find out who she is.

I want her.

TWO

"**WAKE UP, FUCKER.**"

I turn over and bury my head further into the pillow.

"J, wake up. You gotta get going," Aaron says as he kicks one of the legs of my bed.

"Unless you wanna suck my wood or someone's dead, piss off," I groan as I move the pillow over my head to drown out Aaron's annoying voice.

"I'm not blowing you, man. But get the fuck up. Sarge and the prospects are waiting for you."

"The fuck I care if they're waiting? They can keep waiting." I sit up in bed and Aaron's now sitting in the single arm chair in my room. "What do you want?" I look at the time on the clock behind him and see it's just before 8:00 a.m. I groan.

"It's a four-hour ride. You got to get going. On the way to check on the farm, Cain wants you to deliver a rifle to a friend of his."

"What? No, I'm not carrying today. Take a few of the prospects and go. I'm riding straight through and hope to be back early tomorrow." I run my hands over my eyes and then through my hair to try and wake up.

"Well, I'm just passing on the message from Cain." Aaron lifts his shoulders and looks away.

"I'll call that asshole and deal with him," I say as I stand and raise my arms, stretching my back out.

"Don't worry about it, brother. I'll run the merchandise. Just go and see what we need to do with this farm to get it ready for storage." Aaron stands and leaves my room.

I watch as he closes the door behind him, and I fall back into bed not wanting to get this day started.

Last night all I thought about was her. The terrified look she had on her face as she clung to the featureless man beside her. *God, what a damn turn-on, seeing her so frightened.*

The ferociously wild red locks that swept across her beautiful, innocent face.

My cock starts twitching against my boxers with just those memories, which are the only reminder I have of her.

I begin lightly stroking myself, thinking about her untamed red hair. *I want to tame her.*

Thinking about what could be, if only I could find her again.

Closing my eyes, I move one hand to cup my balls and pull them down as I knead and squeeze them. The other hand strokes my cock from tip to shaft in long, even caresses, and on the upstroke I flick the tip with my thumb.

In my imagination, her lips come down on my cock. With the softest of touches, she sweeps her tongue across my slit, licking all the pre-cum off. Her tender blue eyes look up at me and she smiles with pleasure as she sucks me into her mouth.

I weave my fingers through her hair and begin to move her head in the way I want her fucking me.

Yeah, Red. Keep that going.

She removes her mouth and with a small giggle, she plunges my balls between those swollen, pouty, pink lips. I hold her head there and let her keep pleasing my sac with her mouth. Red lets out a tiny groan that vibrates through my balls, all the way up my spine. I shudder with a euphoric, horny craving to bury myself down her throat.

My mouth falls open and I can hear the groans escaping my rumbling chest. My stomach coils and my sac tightens.

"Pull hard on my balls, Red. Don't let me come yet."

I feel her warm hand grab my sac and pull down with just the right pressure to stop me from coming. It's painful, but my hips are rolling on their own, wanting the pleasure to last a bit longer. My cock aches to shoot my cum down Red's throat. I burn for her mouth to swallow me.

A bolt of electricity shoots up my spine as Red swallows my cock. She tortures me with her hand as she stretches out my sac. "I'm gonna come," I murmur as pure ecstasy rips through my body.

With powerful thrusts that lift my hips clear off the bed, hot cum spills from the end of my cock. I feel it coat my hand and my lower stomach as I keep tugging, draining every last drop.

I open my eyes and just lay on my bed looking up at the ceiling. Damn, even in my fantasies, Red can certainly suck cock.

I let my heart regain its normal rhythm and finally get up and walk into the bathroom. My hand and stomach are coated in cum. I could get one of the club whores to come in and lick it up, but I suppose I should get my ass into gear so I can get to the farm.

Turning the water to an almost scorching temperature, I step in and wash away the sticky liquid. Ten minutes later, cum rinsed off and freshly washed, I wrap a towel around my waist and brush my hair so the excess water flicks off.

I walk out of my bedroom and down the hall. I can hear the members talking and some of the skanks giggling. When I hit the bar area, Candy, or Cindy, whatever her name is, looks up at me from the sofa she's sitting on.

"Cindy, my sheets need washing."

"I'll do it for you, Jaeger. It's Sandy though. Remember? I told you last night," she says, then giggles and skips to my room.

What-the-fuck-ever.

"We'll be leaving in fifteen, Sarge." I look over to our Sergeant-At-

Arms and he gives me a small nod. Sarge doesn't say much. He's quiet when it comes to interaction. But he'll slice your throat open without even batting a damn eyelid.

One of our smaller rivals was trying to create a problem for us a couple years back. Sent one of their own over to our clubhouse to 'pay us a visit'. Sarge calmly watched from the monitors as the guy snuck through a hole in one of the fences. He sat quietly, not saying a word as the guy came right into the compound.

Then Sarge got up off his seat, walked outside in broad daylight, clapped a hand over the guy's back and started leading him in toward the bar.

I was smiling as I watched this, because I know that Sarge lives for the Hunters.

As he was walking the guy over, he gutted him. Took a hunting knife out of the waistband of his jeans and stabbed the cunt in the ribs then slid the knife across his gut.

The asshole had no idea what the fuck happened. He went down like a bag of shit. His intestines spilled out, and Sarge simply scooped them up, stuffed them in a plastic shopping bag and took off down the street in the direction of the MC trying to cause us trouble.

Sarge came back two hours later covered in blood and smelling like gasoline.

The members disposed of the guy Sarge had gutted like a fish, and the prospects got rid of all the blood.

All that time, Sarge never said a fucking word. But the other MC disappeared and the hole in the fence was fixed.

I asked Sarge once why we barely ever hear him speak. He just smiled at me and said, "J, just 'cause we got a voice, it don't mean we should use it." From then on, when Sarge spoke, I listened to him carefully.

I walk back into my room and Sandy's still making my bed. I drop my towel on the floor and put my jeans on. Sandy audibly gasps as her eyes roam my body from top to bottom before she turns away and fumbles with the sheets.

"I'm done now, Jaeger. Want me to do your laundry too?" she asks with the biggest fucking smile I've ever seen. Who gets happy about washing someone else's dirty clothes?

"Yeah, thanks Sandy." I tap her on the ass as she walks past me to the bathroom. She fucking giggles, *again.* I roll my eyes and keep getting dressed.

"I'll have them ready for you by this afternoon," she adds cheerily as she carries my laundry basket out.

Dressed in my jeans, a white t-shirt and my club cut, I waltz out to the kitchen area to find Sandy standing near the coffee machine.

"Would you like coffee, Jaeger?" she asks, so damned perky. What is there to be so happy about? Man, this chick needs to stop getting laid if that's what makes her such a damned chirpy motherfucking bird all the time.

"Yeah. Black. Make me something to eat too," I tell her as I sit at one of the chairs of the table.

"Sure thing. Anything in particular or is toast okay?"

"Whatever, just hurry up." I pick up my tablet and start flicking through the news of the world. Nothing interesting, no one got killed around here. Really, I'm just skimming through it so I don't have to make small talk with Little Miss Sunshine.

Sandy brings my coffee and sets a plate in front of me with two pieces of buttered toast. I quietly eat and thankfully, she leaves after cleaning the mess she made in the kitchen. *She must be washing my dirty clothes.*

Sarge's heavy footsteps can be heard coming down the wooden hallway. His boots are weighted below his body and he drags one leg. He told me once it was a war wound from before I met him, but the fucker never told me what sort 'war' he fought. I guessed it had to do with his military service, so I never asked.

Don't concern my club, it don't concern me.

Sarge plonks his ass on one of the chairs, looks at me, and gives me a nod.

"You ready?" I ask between bites of my toast.

"Hmmm," he replies, meaning 'yes'.

"You packing?"

"Hmmm."

"Look, we're crossing a state line. I want you to leave it here."

"Huh?" Sarge's brows are furrowed together.

"Leave it here. Make sure the prospects aren't packing either. I'll be out in ten."

Sarge stands and makes his way out toward the shed that houses our bikes.

I finish off my breakfast and follow Sarge.

Something's gonna happen today; I can feel it. I just know crossing state lines is going to cause some sort of shit.

What the fuck is today going to bring for me and my club?

THREE

SARGE IS FLANKING ME TO THE RIGHT AND THE TWO PROSPECTS, JASON and Lion, are three car lengths behind. We've crossed the Nebraska state line into Wyoming, so we need to play by the rules here.

Nothing worse than...

Fuck me.

'Nothing worse' is just about to happen.

I see the flashes of red and blue lights behind the prospects and they pull over to the side of the road. Behind that police cruiser is another with its lights flashing. They speed up and motion for Sarge and me to pull our Harleys over.

Sarge cuts in front of me and parks his bike. I come up next to him on the dirt shoulder and do the same.

We shut them down, get off the bikes and take our helmets off, hanging them over the handlebars.

"Stay where you are," the cop says over his loudspeaker.

You have got to be fuckin' kidding me with this shit.

"You left your piece behind?" I ask Sarge.

"Hmmm," he replies.

"The prospects?"

"Them too," he says angrily.

"We're in their territory. Just don't kill the pig and we'll be right."

"Hmmm." He chuckles.

There are three cops in the cruiser, and they all get out at the same time. With hands on their guns, they cautiously walk over toward us. I look down the half-mile gap between us and the prospects and see that the cops are frisking the boys against their car.

"Licenses?" one arrogant ass asks as he steps closer to me. "Straying away from home aren't you? Got business in my backyard?"

We hand over our licenses and I watch as the other two cops form a protective triangle behind Officer Arrogant.

"Nah, nothing like that. Just going to see a man about a dog." I chuckle at my own joke. This is the standard line we use when we get stopped outside our territory.

"Who's the man?"

"Don't know him."

"Where's he live?"

"Don't know, meeting him at a park."

"Where's your dog carrier?"

"Might not like the mutt. I'll come back and get him if I do."

"What park you meeting him at?" Officer Arrogant Ass asks.

"You wanna join us for a coffee too?"

Sarge lets out a bellow of a laugh and the two other cops step in closer to us, flipping the straps on their holsters up. I think they're trying to intimidate us. But instead, they look like they're scared to death.

"What's the issue? Do you wanna do a sobriety test on us? Were we speeding? Are you booking us?"

"Hands on the car and spread your legs."

I look at Sarge and see his anger building rapidly behind those calm eyes. I give him a small shake of the head, signaling him to back off and play it cool.

"If you're so desperate to become intimate with me, you should at least buy me a drink."

"You're a mouthy one. Now spread those fucking legs before I take you down to the station and ruin whatever plans you have."

Fuck.

I lean up against the car and spread my legs and Sarge does the same thing. We're being frisked by one cop as one of the others goes over our bikes, checking them out like they're some sort of guaranteed moving violation.

In the distance, but closing in at rapid speed, I hear the sound of a V8 engine hurtling down the empty highway. I look up in the direction of the noise, and an older, faded yellow F150 is approaching. For an older truck, that thing can really move. The truck has to be doing at least ninety miles an hour, and it doesn't look like it's slowing down either.

"Looks like your girl's in a hurry," one of the cops says to Officer Arrogant.

"Yep, must be going home to cook me a feast," he says with a chuckle.

The others laugh and I tighten the hold on my temper, trying to avoid smashing the fucker's head in. They're taking too long.

"We got word of an MC coming through today. Intel said they're here to create problems. Are you here to cause me problems?"

"Nope," I say as I turn around and lean my ass against the cruiser once he's done searching me. I look over at Sarge, and he's stepped away from the cruiser altogether. His hands are shoved deep in his pockets. I can tell he's doing everything in his power not to kill them all.

"Go see about your dog, then get the fuck out my state. But while you're here, I'll be keeping a close eye on you." He turns his back on me. *Mistake number one, fucker. If this was a fight, you'd be dead by now.*

I move off the cruiser, and all three officers get back in. They turn off their lights, make a U-turn, and leave. The other cop car follows. The prospects come up to us, and Sarge and I lean against our bikes.

"What happened?" I ask Lion and Jason.

"Nothing. They pulled us over, frisked us, and asked us where we're headed. Told 'em we were checking out a dog. Then they just sat back and asked us about our machines," Jason answers, shrugging as he lights up a smoke.

I study Jason for a moment before I clap a hand to Sarge's shoulder and we walk away from the prospects.

"That was a target on us," I say as I look at Sarge. He nods his head in agreement. "Someone knows our business, or..." I stop talking and let the worst case play out in my head. "We've been sold out."

"Fuck," Sarge mumbles heavily.

"Look, for now it stays here with you, me, and the prospects. No one breathes a word." Sarge is nodding and I turn to look at Jason and Lion.

"You two, not a fucking word about the cops."

"Sure," they both reply in unison.

"Let's get to the farm and see what's on it. I don't remember seeing a barn, but we can bring in a storage container if there isn't one."

The prospects get on their pissy little Harleys and Sarge and I pull out onto the empty highway.

With a good forty minutes left before we get to the farm, there's not much else to do but think about the cops pulling us over.

It feels like the moment we crossed state line, we were targeted. With the cops breathing down our backs and making it clear they were going to stay on us, I have this sinking feeling that our club's luck is about to turn to shit.

We get to the farm and the prospects hang back as Sarge and I ride down the long dirt driveway. It's a good mile in from the main road, and the house is set far back across open, flat fields.

The house itself is white and looks small from the outside. As we get closer, I see the old yellow pick-up sitting in the driveway along the side of the house.

No fucking way.

Old man Ward lives here. Officer Arrogant Ass is his son Dillon? What the fuck?

We stop next to the pickup and peg our bikes.

"You stay here," I tell Sarge. He nods and leans back on his bike.

I go to the front of the house and take the four creaky steps leading to the front door.

I knock twice and step to the side of the heavy wooden door, covered by a flimsy screen door.

The big, solid wood door creaks open, and the first thing I see is a double-barreled shotgun pointed at my face.

My heart instantly reacts, and is beating faster and faster, until it's thumping so hard I can hear it in my ears.

The hair on the back of my neck stands at attention with a shock of excited anticipation.

My blood begins to boil, pumping hard. Electricity touching every nerve ending in my body.

My mouth dries out completely and it's difficult to swallow around the huge lump sitting at the base of my throat.

Not because I'm staring down a double-barrel.

Not from sheer terror of my possible death.

Not for any logical reason.

My body is reacting because I'm fucking turned on.

It's her.

Red.

FOUR

"IF YOU VALUE THAT PRETTY-BOY FACE OF YOURS, I SUGGEST YOU TAKE your little pack of animals and leave," Red says.

Well, fuck me.

Looks like she's not as shy and retiring as I originally thought. And that's even more of a damned turn-on. *God, I hope her pussy is delicious, 'cause I can't wait to taste her.*

I slowly lift one foot and take a small step toward her.

"Today a good day for you to die?" She releases the safety on the shot gun. I retract my step and put my hands up, showing her I'm not here to hurt her.

"Come on, Red. I don't think you got the guts to kill an unarmed man."

"Self-defense. I can get away with that. Now take your trained monkeys and get off my farm."

Her farm?

Who the fuck is she?

I own this farm.

"Look, I'm just here to talk to Chris. He's got business with me that we need to sort out."

"What business have you got with my father?" She pushes the

old screen door open with the shotgun and takes a few steps forward until she's standing outside.

I can't help raking my gaze down her enticing body. Damn. My cock springs to life, but this is definitely the wrong time for that, seeing as she has a shotgun pointed at my head.

Her wild red hair is exactly as fierce as I remember it being that first night I saw her. Her intense, clear blue eyes scream that she's most certainly capable of pulling the trigger her finger is hovering over. Her tits are just visible through the white t-shirt she's wearing and her legs... Man, those long fucking legs. She's wearing jeans that hug her luscious body and leave nothing to my deviant imagination.

God, I can't wait 'til those legs are wrapped around me as I fuck her like she's never been fucked before.

"Do you wax?" I ask her.

"What!?" She looks bewildered and fucking angry. *Sexy.*

"Do you wax? It's an easy question to answer, either yes or no. I'm hoping it's a yes 'cause I love a smooth pussy. But don't get me wrong, I'll fuck a hairy one too. I just won't eat it." I take a step closer to her. *I'll get her to shave if it's covered in hair.*

Red keeps her eyes on me with a look I can only describe as seething. Her eyes dilate and her jaw tightens as she takes a step closer to me. She swings the shot gun to the side and lets a round off.

"Fuck, you could've hit me!" I yell at her, but don't move.

"The next one will. Now take your pack and leave." Her tone's turned icy and I know now she means every word she's saying.

I hear Sarge's footsteps come running up behind me and without even turning around I raise a hand to stop him before he kills Red.

She points the gun at me and the moment her eyes make contact with Sarge, she swings the gun to him then back at me. Her shoulders are tense and her back has straightened, but her hands are the most steady I've ever seen on chick holding a gun.

"He won't hurt you, and neither will I," I say as my hands go up in surrender again. I retreat a step, only because I've seen that look in a person's eye before. She's confident she'll be able to let that round off and kill one of us before the other can take her down.

"You have no business here. Now leave."

I go to take another step back, but I hear motorcycles roaring down the dirt road toward us. I turn to see Lion and Jason roaring at us. I look to Sarge who understands what I'm asking him without saying a word. Sarge meets the prospects and I deal with Miss Temper.

"Look, I just wanna talk to Chris," I say again. "This has got nothing to do with you or your brother."

"My brother? I don't have a brother."

"Then who's Dillon?"

"That would be me, and unless you wanna tell me what this business is that you claim to have with my father, get off my land!" she shouts the last part. *Like that'll scare me.*

"J," Sarge calls from over the railing.

I turn my back on Red and walk away from her. If she really wanted to kill me she would've done it by now. I know she *can* do it, but I also know she won't pull that trigger.

"What's happening?"

"Crowes," Sarge says.

Fuck.

"They're here too?"

"Hmmm."

What the hell are the Crowes doing here?

I turn back to Red and walk over toward her.

"Get inside and lock the door. Don't come out, regardless of what you hear until I come looking for you."

"What? What the hell's going on?"

"Just listen to me. Get inside and lock the fucking doors. I'm sorry, Red, but I'm gonna be kicking this one in."

"Then why am I locking it?"

"To make it look like there's no one here. Now get inside."

The gun is still pointed at me, but I can see her resolve is starting to waver and the angle of the gun is lowering. I step into her and push the gun to the side.

"Dillon, we aren't gonna hurt you, but the guys who are coming, they will. I need you to go inside and stay away from the windows."

"I can protect myself," she says as she raises the gun to show me.

"No doubt. But if they get to you they'll torture you before they rape you, and then if you're not dead, they'll sell you to the highest bidder. If you think you wanna take a risk with that, then by all means, we'll leave you to fight it out."

Her blue eyes soften and her mouth pops open as she starts to struggle for breath. "Torture?" she says through a gasp of breath. "Rape?" And her stunning eyes fill with tears. "What's he done?" she says in an almost whisper.

"Just get inside." I take the gun out of her hands and open the weak screen door and push her through. "Dillon." I try and get her attention, because her expression has glassed over completely and she looks like she's about to panic. "Dillon!" I say louder. She looks up at me and stares intensely into my eyes. "Lock all the fuckin' doors and *hide*." She simply nods and closes the door. I hear the click and know she's locked it.

Without a moment's hesitation, I lay a swift boot into the wood as it swings open easily and freely. I can't see Red, which means she must be hiding somewhere.

The sound of the Crowes' bikes coming down the long driveway tells me that they outnumber us and probably outgun us. Our arsenal consists of one shotgun and the one round left in it. I cradle the shotgun in my arms and stand next to Sarge, who's already taken off his cut and is ready to fight to the end.

"Let's not give them a reason to kill us," I say to him quietly.

Sarge looks at me and nods. But the killer glint in his eye tells me he's ready for anything the Crowes want to throw at us.

The five bikes all roll in together, two in front and three behind. They come to a stop and peg them up. Black gets off his bike first and Spit follows closely.

I nod at them and step forward to shake the hands of Black, the Crowes' VP and Spit, their Sergeant-At-Arms.

"Jaeger. What brings you out to Freedom Run?"

"Here to see the old man. He owes me a debt."

"You too, huh?"

Fuck. The old man isn't in hock to just me, which now complicates matters even further.

"What's he into you for?" I ask, knowing I'm not going to get an answer.

"That's club business, Jaeger. I'm sure you won't tell me what he owes you either. Look, he's got a sweet little piece of pussy I can take for what he owes us if he doesn't have the cash. The boys and I need a fresh cunt around the clubhouse and she looks like she can take a few of us at once."

"Yeah, I hear ya, but I've been knocking and no one's home. So I smashed through the front door," I turn to show him the wide open door, "and checked the place out. There's no one in there. The boys have been through it too. No one home."

"Fuck, where the hell is he?" Black asks, looking around as he runs a hand through his hair.

"Look, if he owes both us and you, then I assume he owes others too."

Black nods his head and turns to look at Spit, who's chewing gum and looking like he doesn't give a shit. But I've seen Spit work before. That guy could almost rival Sarge. *Almost.*

"You've been through it? Spit, wanna walk through and see what's there?"

Fuck, if they find Red, we'll have to take them on unarmed. I hope she's fucking hidden well.

Spit walks up the few creaky steps and swings the weak outside door open as he looks at the wood that I've just kicked in. He examines it and then looks over to Black and gives him a small nod.

"Truck's here." Black points to the old faded pickup sitting around the side.

"Yeah, I saw that too."

"What are you gonna do, Jaeger? Bastard's fucking ghosted, and looks like he took that tasty pussy with him."

"I'll take it back to the table, same as you."

"Don't try and fuck me over," Black says as his body language changes. He straightens his back and a snarl crosses his mouth.

"You telling me that Skinny's okay with you screwing this up?" I gotta try and get the Crowes out of here so I can find out what the hell is going on.

"Prez will wanna run it past the club."

I shrug and take a step back. "We all want what's owed to us. Fuck knows who else is coming."

Spit comes through the front and just shakes his head once, indicating no one's inside.

"Later, man," Black says as he and Spit and their boys get back on their bikes and take off up the dirt driveway.

"What the fuck you protecting the bitch for?" Sarge asks. "You should've let 'em have her and we could've had the fucking farm."

"No way is that shit happening. We're taking the farm, and I'm taking the girl." I look over to Sarge and he shakes his head.

"Hmmm," he mumbles.

I walk up the creaky stairs and go inside the house.

It's small, and fucking old, with that timber paneling shit on the walls. The sofa looks ratty and well-used. The kitchen is just to the side, really small and old-fashioned. But it's clean. Fuck living here though.

"Red," I call for her. I get no response, as I keep walking through the tiny house. "Red," I call again.

She comes at me with fists up high and takes a swing, hitting me square on the chin. Lil' thing can pack a punch, that's for sure. But her second swing isn't set up right and I step out of the way and grab hold of her wrists.

I can't fucking help myself as I run my thumbs over the soft skin on the inside of her wrists.

"I'm not gonna let go 'til you stop fighting me." She tries to struggle, but gives up when she realizes she ain't gonna win this round.

Her shoulders slump in defeat and her eyes lower to the floor as big, fat tears roll down her pink cheeks and slip off her pretty face.

"What does he owe you?" she asks in a tiny, crushed voice. She moves her hands from within my grip and sits on the worn sofa.

"He defaulted, so he owes me his farm."

"What!?" she shouts. "He signed the farm over to you?" She brings her hands up and buries her face into them and cries. I hate crying. It's just not necessary. Just get over that shit already. But I cut her a bit of slack seeing I just gave her an eviction notice. I know how that feels.

"Yeah, something like that."

"What does that mean?"

"Red, this isn't really something that concerns you. I just need to speak to your dad."

"You can't," she sobs.

"Why the fuck not?" I ask as I come to stand in front of her.

"'Cause he's dead."

What the fuck?

FIVE

"WHAT DO YOU MEAN HE'S DEAD?" I ASK RED AS I LOOM OVER HER slumped, crying form.

"Are you slow? How else can somebody take that? Dead, as in I buried him two weeks ago," she says as she looks up at me with puffy, tear-filled eyes.

Shit, so that's why he missed his payment to me.

"How did he die?" I ask, clearly pissed off.

"Ran off the road and he hit a tree. His car exploded on impact and he died instantly." Red wipes the fat tears off her cheek and focuses on something on the wall. Her eyebrows knit together and her shoulders slump as she continues crying.

Man, why do chicks do that? Are tears cathartic for them or something? Fuck, that shit annoys the hell out of me. They start sobbing and getting all emotional and shit, and it sends me fucking insane.

Why can't they just punch someone's face in, and be done with it? When they cry they're just so…clingy.

"Look, it's fucked up that your old man died. Well, fucked up for you. I don't really give a shit. But now he owes me money, and those guys that were here before? He owes them money too. And if they don't get their cash, guess what they're gonna take?"

Her blue orbs find mine as she lifts her head to look at me. "My farm," she says as she regains her composure.

"Not exactly, Red." I grit my jaw together and shake my head to her.

"Dad didn't have anything else of value. Just the farm," she says as she stands and begins to pace her tiny little family room. "He already sold the cattle."

"I'd think closely about that. I'm sure you're old man had one thing he'd die for."

"There's nothing else…" She pauses, becoming silent and still. Dillon turns to face me, her face drained of all color, her mouth open to reveal a perfect O. "Me? They're going to take *me* when they find out there's nothing left here?" She collapses to the floor in a small heap and brings her knees up into her chest and wraps her arms around them.

"Red, they aren't gonna take you, 'cause I'm not gonna let them." I stand with my feet hip-width apart and cross my arms in front of my chest.

"Why do you want to help me?" she asks cautiously.

"Oh no, Red. I'm not gonna help you. I'm gonna bring you back to my clubhouse."

"The hell you are!" she screams at me as she rapidly gets to her feet.

"I'm giving you your eviction notice and taking your farm. You're coming back with me," I tell her in my 'don't fuck with me' tone.

"Ha! Well, you really are slow then, aren't you?" She shakes her head at me and walks toward the small hallway.

"Come back here, I'm not finished talking about this," I yell after her.

"Seeing as you like the sound of your own voice, you keep talking. I'm going into town."

"The hell you are. If the fucking Crowes see you, they'll grab you. And I'm telling you right now, you don't belong to them. You fucking belong to me."

I'm met with silence.

I hear nothing.

No scuffing of shoes against the creaky floorboards, no sassy replies from her smart ass mouth, nothing. Not a single damned word.

"Red," I yell but get nothing. "Red," I yell a little louder.

Nothing. Again.

"Red!" I shout.

I hear her padding back down the hall toward where I'm standing, and I'm met with another fucking gun in my face.

How many guns does this girl have? She's seriously beginning to piss me off.

"Look Red, this whole pointing guns at me thing, it's wearing thin," I say as I take a step closer to her and reach for the pistol that's pointed at me.

"Maybe you'll take the hint and leave before I put a hole in some part of you," she smirks from behind the dark metal.

"I'm not going anywhere. Now make me a coffee so I can think." I go and sit on the sofa as she lowers the gun and shuffles her feet to stand beside me.

"I'm sorry…"

"You don't have to be," I say pleasantly, cutting off whatever she was about to say.

"Oh I'm not. I was just going to say that this is not your pathetic little clubhouse. I'm not one of the pathetic little club whores you can order around. And *you* are an asshole. So, please leave, before I shoot you," she says with an 'eat my shit' grin.

Man, she's really pissing me off. Does she not understand that I'm not going anywhere and that I'm trying to help her?

"Red…"

"Stop calling me that. It's not my name. And seeing as you're an asshole, you'll be lucky if I let you call me Ma'am."

"As I was saying, Red," I emphasize 'Red' so she knows she hasn't gotten under my skin. But I'd definitely like to be under her as she rides me, nice and hard. Moving those delicious small hips in circles as I lay back and watch her tits swing. Fuck, what I'd give just to suck on a nipple until she screams for me to pull that long red mane and fuck her 'til she can't breathe.

"Stop looking at me like you want to have sex with me," she half-yells at me.

"Well, I do. So unless you're gonna get on your knees and wrap those pretty lips around my cock, I'll imagine you any way I damn well want."

The look on her face is one I've seen many times before–horror that I actually said that aloud.

"You really are a dick. And you should learn to shut your mouth."

"Why? Maybe you're one of those girls that gets wet when someone like me tells them what to do. Or maybe you pretend to be offended, but still get wet over it. Or maybe you're nothing like those girls and actually do think I'm a dick. Either way, I've got a sixty-six percent chance that you'll fall to your knees and suck me off and only a thirty-three percent chance you won't. No skin off my nose, 'cause I'll just go in town and find a sixty-six percent girl and have her suck me off."

"Do you even hear yourself? Are you truly so conceited that you believe women, not girls, but *women* are like that?" Her eyebrows shoot up and she tilts her head to the side.

"I've got a clubhouse full of 'women' that *are* like that," I air quote "women", almost teasing her, as I respond.

"Then I'm amazed you still have a cock and clam chowder hasn't claimed it yet."

"I might like to fuck, but I'm not an idiot. I wrap it so I don't get anything those sluts might have," I say angrily. "Anyway, what the hell do I call you seeing as you don't like Red?"

I see her chest heave out a huge breath as she knits her eyebrows together and does this strange, yet fucking sexy thing with her mouth. She sort of screws it up, trying to look all tough girl, oops, tough *woman* toward me, but it looks more like a sexy snarl. One I definitely can't wait to have wrapped around my…

"You're truly demented. You're sitting there getting a damn hard-on." She points to my crotch, "and all I want to do is throw you and your stupid little gang out of here so I can figure out what to do."

"You don't have to figure out anything, Red. All you have to do is get in that truck and come back to my clubhouse."

"I'm not going to do that, and if you insist on addressing me, call me Phoenix."

"But your name is Dillon, why the hell would I call you Phoenix?"

"Because I hate Dillon and I've been called Phoenix, or Nix, ever since I can remember." She's still holding the gun, although now it's more casually, just against her thigh.

Progress?

At least she's not pointing that thing at me, wanting to kill me. For now I'll call that progress.

"Look, Phoenix," I accentuate the name she prefers to be called. "The Crowes are a serious MC; we've had dealings with them in the past. But your dad has put this farm in hock to me, to the Crowes, and God only knows who else. You can't handle this on your own. And besides, it's no longer your farm. It belongs to me now." I sit back on the springy sofa and bring the ankle of my left leg up to sit on my right knee.

"Like hell this belongs to you! I've worked the damned land, looked after all the cattle until Dad sold them off, and did it all on my own. I've been killing myself to get some money together so I can pay the bank."

"Taken care of," I say as I flick a hand in the air, dismissing the entire notion of the bank.

"What? You just got here. How can that be taken care of?"

"I'll take care of it when the bank opens in the morning."

"Why?" she asks, leaning up against the wood-paneled wall.

"Because I want to."

Phoenix lowers her gaze, suddenly a very humbled and apologetic look flashed across her face.

"I don't know what to say," she murmurs, but her eyes continue to look toward the ground.

I stand and walk over to her. Slowly, I take the gun from her and tuck it in the back of my jeans waistband. With a measured, delicate touch, I put my hands on her hips. She snaps her eyes up to mine and puts a hand to my chest.

With the light pressure, she pushes me away. Her push is so weak that it's almost non-existent.

"Because," I start saying as I lean in to her to run my cheek against hers. Phoenix's breath catches as my skin touches her warm shin. She's breathing rapidly and moves the lower half of her body closer to mine.

Fuck, yeah. I push my hips into hers more. She can definitely feel my rock hard cock straining against my jeans as I push into her further.

"Because," I say again as I smell her hair. God, it's just as fantastic as I thought it would be. I bring my right hand up to weave in her wild red curls, and hold her by the nape of the neck with my fingers entwined in her softness. My thumb just skims the supple skin beneath the hairline. "I now own this farm," I say as I lean in to kiss her.

Phoenix brings both hands up to my chest and pushes me away with all her might. Damn, that girl is strong. I take a step back and hold my hands up to her. "Not gonna hurt you, Phoenix."

"You arrogant asshole, get out!" she shouts at me.

"Jaeger, got a problem," Sarge says as he comes to front door.

"What?" Phoenix and I both say at the same time.

"The boyfriend's on his way," Sarge answers.

"Whose boyfriend?" Phoenix asks, looking between Sarge and me.

"Yours, Nix," I reply, knowing the cop is on his way down the driveway.

"I don't have a boyfriend," she says, frowning.

"No fucking wonder, 'cause you're a ball-buster. The cop, he's on his way." I turn to see Sarge is gone.

"He's not my boyfriend, and I'm not a ball-buster," she yells, clearly pissed that I called her a ball-buster.

"When he pulled us over earlier today and you drove by, he said you were probably on your way home to make him a feast for dinner."

"What the hell is he talking about?"

"Hey, baby."

Phoenix and I turn to the door to see Officer Arrogant standing tall, looking all protective as he sweeps his eyes over me and frowns.

"Don't you 'baby' me, Liam. Who the hell do you think you are, telling him that you're my boyfriend?" Phoenix says as she points to me.

She is a firecracker. I take a step back and let her deal with the cop. It doesn't look like she needs me to save her ass with him. She's already made him step back onto the verandah.

"Baby, come on. Don't be like that," he says, though his voice wavers with a zap of fear.

"Where the hell did you put my gun?" she asks me as she turns to look at the table. I throw my shoulders up and shrug at her. I'm not giving her a loaded weapon. She'd damn well use it, then there would be cops everywhere.

"Nix, can I come inside?" the cop asks.

"No! And for being a jerk, you can call me Dillon. Now get back in your car and leave."

"But you hate being called Dillon," he says, confused.

"And at this moment I hate you, too. Leave! And don't come back!"

He turns hot on his heels and steps off the verandah.

Pussy.

I'd stay here and fight it out with her.

As a matter of fact, seems like a good plan.

"You too," she says as she turns to me.

"No can do, Nix. I'm here to stay," I say as I give her a smug smile.

I know what I'm doing. I'm irritating the fuck out of her, and having a ball doing it.

"Fine, stay. You can sleep out in the barn. There's a room in there with a bed. Just get out of my home."

I chuckle at her as she turns to go toward the back of the tiny house.

"What's funny?" she asks with her hands on hips while gritting her teeth.

"I ain't sleeping out there, and I ain't sleeping on that." I point to the barn and then the uncomfortable sofa.

She's fighting with herself, I can see it. Her face flushes red enough to match her hair. Her shoulders tense up and she's grinding her jaws together hard.

"Fine," she spits toward me. "You can sleep in Dad's room," she says through clenched teeth.

Oh yeah, this is gonna be fun.

SIX

Phoenix

LYING IN BED, ALL I CAN HEAR IS THAT ARROGANT ASS SLEEPING IN THE room next to me, or should I say *snoring* in the room next to me, and damned loudly too.

What the hell am I going to do?

The bank is about to foreclose on my farm, and I have people–or should I say thugs–that are after it. And if they can't get it, then they'll take me as payment instead.

Dad died and left me with no life insurance and a farm that's in more debt to the bank than it's worth. And I only have two thousand dollars in the bank, the little that's left of my college fund.

I stare up at the ceiling and listen to the familiar sounds of the land. The crickets singing outside, the wind as it moves branches to tap on my window, the stream that runs a half a mile away.

All these sounds are incredibly hypnotic, and usually lull even the most alert person into a comforting sleep.

But I'm far past being alert, I'm incredibly stressed and I'm truly at a loss for what to do.

There's no one I know that I can ask for help. Milina, my best friend, is the only person who knows that the bank is going to take the farm. But now there are other problems to add to the mix, and I just have no idea what to do.

I turn over and lie on my side looking at the door, wondering what made Dad bet the farm. Why would he leave me in this situation?

I have no one to turn to, and now it appears, once the bank takes over I'll have nowhere to go.

I could call Uncle Patrick for help, but I know he likes to bet on the races, too. What if he's in debt as bad as Dad was? He took me to an underground fight all those years ago. I was staying with him when Dad asked me to give him some time alone after Mom died. That was horrific. I freaked out when those two guys started fighting, and almost passed out. I made him take me home.

The more I think about it, the more I'm convinced that Uncle Patrick is in it as bad as Dad was. He won't be any help to me.

Then there's Liam. He's been after me for as long as I can remember. We went out on a date once back in high school, and that was nothing more than me fighting him off. Now he's a damned cop, and I still have to fight him off.

Though now he does keep his hands to himself, he's forever showing up here wanting to eat dinner with me. And when Dad died, he was here every moment of the day trying to get me to 'cry on his shoulder'. But I don't want his shoulder to cry on.

Jaeger rode in on his damned motorcycle, and from the moment I opened the door I knew I was in trouble.

He looked at me with those molten brown eyes; his shaggy light brown hair that flopped over one of his eyes before he shook his head and moved it away, and that's all it took. His body…wow, his body. His six-foot frame has the most delicious, broad shoulders I've seen. His shirt hugged his chest, highlighting his taut, strong pecs and the muscles that strained the arms of it.

But then he opened his mouth. And damned if he's not the biggest asshole I've ever met. Asking me if I shave or wax my sex…how rude! The more he spoke, the angrier I got.

And then he almost kissed me. If he hadn't opened his mouth I think I would've let him too. Thankfully, though, he did speak, and it saved me from making the worst mistake of my life.

I turn over again and face the wall. I tuck my hands under the pillow and close my eyes, trying to find some peace after this crazy day.

My mind begins to drift, slowly shutting down. I decide not to worry about tomorrow, what it may bring, what might happen, or who else may turn up.

Slowly my body gets heavier and everything relaxes, letting me get that desperately needed rest.

The roar of the bikes wakes me as I hear them barreling down the dirt driveway.

"Phoenix, get up. Now," Jaeger yells as he bursts through my bedroom door and comes straight for the bed, ripping the covers off me and grabbing me by the shoulders.

"What the hell?" I say as he pulls me up and I try to steady myself on my feet.

"Now. We need to get out, now," he says in a low, but urgent voice.

"What's happening?" I ask as I grab a jacket and try to slip into my jeans.

"No time for that, grab it and let's go."

"Where?"

"I've got to get us out of here. Is there another way out?" he asks as he's pulling me out the door and toward his bike.

"Down by the barn, follow it straight out and it'll take you to the highway."

"*Us*. Now put the helmet on." He hands me a black helmet.

"I'm not going," I stubbornly say.

He grabs me by the shoulders and tightens his grip on them, shaking me. It's hurting me, but I think that's his point. "Listen to me. If you stay, you will either die or you become a club whore. And that's not gonna happen. Get your bony little ass on the bike, and for the love of God, shut the fuck up."

Jaeger swings his leg over his bike, starts it, and then reaches for my hand to help me on.

"I know how to get on," I say to him as I pull my hand away from his.

I get on the bike and he turns his neck to give me that smug smirk, "Hold on, Nix, we're getting out of here fast."

I wrap my arms around his waist and he bends his arm around to my back and pulls me forward, so my chest is flat against his back. "That's better," he says as he takes off down past the old red barn.

Looking back at my home, I see in the distance a group of small headlights coming up quickly. I keep trying to look when I hear the gun shots. A spray of them, most likely toward my home, destroying the last hope I have of dealing with this on my own.

I rest my head on Jaeger's back and I can feel tears welling behind my closed eyelids. How did I end up in this situation? I'm twenty-two and should be living life, not living in fear of what my father's gambling has gotten me involved in.

I feel one of his warm hands close over mine as he navigates down the dirt track in the direction of the highway. He gently squeezes my hand as I quietly take these minutes to cry.

I don't want him to see me as a typical, feminine, blubbering damsel that falls apart when shit gets difficult. He doesn't need to see what a wreck I am right now.

Damn it to hell, what am I going to do now?

SEVEN

FUCK. I HATE IT WHEN CHICKS CRY, UNLESS IT'S AFTER GREAT SEX. NAH, not even then, 'cause they start to get all mushy and emotional and shit, wanting to share feelings and all that crap.

How many times have I rolled my eyes and gotten up to leave them and their tears while I go and trash the condom? I'd take way too long in the bathroom, hoping they'd either be asleep or gone by the time I got out.

But this chick, there's something about the way her body is trembling against mine, and how she has her arms tightly clasped around my waist. All I want to do is get off this bike, kiss her and tell her everything's going to be okay. I can feel her tremors as she cries as quietly as she can.

Once we make it out onto the highway, the roar of the bike drowns out her noises, but the quivers coming from her body, and the fact that she is leaning her body against mine speaks volumes.

I have to say, I do feel sorry for her. She's been dealt a fucked-up hand, but hey, I'm just a guest at this table. I didn't orchestrate the circumstances; I'm merely playing the game that someone else has arranged.

I knew the Crowes were going to cause a problem, but I wasn't expecting them back as quickly as tonight. But what the prospects said when they called to warn us was that the entire MC was there. We wouldn't have escaped; they would've killed all of us.

"Where are we going?" Phoenix asks as she moves her mouth closer to my ear so I can hear her.

Damn, she feels so good wrapped around me.

"Back to the clubhouse," I say, hoping she doesn't totally freak out.

I feel her take a huge breath in as her tits push against me, then she exhales and her warm breath only just touches the side of my neck. She does though, remain quiet for a distance.

We cross the state line back into Nebraska without much of an issue. Riding back toward the clubhouse, I feel Phoenix become too heavy against me.

I pull the bike over and peg it up, hold onto Nix's hand as I turn to look at her.

"Hey," I say loudly enough that I wake her.

"What?" she answers, all grumbly.

"You can't go to sleep. I'm doing sixty-five. If you fall off, it'll kill you."

"Who cares?" she mumbles so low that I'm sure she didn't mean for me to hear.

"Hey, this self-pity bullshit doesn't fly with me. Get over yourself. I told you, I own the farm now, so don't worry that pretty little head of yours."

"Fuck you," she shouts at me as she gets off the Harley and starts walking away.

Well, that woke her up.

"Where are you goin'?" I call as I watch her walk down the road.

"I don't know," she says. There's definite wrath in her sharp voice.

"Get back here," I command. What the hell is she doing? We're still a good two and a half hours away from the clubhouse. "Get back here now before I throw you over my shoulder and carry you back."

She swings around and looks at me, "Again, fuck off," she yells as she puts her hands on her hips and flares her arms out.

What a sight, a hilarious one at that. Dressed in nothing more than a skimpy pajama short set thing, a jacket and a pair of cowboy boots, she's taken off down the road. She's bound to get herself into trouble walking along the road like that in the middle of the night.

"You're gonna get yourself killed out here," I yell after her. She's turned away and started walking again.

She flips me the bird behind her back and keeps going.

She's as stubborn as they come, the most headstrong person I think I've ever met. And by far the most courageous too. She's already stood up to me countless times and was even willing to take on the Crowes.

And she makes me hard. Just thinking about her determined ass trying to handle this on her own does it for me.

She's a few hundred feet down the road and I look around to see just how deserted it is out here. Sarge and the boys are hanging back having a smoke while they let me deal with Phoenix. I look at Sarge and he chuckles and shakes his head at me.

Here we are, middle of the night, secluded highway, her dressed like *that*, and she decides to walk off.

"Phoenix," I yell at her again. But she ignores me and keeps going.

I get on my Harley, start her up and roll down the road to where she's walking.

"Get on," I say as I cruise beside her.

"Go away," she responds with furrowed eyebrows and squinting eyes.

I pull over again, peg the bike up, get off and catch up to Phoenix in three long strides. If she wants to act like a spoiled brat, then I'll treat her like one. I reach her, turn her around, lean my lower half down and throw her over my shoulder. "You want to be a child? Fine," I say as I smack that pert little ass.

"Put me down, you Neanderthal." She hits me on the back, and I laugh 'cause upside down her strength is shit.

"Not until you're on my bike," I say. God damn it, why am I getting hard holdin' her like this? Maybe 'cause if I turn my head I can bite that ass of hers, or possibly because I wanna fuck her on my Harley.

"Put me down. I can walk."

"No can do. You're comin' back with me, and that's final." I give her another smack on the ass to reconfirm it and she jerks just enough to tell me I've smacked her too hard.

"Fine," she finally concedes. I pull her down over my shoulder, letting her hot body slowly slide against mine. Riding with wood will be difficult, but Nix will have her arms around me, so I'll take that. *For now.*

"You really are an arrogant jerk," she says as she straddles the bike again.

"Yeah, yeah. I've heard it all before, and I'm sure I'll hear it again. So unless you've got something new to tell me or you wanna reconsider wrapping those pink lips around my cock, I'd keep my mouth shut if I were you."

"Ass."

"Pig-headed," I fire back.

She closes her mouth and smashes her lips into a thin line. It's clear to me that she's pissed. I stand and look at her, waiting for the next smart-ass comment to fly out of her mouth. But she remains quiet.

"You done?" I ask.

She doesn't say anything, just looks away and rolls her eyes.

"Good, now hold on tight, 'cause you just put us behind by twenty minutes and I wanna make that time up." Really I just want to scare the shit out of her, let her know that this is the major leagues. If she's so insistent on being a pain, I'll happily take the lead.

No girl... oops, woman, is going to top me as alpha.

No fucking way.

EIGHT

THE REST OF THE TRIP GOES FINE. PHOENIX SHUT UP AND DIDN'T SAY A single thing. Her arms remained tight around me and damn, that felt awesome.

There's something about how she feels, so close to me, that makes me want to keep her there a while longer.

We roll into the clubhouse at around three in the morning. Sarge must have called ahead because four of the prospects are waiting for us so they can roll the gates back and let us in.

I chance a look over my shoulder and Nix's eyes are wide open, looking around the compound. Her arms tighten more around me. She must be feeling insecure; this is far from her normal surroundings.

"Relax. I can protect you here," I say in a low voice over my shoulder.

The look of fear eases a touch when I say that to her, and her arms relax. But I don't let her off that easily. I grab her hands and keep them tight around me for just those last few seconds as I park the bike.

Aaron walks out and stops as he checks Phoenix over.

She gets off the bike first and timidly stands behind me, but not entirely, trying not to look frightened.

Where's my tiger gone now?

"Aaron, Phoenix. Phoenix, Aaron," I say introducing the two.

"Damn," Aaron says. He takes her hand and bends over to kiss it.

"Spoken for," I say. A nice, gentle warning that he's not to touch her, and neither is anyone else in the clubhouse.

"Understood," he says as he bows his head and kisses the back of her hand.

Prick. No one would guess that this Romeo is actually Casanova in disguise, not when he's all attentive and pussy-like.

"I'm not spoken for," Phoenix pipes up as she looks at me.

God damn this chick. If she hadn't gotten under my skin all those years ago, and if I didn't want her so much, I would've dumped her ass and let her fend for herself.

"Why the hell do you have to make everything an uphill battle?" I ask her as I grip her upper arm and drag her away from everyone. "You're forever undermining everything I say."

"No I'm not," she fights back, proving my point.

"You're doing it right now."

"I am not."

"Listen to yourself, you're fighting me without you even realizing that you're doing it. Are we going to fight the entire time you're here?"

"I'm not staying long, just a day or two until I can make other arrangements."

I'm starting to lose my patience with her. There's only so much stubbornness one man can take.

"You're wearing the last of my nerves thin, Red. Just shut up and let me take care of things. Tonight is not the night to fight, and it's not the night for you to show everyone what a hard-ass cowgirl you are. It's the night you say, 'thank you, J, for saving my butt,' and shut up until we get some sleep and figure out what to do tomorrow."

Finally, she gets it.

I hope.

"Fine," she says as she lowers her gaze.

"Are you hungry?" I ask as I lead her toward the clubhouse.

"Yeah, I am."

I swing the door open, and it seems most of the club is here. A few skanks are lounging around on the sofas. Sandy, I think that's her name, jumps up off the sofa and runs over to me. She leaps into my arms and wraps her legs around my waist as she kisses me.

I push her away, almost throwing her off me to the ground, "What the hell are you doing?" I say as I turn to look for Phoenix.

She dropped my hand the moment Sandy barreled over, and when I reached for her, she didn't take my hand.

"I'm sorry, Jaeger, I just missed you so much. Maybe I can help relieve some stress," she says as she steps up to me and moves in to kiss me again.

I step back and hold my hand up to her. "No, that's not necessary. But you can make us something to eat if you want?"

"Who's 'us'?" she asks, as her eyes defiantly dart to Phoenix and then back to me.

"All of us. Sandwiches will do," I answer in a clipped, pissed-off tone. Sandy gives me a small scowl and sneers toward Phoenix then skips off to the kitchen to make us something to eat. "Come on," I say to Nix as I hold my hand out to her.

I introduce her to all my brothers and they all look her up and then down and then over to me. She misses the head shake I give them, subtly telling them to keep their hands to themselves. She's mine and if they fuck with her, they'll end up hurt.

"Come on, let's have somethin' to eat then we can get to bed," I say as I place my hand on the small of her back and guide her toward the kitchen.

I subtly slide my hand under her jacket, but her thin, flimsy pajama top still poses a barrier. But at least I'm one layer closer to touchin' her soft, warm skin. Maybe when we get into bed I'll get to cop a feel, *or a fuck*.

Three of the four chairs are already occupied around the kitchen table and I look at one of the prospects and twitch my head to the side, telling him to move.

"Oh no, it's okay. You don't have to do that," Nix tells him, and the fucker sits back down again.

Fine with me.

I sit and grab her around the waist and plonk her cute little ass on my thighs.

"What are you doing?" she says as she looks over her shoulder at me.

"You're not standing."

"I'm fine," she fires back.

"Will you just shut up and sit?"

Sandy walks over with two sandwiches for Jason and Lion, and then comes back with a stack of sandwiches for Sarge. Sarge grunts his thanks and attacks them like he hasn't eaten in a week.

She comes back with a sandwich for Nix and two for me.

"Thank you," Phoenix says as she picks up half of the sandwich to take a bite. But Sandy smirks at her and leans back on the kitchen counter, relaxing her body as she watches Nix just about to take a bite.

"Stop," I yell as I smack the sandwich out of Phoenix's hand. I look at Sandy who's suddenly looking guilty. "Here. Swap with me," I say and switch the plates.

"Oh," Sandy says as she steps forward and bites her nails.

"Thought so." I move Phoenix off my knee and stand up, and just by crooking my finger, I beckon Sandy and point to my office.

She hangs her head and stalks off in the direction of the office. She looks like a prisoner going to their execution.

In the office she stands beside the desk, looking embarrassed and ashamed.

"What did you do?" I ask as I sit in my chair and bring my boot-clad feet up on the desk, crossing them at the ankle.

"I spit on her sandwich," she admits openly.

"Why?"

"Because. Who is she? Why is she here? It's tough enough getting you to notice me with all the other girls around, and now you've added another one, which will make it tougher still." Her hands fly out as she points past the door, and tears are have started to roll down her cheeks.

What the hell is it with these chicks and their tears?

"I know exactly who you are. But if you're waiting around for me to make you more than just a club slut, well darlin', that just ain't gonna happen."

"But I do everything you want me to," she whines as she starts to sob.

"If I wanted a lap dog I'd go buy a chihuahua."

"You mean that you don't want me?"

"I want you around 'cause you're a good girl, but there's nothing permanent between us. You suck cock alright, keep us fed when we're hungry, and do my laundry. But other than that, forget it. You'll never be my old lady."

"But she will?" Sandy says bitterly, pointing toward the door again. She means Phoenix.

"What?"

"I saw how you looked at her, and it's not like you look at me. You want her."

"Darlin', what I want or what I'm gonna get is none of your fuckin' business."

"Maybe I should I leave then?" she says, more of a question than a statement. Maybe she's waiting to see what my reaction is going to be.

"Sounds like a good idea." What else am I supposed to say?

Her weeping becomes uncontrollable and she starts that whole chest-heaving, can't-breathe-properly, ugly-girl cry.

She turns on her heels and flings the door open and runs outside.

I get up and walk out to the kitchen. Sarge has demolished his sandwiches already and the prospects are sitting back casually making conversation with Phoenix.

She's laughing at something that they said, and I immediately get pissed off.

Why does she constantly have to be so angry when I'm around? Why can't she laugh with me too?

"Sarge, make sure Sandy gets home. You two, go with him."

"I don't need an escort," Sarge actually speaks.

Jason and Lion stand and then sit back down again when Sarge barks his objection.

"Then go clean the garage out," I say to them, narrowing my eyes and warning them not to flirt with my woman.

Both of them get up and walk out of the kitchen. Sarge leaves to take Sandy home, leaving Aaron and the rest of the club members in the bar area with a few skanks still hanging around.

I sit beside Phoenix and pull my plate over and eat what she didn't. "Not hungry?" I ask, because she's only had half a sandwich.

She leans her elbow on the table, rests her cheek on a closed fist and gives me that look again. Here we go, another argument.

"Before you say anything, I just asked if you were hungry. I don't want a fight, I don't want the snarky, bitchy you to mouth off. I just want to know if you're hungry."

Her eyes change from that intense hard blue, to a softer, more accepting shade within seconds. Her face pales and her features drop, telling me she had to pull herself back from being a bitch.

"No, thank you. I'm not hungry. I had half a sandwich but truthfully, I'm just tired and want to go to sleep."

"Okay, I'll show you to my room."

"Where will you be sleeping?" she asks as I stand and hold my hand out for hers.

She looks at it, then reluctantly places her small, warm hand in mine and stands.

"In my room."

"And where will I sleep?"

"In my room."

"In the same bed?"

"Unless you want to sleep in the chair, or out here with everyone else, yes, in the same bed."

I see her visibly stiffen, but thankfully, she shuts up.

Hallelujah, the woman *can* keep her mouth shut.

"Thank you for letting me stay here until I can figure out what I'm going to do," she says in a flat voice.

I won't bother to correct her tonight. I just want to go to sleep.

But hey, if she wants to suck me off to help me sleep better, I won't say no.

"Bathroom's over there, and those are clean sheets. There's a spare toothbrush under the sink in the bathroom." I show her into my room and she stands looking lost.

"Can I use the bathroom first? I want to wash some of the road grime off me."

"Sure. Towels are on the rack in there."

She takes a few steps toward the bathroom, but hesitates before she gets inside. She turns around, brings her leg up and takes off her boot, then repeats the procedure with the other leg.

"Jaeger?"

"Yeah."

"Thank you."

Man, that must have felt like razor blades in her mouth.

"You're welcome."

She turns and goes into the bathroom and closes the door. I hear the shower start.

Slipping into bed I lie on my back and listen to the shower, knowing full well she's just on the other side of the wall.

Naked.

Wet and naked.

She's not in there for long before she turns the water off and comes out of the bathroom dressed in her sexy little pajamas.

"Would you like some clean clothes?" I offer before she gets into bed.

"Thank you. I'd love something fresh to change into."

I get up out of bed, and her gaze travels over my chest and all the way down my body.

Her eyes are glued to me, and her mouth pops open when she gets to my crotch and sees I'm sporting wood. Damn, it feels like I've been hard since the moment I met her.

"Oh I um..." She turns her head and scratches her neck, avoiding me at all cost.

I open my top drawer and give her a pair of boxers that are too small for me, and a t-shirt from the drawer below it.

"Thank you," she says as I hand them to her.

She disappears back into the bathroom, and I settle back into bed. It's good to know that I affect her as much as she affects me.

Maybe if we just fuck, we can get over whatever this is that's making us both so damned insane.

The door opens and she walks out in my clothes.

That has *not* helped with my situation. She looks fine in my clothes and I want her to keep wearing them so my scent is all over her, marking her, telling everyone she's my property.

She gets into bed beside me and turns on her side away from me. I turn on my side so my front is to her back, and I scoot over. I'm not touching her, but surely she can feel me close to her.

"Goodnight, Jaeger," she says then lets out a huge yawn.

"Night, Red," I reply.

She sighs and I see her shake her head a little. I can only imagine she rolled her eyes too.

I turn over and reach out to turn the light off beside my bed. When I turn back again I put my hand on her hip, and pull her close to me.

She doesn't say anything, but she does wiggle her butt back, letting me get her close to me.

Progress.

Maybe tomorrow, she'll suck me off.

NINE

Phoenix

Jaeger pulls me closer to him, and I'm fighting with myself to keep from yelling at him not to touch me.

But this does feel nice.

With his chest to my back and his hand on my hip, his breathing evens out and he begins to relax behind me.

My own eyes are closed, and my body synchronizes with his. Our breathing matches and my mind begins to drift. For the first time in a long time, I feel safe.

Jaeger moves his arm around my waist and pulls me in closer to him, as he slips his hand under my t-shirt and possessively splays his fingers across my stomach.

"Hmmm, you feel good," he mumbles behind me.

Ass. He's still awake? He's half-snoring in my ear, but still manages to try and sex me up.

He's a walking, sexy, testosterone-fueled hornbag.

When we came into the clubhouse and that bitch Cindy, or whatever her name is, jumped on him, I couldn't help but feel a tinge of disgust.

He must screw everything that walks. And he has to have some serious shares in Trojan to ensure his junk is kept wrapped.

GRIT

Otherwise, he'd be a two-legged STD.

Jaeger moves his hand up my body. Now it's sitting between my belly button and my breasts. If he moves it any further up, he's going to get the shock of a lifetime when I smack him one.

But my mind blanks out completely and a peaceful darkness descends, allowing me to sleep. I hope to God that the people shooting up my farm haven't followed us to the clubhouse.

···✦···

Strong arms envelop me and I hear a delicious, low groan.

I turn over and snuggle into the warmth. A wisp of chest hair tickles my nose and I swipe it away.

A hand rests on my butt.

A kiss lands on my forehead.

A leg scissors between mine, and the top of a muscular thigh feels exquisite against my sex.

Hmmm, he's so warm and feels so right. I'm safe for what seems like the first time in years.

Am I asleep?

···✦···

"Baby," I hear a deep voice call.

"Hmmm," I answer. I must still be dreaming.

"I'll be back in a little while."

"Hmmm."

Warm lips brush over mine, and moisture sticks to my mouth.

That feels awesome. Whoever he is, he must be so damn sexy. What a fantastic dream.

I never want to wake up.

···✦···

I blink my eyes and try to focus on where the hell I am.

I struggle temporarily to identify my surroundings. I run my hand over my eyes to rub the sleep away and look around the room.

Oh shit, that's right. I slept with Jaeger last night. Not *with* Jaeger, but in Jaeger's bed.

He's gone now and the door to his bedroom is shut.

I look at the digital clock that sits on the nightstand and big red digits proclaiming it to be 10:18 a.m. stare angrily at me.

What the hell?

I haven't slept this late since I can't remember when.

I shoot out of bed, and fling the door open as I pad down the hallway toward the family room, or whatever it is they call it, but only Jason and Lion are there.

"Morning," I say, "where's Jaeger?"

"Prez is behind closed doors," Lion says as he points to a door that's shut.

"Thanks." I walk over to it and grab the door handle.

"Hey, you can't go in there. It's club business. You're not invited," Lion says as he jumps up off the stool and comes after me.

I turn the door handle and see Jaeger at the head of the table. "...Ward," he is saying and stops the moment I come into the room.

Everyone at the table turns to look at the interruption and suddenly, I feel twelve pairs of eyes burning into me.

"What the hell were you talking about?" I ask Jaeger as I step further into the room.

"What the hell are *you* doing in here?" he scowls at me as he stands and leans his fists on the table in front of him.

"I heard my name. If you're talking about *my* land, then I should be here."

All the guys chuckle, and look back to Jaeger.

"First, you will not walk around looking like that." He points at me, and I look down to make sure nothing's slipped off me. "Second, when the door's closed, you don't enter." I put a hand on my hip and give him my best 'fuck you' glare. "And third, like I told you last night, don't worry that pretty little head about it."

My blood is beyond the boiling point. I can feel myself just about to snap and rip his God damned head off.

"Fuck you and the silver horse you rode in on. That is *my* farm, and if you didn't hear the first time, I'll repeat it so your slow brain can keep up. That. Is. *My*. Land."

Jaeger picks up a gavel and slams it down on the table. He's by my side in three very angry strides, grabs my upper arm and pushes me outside the room.

"What the hell is wrong with you, Nix?" he asks. He pulls me down the hall and into his bedroom.

"Me?!" I shriek. "What is going on with you?"

He pushes me into his room and slams the door with so much ferocity the book case holding a few knickknacks bumps up against the wall.

"You're a damned pain in the ass," he yells at me as he pushes me onto the bed. "I'm trying to protect you and all you do is try and fuck it up."

"Protect me? How, by taking the only thing I have left away from me?" I shout back as I stand from the bed and take a step closer to him, going head-to-head.

"You don't own it any more. I do."

"No you don't. Stop trying to snatch it away from me!"

"I own it."

"No, you don't."

Jaeger turns and crashes his fist into the drywall, putting a hole straight through it. "Fuck!" he yells as he quickly turns and looks at me.

"You're a crazy person," I say as I try to step around him and leave.

"And where do you think you're goin'?" He tightly grabs my arm before I reach the door.

"To find a way to get out of here and back to my farm."

"Not dressed like that." He points at my clothes again, well, his clothes.

"I'll change, you can have your stupid t-shirt and boxers."

"You are by far the most annoying woman I've ever had to deal with." He runs a hand through his hair, and then pulls me further back into the bedroom.

"I'm not staying here. I'll call Milina to come get me so she can take me home."

"You really don't understand, do you?"

There's a certain reasonable tone to his voice which stops me cold, even if it's only just for a moment.

"What don't I understand?"

"You already lost your farm to the bank. I called them this mornin' and told them to start drawing up the papers so I can buy the land from them. They'll be ready by tomorrow."

Jaeger lets my arm go, and I back up a step, not really sure what I just heard.

I back up another step, and another, until I feel the coolness of the wooden door touch my heated skin.

With my back against the door, I slide down until my butt is on the floor. I bring my legs up and wrap my arms around them tightly, searching for comfort.

A whirlwind of emotions swirls around deep inside my head.

Reality hits hard. The bank foreclosed. He's legally buying my farm, and there's nothing I can do to stop it. Now I really have nowhere to go.

"What am I going to do?" I say, rocking back and forth, trying without success to convince myself that everything's going to be fine.

"You can stay here as long as you want," Jaeger says. I snap my eyes up to meet his and I think he surprised himself by saying that.

"And do what? Be one of those sixty-six percent girls? Sorry, Jaeger, but I'm not going to service your entire crew 'cause you made one cry and leave last night."

"If those lips of yours, or any part of your body, goes anywhere near one of my brothers, I will kill them. Don't test me, Nix." His face morphs into anger as his hands become fists. Obviously he's trying not to lose it again.

He can't keep punching the wall every time someone challenges him. I look around and notice, other than the hole he's just created, the room's light green walls are relatively unscathed.

I stand to my feet and look at Jaeger.

"I'll call Milina to come get me. I'll be gone as soon as she gets here."

"Phoenix," Jaeger says as he takes a step toward me.

My eyes don't leave his. His steps are cautious. I can see his chest rising and falling rapidly. His mouth parts as his eyes go to my lips.

"Jaeger," I let his name roll off my tongue softer than my ordinary voice.

Jaeger has an uncanny effect on my body, the way he can spark the wildest of emotions in me. One moment I want to slap him, and the next I want nothing more than to have his taut, strong body hungrily envelop me.

"Phoenix," he says again, stepping into my personal space.

His mouth lowers and skims my lips lightly, just passing over them, as he leans his arms on the door, trapping me in his human cage.

"Stop fighting me," he almost whispers before his wet lips connect with the column of my throat.

My eyes close on their own. I tilt my neck to the side, giving Jaeger more area to discover, hopefully with his tongue.

He accepts the invitation. His tongue strokes a fine line from my ear to my jaw, as he pushes his hips into me. My right leg hooks around his waist and Jaeger moves his left arm down so he can grab my leg and lift it higher.

Jaeger thrusts against me. The lush feeling of wetness as my sex calls for its partner in this sexual tango is beyond anything I've experienced before in my life.

"God, yes," Jaeger moans as he forcefully grabs my wrist and slams it up against the door I'm leaning on.

Damn it, why do his cave man ways turn me on so much?

"I wanna fuck you," he says, his mouth still discovering the skin of my throat.

Shit, I want this so much.

"Jaeger you in there? We got an issue," someone calls from the other side.

A bucket of ice water may as well have been thrown on us, because Jaeger lowers my leg and steps away and I'm left up against the door, nearly breathless.

"Yeah, give me a minute," Jaeger replies, but doesn't take his eyes off me. "I've got to go, but we'll finish this tonight. And you're not going anywhere."

"That was a momentarily lapse in judgment. We aren't finishing anything tonight." With wobbly knees I step away from the door so he can leave. "And I'll call Milina to come get me."

Jaeger shakes his head as he clears his throat and runs his hand through his shaggy hair. When he opens the door, Aaron is leaning up against the opposite wall with his legs crossed at the ankle and his hands behind his butt.

"Make sure she doesn't use the phone," Jaeger tells him and disappears down the hallway.

Jerk.

Sexy, fucking hot even, but he's still a jerk.

TEN

Damn woman, what's wrong with her? Doesn't she get that all I'm trying to do is make sure she's safe?

Is there a self-preservation gene missing in her make-up that convinces her she's going to be fine out there with nowhere to go? She's a hard-ass though, fighting me every moment she can, always trying to show me up.

Well, fuck her. If she thinks for one minute I'm going to let her walk out of here without so much as a God damned fight, well she certainly has another thing coming.

And that almost-kiss…I swear I heard her moan. I bet she doesn't even realize that she grabbed my shirt and pulled me closer to her. The heat that radiated off her was so scorching it would have burned my soul. If I had one to burn, that is.

Her hot, tight body uncontrollably writhing against mine, she was pushing her tits into my chest, making me want her more than I already do. She's driving me beyond crazy.

"What's happenin'?" I ask Aaron as we walk back into the meeting room and I sit at the head of the table. Aaron closes the door and takes his place beside me.

"We just got a call from Cain. He wants to come visit. Said he has an offer for us."

"What sort of offer?"

"I think it's the same one as before."

I take a huge breath and look around at the members, "I don't want to start mulin'."

A few of the members shake their head, and a few more look like they're considering the risk of hauling Cain's drugs around.

"This is a big risk, boys."

"Think of the money," Aaron says, taking me aback. Up until this point, he's never really said anything that makes me think he wanted to go down this route.

"The money would be great, but the guns are enough. This is something that involves big players, and we could easily get wiped out."

"But the money makes it worth it," one of the guys down the other end says.

There are a few heads nodding, and a few heads shaking 'no'. Looks like we're a table split from where I sit.

"Unanimous or things remains as-is," I remind the table.

"Let's hear Cain out and see where this leads," Aaron says as he looks around the table.

Everyone nods their head, willing to at least be open to a discussion.

"When did he say he was coming?" I ask Aaron.

"On his way," he replies as he sits back in his chair and crosses his arms in front of his broad chest.

Shit.

He's on his way now? I don't want him knowing that Phoenix is here, because I've seen how he treats the girls. And she's not to be touched, by anyone, especially him.

"Anything else on the agenda?" I ask as I look around the table.

Everyone shakes their head, I pick the gavel up, smack it down once and immediately, eagerly go find Nix. She's exactly where I left her, in my room lying on the bed.

"Hey," I say, announcing myself as I walk through the door.

Her long legs are out stretched in front of her, her hands beneath her head, just resting as she looks up at the stark white ceiling.

"Hey," she responds without turning her head to confirm that it's actually me.

"What are you doing?"

"Thinking."

"About what?"

"A plan of action for my fucked-up life."

"And what have you come up with?"

"That at the moment, I'm screwed." She moves her head to see me leaning against the door jamb, ogling her legs.

What I would do to have those legs wrapped around my waist, or better still, hooked over my shoulders, digging into my back, urging my mouth closer to her pussy. I really hope she waxes. Nothing better than a smooth pussy.

I take a step closer to her and see my shirt's riding high on her belly. There's a gap showing around her belly button and I can feel my eyes glued to the milky, fair, untainted skin. I wonder if I just lean down and lick her, how she'd react.

I'm sure she wants me as much as I want her. Maybe if I wrap my hand around her...

"You really are an ass," she mumbles, snapping me out of my daydreams about what I want to do to her. She sits up in bed and pushes off with disgust clearly emanating from every pore of her body.

"Whatever," I say as I shrug at her stubborn ways. "Where are you going?" I ask before she gets a chance to leave the room.

"And this is why I call you an ass. You didn't hear a single thing I was saying. Instead, you were looking at me with that 'I'm going to screw you hard' look. If you were listening..."

Why can I only focus on her lips, and how pouty her mouth is? What is it with her?

Fuck this, I'm not going to wait.

She's only six inches away from me, pointing a finger in my face, saying some shit I really don't care about.

I take a step forward. She scrunches her eyebrows together and her mouth stops moving as she starts to take a step back.

Before she can move, I reach out and weave my fingers hard through the hair at the back of her neck and bring her face to mine. I don't wait for her to tell me that it's okay, because all she'll do is argue, which will make me harder and her, most likely, soaking wet.

I'm not gentle. I crash my mouth against hers and force my tongue inside her mouth.

But surprisingly, she doesn't fight me. She's ready and willing to accept me as she steps into me and smashes her tits against my chest.

I put my arm around her to bind her body to mine. Phoenix lets out a grumbling noise from the back of her throat. She may believe that she doesn't want me, but her body doesn't lie.

The shirt she's wearing is thin and I can feel her nipples tighten beneath it as she presses into me.

Lowering my hand, I find the bare skin under the t-shirt and trail my fingers up her ribs, gently making my way toward those hot tits of hers. I can't wait to see and taste them, maybe even fuck them.

Screw this, I want nothing between us.

I kick the door shut and without breaking that all-consuming melding of our mouths, I grip her shirt and raise it over her head.

Phoenix pulls away just enough to let me take it off her and drop it carelessly to the ground.

I take a small step back and look at her tits. Damn, she's not wearing a bra. They're full and they slightly sag. Not much, but my God, they're such a perfect mouthful.

"I'm gonna fuck 'em," I say loudly, which snaps Phoenix right out of the horny state she was in.

She pushes me away, takes a step back from me and bends to get the t-shirt, swiftly covering herself up again.

"Why do you have to look like that," she says as she waves her hand from my head to toe then back again, "but the moment you open your mouth you screw everything up." She sits on the bed and looks up at me.

"I'm a guy." That's a defense, isn't it?

"How on earth a woman hasn't killed or severely maimed you yet is beyond me."

"'Cause I don't do the relationship thing," I answer her honestly. "I like to fuck, and I like to fuck a lot, with many different women, sometimes separately and sometimes together."

"But you come in here and jump me the moment the testosterone kicks in, and think that I'll gladly open my legs for you. Why, because you believe that I'm one of that sixty-six per cent of women who'll get wet over you acting like an idiot?"

"Well, yeah."

"And your success rate?"

"Pretty good, because if one slut doesn't put out, then there's plenty more to choose from."

"So go find one of those, because although you're incredibly–" She stops herself from saying anything that I can use against her.

"Incredibly what?"

"You're wasting your time with me. I'm not a slut."

"But your pussy is probably drippin'. And I didn't say *you* were a slut." I take a step forward so I can feel it for myself.

"No, I'm not and I'm glad you cleared that up. But it's still not happening." She closes her legs tight and straightens her back, defiant again. Her arms fold across her chest.

I hold my hands up as a sign of resignation and take that step back. Lady said 'no' and clearly means it, *for now*.

But soon she'll say 'yes', and then I'm going to feast on her until she can't take it any longer. And I'll start all over again and screw her until she's nothing but a rag doll in my arms. If she's lucky, I might stop, but I certainly love to eat a well-pounded pussy.

"You're doing it again. Stop thinking about having sex with me, because it's not going to happen." She crosses her legs and her thighs tighten in the smallest, most discreet movements, and then quickly release. Like hell it's not going to happen. I bet she's dripping for me right now.

But I won't push it any more. Well, for now at least.

"I came in here to talk to you," I start, trying to defuse the false anger she's projecting.

"But you attacked me instead."

"Which you wanted too. I just made the first move."

"Ass," she murmurs and looks away, confirmation enough to me that I'm right.

"You have to stay in here."

"Why?"

"Because I said so."

"You're not my father."

"Clearly not. I'm trying to protect you, and he couldn't give a shit about you."

There's an audible gasp and I think this is one of those times I probably shouldn't have said what's on my mind. But hey, I did anyway.

"Could you muster just the smallest amount of compassion?" she asks as she sits and puts her elbows on her knees, dropping her head into her hands.

"Why the hell wouldn't I tell it like it is?"

"Really? After all the crap you've seen me go through, you still can't shut your damned mouth just once?"

"Darlin', it sucks that you got fucked over, well not yet, but soon, *I hope*." Her eyes fly to mine and there's genuine hatred this time. Her orbs are filled with angry tears and any moment she's going to start the water works again.

"Just once," she pleads with me.

I take a huge breath and step closer to Nix; I sit beside her on the bed and reach out to put an arm around her shoulders. She tenses at the contact but slowly relaxes.

She stays still for a moment. No tears, no smart-mouthed

responses. Nothing, just a room filled with a comfortable silence.

Phoenix slowly leans into me until her head is on my shoulder and I've got both my arms wrapped around her, protecting her against anything that might hurt her.

"Can you stay in here, please?" I add the please as an afterthought, hoping she doesn't question me.

"Why?" Yeah, like the 'please' worked.

"Someone's coming here and I don't want him to see you."

"Why?" she asks, lifting her head from my shoulder so her intense big blue eyes can stare at me.

"Because he's not a man you should ever know."

"Would he hurt me?"

"Possibly."

"Will he hurt you?"

That question takes me by surprise, and I don't really know how to answer it. I've never really thought about it, or cared.

"Probably," I say, because unfortunately, it's most likely the truth.

"Then I'll stay in the room, and no one will even know I'm here."

"Thank you," I whisper.

I go to stand and leave, but her hand is closed tight around my shirt.

She pulls me down to her and before I know what she's doing, she gives me a gentle, girly kiss on the lips. No tongue, just a closed mouth kiss. *Damn it.*

"Thank you," she says as she lets go, freeing me to leave.

But I don't want to leave. I want to stay here with her, and protect her from the evil of Cain.

ELEVEN

STANDING BEHIND THE BAR, I GRAB A BOTTLE OF JACK, A SHOT GLASS and twist the top off it. Fuck it, I should just swig it straight from the bottle, but with Cain, I need to keep my cool.

Sarge walks over, and sits on one of the bar stools opposite me.

I don't ask, simply grab another shot glass and put it beside mine. Filling the glasses up, I give one to Sarge and give him a small nod.

We down them in unison and go for seconds, then thirds, in complete silence.

"J," Sarge says as he eyes the bottle again.

I hand it over the bar, but take my shot glass away, clearly telling him I won't drink any more.

"You don't want this, do you?" Sarge asks me. I narrow my eyes and look at the bottle. "Cain," he clarifies.

I look over my shoulder toward my room and then back to Sarge. "Something's going on and I don't like the direction."

"Hmmm," Sarge gives me his normal grumble.

The club house door swings open and Sandy walks in, looking quite sheepish and apologetic. She walks up to the bar area and lowers her gaze, "J, can we talk?" she says in her meekest voice.

"Not now, Sandy, maybe later."

"Please?" she begs, eyes brimming with tears.

Oh shit, here comes the damned water works again.

"Sarge," I say as I take a deep breath. Sarge gets up and leaves, allowing Sandy and me to talk privately.

"Drink?" I ask as she sits on the stool Sarge just vacated.

"No. I just wanted to say that…" She composes herself and straightens her back, "I'm sorry for what I did and said yesterday."

"Alright." Good. Done and dusted.

"I just thought," *Oh come on. Shut up, Sandy.* "…that maybe you and I could end up together. But now I know that's not going to happen."

"Fine." I turn to walk out of the bar and toward the meeting room.

"I should apologize to the new girl too. I was feeling lonely and I thought we had a connection." *For the love of God, shut the hell up.* "But now I know that it's always just been sex and nothing more."

"Yep." I try to move away, again.

"I'm just lonely."

"Listen, go to confessional or something 'cause I'm not cut out for this."

Sandy's eyes drop to the bar top and her shoulders droop down, too.

Why the hell am I plagued with uncooperative chicks?

"I understand. I just wanted to say sorry to you and to the new girl. Where is she? I'll apologize."

No way, I don't want her to know where Nix is, especially if Cain comes in and Sandy starts shooting her mouth off.

"I took her back to a motel last night."

"Oh, right," she says and lets out a huge breath. "I'll catch up with her next time." Sandy hops off the stool and comes to give me a hug.

I awkwardly pat her on the back, then dislodge her clamped arms from around my waist and push her away. "Don't worry about it. Just don't do it again." I feel like I'm scolding a schoolgirl.

"I won't. If you want me to suck you off later, just let me know." Sandy is certainly a sixty-six percent girl.

"I'll be fine, thanks." I walk away from her and into the meeting room before she can pout or distract me any longer.

Sarge is sitting in his usual spot and looking outside through the huge window that overlooks the shed and the yard.

"What's on your mind, Sarge?" I ask as I sit at the head of the table.

"Cain," he answers, grimly. I don't think I've seen Sarge look so…lost.

"What about him?"

"Something feels off."

"Yeah I got that feeling too, like we're just about to step straight into a mine field."

"Hmmm."

He sits back in his chair, steeples his fingers together, and brings them to his mouth.

"You got any thoughts on this?"

"Just smells like shit."

"I agree." I tap my forefinger and middle finger on the table, trying to make sense of all that's going on.

All the main pieces to this jigsaw puzzle are missing, so I can't even try and make out what's happening.

"J," Aaron comes to the door and stands beneath the arch.

"Yeah." I swing around and see his urgency.

"Cain's here," he announces. I get up and walk through the clubhouse to the driveway. One of the prospects has opened the gate to let Cain's huge black Range Rover SUV into the yard.

Cain gets out of the back seat, dressed in his usual black suit and dark sunglasses. He adjusts one of his cuff links and looks to the side, then to me.

"My friend," he says as he steps forward and extends his hand to shake mine.

"Cain," I reply, shaking his hand.

"Let's go inside." He claps a hand to my back and I turn to lead the way into the clubhouse.

When we get inside, Sandy is behind the bar. The moment she lays her eyes on Cain, her face reddens and she fucking giggles.

"Hello, my beautiful girl," Cain suavely says to her.

"Hello, Sir. Could I get you a drink?" she asks, flustered and flushed.

Cain's eyes widen and he takes a step closer to Sandy and runs the back of his hand down her rosy cheek. "Whatever you're pouring, beautiful."

Sandy's cute youthfulness and her blushing cheeks are certainly going to attract a man like Cain. He prefers his girls in their early twenties, although he's closer to his late forties.

She pours him a drink. He lifts the glass to his lips and throws it back while maintaining eye contact with her.

"Thank you…" He waits for her name.

"Sandy," she gushes and flutters her eyelids at him.

Yep, sixty-six percent.

"Maybe you'll be around when I finish talking with Jaeger." He's extending her an invitation for sex.

"I think I can hang around."

He leans toward her and whispers something in her ear while he skims his hand softly down her arm. A big smile plays on her lips and she lowers her head, obviously embarrassed by what he's saying to her.

"Yes, Sir," she says as she moves straight past both of us and out the front door.

"Come, we have things to talk about," Cain says as he falls into step beside me.

"What was that about?" I ask and point my thumb behind me toward the door.

"Oh, I told her I want to fuck her and if she wants it to go wait for me in the car. Tell me, Jaeger, does she like being fucked in that tight little ass of hers?"

"I don't know." I shrug. It's not my business what she likes or doesn't.

"No matter. I'll find out soon enough." He stops talking as we enter the meeting room, "Sarge, how are you?" Cain asks as he extends his hand to Sarge to shake.

"Hmmm," Sarge responds and looks away from Cain, essentially telling Cain to shove his hand up his ass. Typical Sarge greeting.

"Ha, nothing's changed. You want your VP in here for this?" Cain looks around for Aaron.

"Nope. Just you and me." And with that Sarge stands and leaves, closing the door behind him.

I gesture to Cain to sit and I take my chair too.

"What business you here for today?" I ask as I lean back in my chair and cross one leg over the other.

"You got that land?"

"Securing it tomorrow."

"Ward?"

"Died. Car ran off the road and hit a tree, killing him instantly."

"The girl?"

How did he know he had a daughter and not a son?

"What girl?" I test him.

"Dillon, the daughter. Where is she?"

I shrug my shoulders and curve my mouth down at the ends, showing him I have no idea. "Didn't know he had a daughter. Thought he had a son. Dillon, he told me the kid's name is."

"Yeah, fucked up that he called her Dillon. But she's a sweet piece of ass, and someone that can be useful to me."

"How?" I ask, wanting to know what he's after, although I have a feeling he's playing his cards very close to his chest. He ignores me.

"Anyway, I want to cook out there."

"No."

"Hunters transport from there to here, fifty kilo a week for sixty a week."

"We aren't drug mules."

"Eighty a week," Cain counters as he adjusts his tie.

"I'll take it to the table, but I don't think we'll agree."

Cain sinks further into his seat and entwines his fingers together.

"Tell me, how would the club survive without running guns?" he asks smoothly as he stares at me, expressionless.

"We wouldn't."

"Good, so take it back to the table and see what your members say." He stands and puts both his hands on the table, "but be sure to mention that you'll lose the guns if you don't agree to the farm and the transportation." He turns and walks out the door.

Fuck me.

Can this shit get any worse?

Cain leaves the club house, and I hear the roar of his V8 engine come to life and drive away.

Sarge is the first to come back in and looks over at me. "That bad?"

"Worse," I answer and shake my head.

One by one the members arrive, and I sit in the meeting room waiting for them. Over an hour later we're all sitting around the table.

Aaron pulls a pack of smokes out and lights one. "What happened?"

"Cain wants to use Freedom Run to cook, and us to transport between there and here. Fifty kilos a week for eighty a week."

Murmurs are heard all around the table.

"That's a fair amount," Aaron says, the first to speak.

"There's something else," I start. All eyes are on me, "If we say 'no', we lose the guns."

A collective "fuck" is heard around the entire table.

"We lose the guns, we close shop," Dark says from the other end of the table.

"He'll screw us over," Sarge asserts but says nothing else.

"We can find another supplier to run guns for," I add in, hoping the table doesn't play into Cain's threats.

For over two hours we all talk about Cain's offer.

But we remain at deadlock with six for and six against.

"Let's take a break," I suggest as I stand and stretch my back. "Meet back here in an hour."

All the members do the same thing and mumble agreement.

I head down to my room and find Phoenix curled up on her side, with her hands beneath her face, asleep on my bed. Her knees are pulled up together and she's lying in a fetal position, perfectly still on the same side of the bed she was on last night.

I take my boots off and mold my body around hers, my knees behind hers, my front to her back. When I drape my arm over her hips, she wiggles back and lets out a soft moan.

"Nice," she sighs as she links our fingers together.

I know she's asleep, 'cause she'd be yelling and cussing at me if she was awake and I tried touching her like this.

My body harmonizes with hers and before I know it, my eyes are drifting closed.

"I'm gonna fucking kill him!" I hear someone shout, rousing me from my sleep. Did I just dream that?

I open my eyes and look around, Phoenix is still asleep next to me, but she must have turned because her head is on my chest and her arm is draped over my waist.

"Dead motherfucker!" Sarge is yelling about killing someone. "What the hell!" I hear a door slam, and this wakes Phoenix.

"Hey," I say as I kiss her forehead.

"What's happening?" she asks groggily.

"I'm not sure. Stay here. I'll go check it out."

"I'll come, 'cause I'm hungry."

We get out of bed, I put my boots back on and I walk out of the room toward the bar area while Phoenix goes to the bathroom.

There on the sofa is a bloody and battered Sandy. Her face is swollen, her clothes are torn and there's blood coagulated around her mouth, still fresh.

Sarge drapes a blanket around her shoulders and I look over her entire body. She's covered in fresh blue bruises and she's sobbing uncontrollably on the sofa. Jason and Lion stand back near the kitchen area with their hands in their pockets and the other members are starting to come back in.

"Sandy," I say as I take a step toward her.

"Don't," she sobs.

"Hey, can I get something to...what the hell?" Phoenix cries when she sees Sandy.

Immediately she flies toward her and kneels in front of her.

"What happened?" Phoenix asks as she puts a gentle hand on Sandy's leg.

"It w-was m-my fault," Sandy tries to stammer out.

"What happened?" Phoenix hisses again, this time in the direction of the male standing closest to Sandy, who happens to be Sarge.

Sarge throws his hands up in surrender, strangely backing down from Phoenix's wrath.

I can tell that she's beyond pissed. She's shaking and mad as hell.

"It wasn't h-him," Sandy cries. "It w-was Sir." She bursts into tears and buries her face into her hands.

I notice a few of her fingernails have been ripped off, her wrists and ankles are bloody where she was tied or cuffed, and there are scratch marks all over her arms.

Cain did this.

And although Sandy is just a club whore, no woman deserves to be raped.

"Meeting room. Now," I snap at everyone. "Can you help her?" I ask Nix.

"I think she needs a hospital."

"NO! N-no hospital," Sandy whimpers.

"It's okay, we'll figure this out." Phoenix comforts her. "Go," she says and flicks her hand to me, dismissing me.

Fucking Cain did this to one of my girls. He laid an unwelcome hand on someone who clearly did not want this.

No one touches my girls like that.
Not even Cain.

TWELVE

Phoenix

"**Hey,**" **I say to the girl as she sobs almost uncontrollably on** the sofa.

She lifts her head from where it's leaning on her drawn-up legs, and her eyes hold so much pain and sadness as she vacantly stares at me.

"Hey," I repeat again as I gently try to move some matted hair back away from her face. She flinches and closes her eyes, obviously preparing for me to lay an angry hand on her. "I won't hurt you," I almost whisper as I soften my tone. "What's your name?"

"S-S-Sandy," she says as she takes a deep breath. Tears cling to her cheeks and her eyes are bruised, puffy and red.

"What happened, Sandy?" I ask as I sit beside her on the sofa.

"It w-was my f-fault." She repeats and buries her head against her legs again, putting that barrier up.

"I'll have to call the police."

"NO," she shouts, but doesn't lift her head.

"Then you need to tell me what's happened, and tell me the truth."

"He s-seemed so nice, and so, y-you know..." She stops talking and continues to hide away from me.

"No. What do you mean?"

"You know." She urges me without saying anything.

"No I don't, you need to tell me."

"He was s-so sexy and all d-dominant when he walked in here." Her sobs grow louder. "And he told me how b-beautiful I am, and I believed h-him." She stops and takes a few deep breaths. All the while, her eyes are focused on her bent knees.

"Go on, Sandy," I gently encourage her.

"He was so sexy, so c-commanding, and it made me..." Sob, sob, sob. "...so excited. I couldn't w-wait for him to finish talking to J so he could take me away and make love to me."

I swallow a huge lump in my throat. The more she says, the angrier I get.

"I j-just want to be loved, and I know J d-doesn't love me."

Damn, her words rip at me. I want to hug her and tell her everything will be alright.

"I w-waited in the car for him, and when he got into the car he r-reached over and started kissing me w-with so much passion, I just melted."

Sandy swipes the tears away from her heavily bruised face and winces when the back of her hand, wet with her salty tears, makes contact with an open wound.

"He was doing everything I n-never knew I wanted. He told me to suck his c-cock in the back of the car, and the way he said it, I just couldn't wait to get to him."

I can see the effects of the situation, but she needs to tell me.

"He told me to put my hands behind my back, and he put handcuffs on me. I thought he was going to do some sort of kinky shit to me, but he..." She can't finish the sentence. The wailing breaks through her tears and now she's struggling to breathe. "He h-held my head d-down and fucked my throat until I p-puked on him. We w-went somewhere. I think it was a f-factory building. He m-made the d-driver carry me inside and s-strap me to a cross."

The more she talks, the sicker and more pissed off I'm getting.

"He...he...he let..." She stops, and I'm damn thankful that the room is empty except her whimpering.

"It's okay; you don't have to tell me anymore."

"He w-was so m-mad that I threw up on him. He told me I'm exactly like every other slut he's had."

Closing my eyes I bring my hand to my face and run it over my eyes. What the hell do I do here?

I feel an obligation to go to the police and report it, but if Sandy refuses to confirm it by letting me take her to the hospital, then I'm fighting an uphill battle with her.

I sit back on my haunches and look up at a broken Sandy.

"Sandy, we need to go to the police."

"You can't," she says in an eerily calm voice. "You just can't."

"Tell me why."

If her reason is weak, like she's protecting the club, then I'll drag her down there by the damned hair and make her tell the police what happened.

"Because h-he's got my address and a p-picture of my daughter. He told me he'll s-sell her." She begins wailing again.

This changes everything. She has a kid?

"She's eighteen months old."

Well, fuck me.

"How old are you, Sandy?"

"I'm twenty-one."

The anger inside me is bubbling away, but now it's directed toward both that prick and Sandy. I can feel my blood at the boiling point and I'm about to rip into her.

"What the hell are you doing hanging around a place like this if you have a baby at home?" I ask her sharply.

She recoils at my words and I see someone dart out of the meeting room. I turn my angry stare to see that Jaeger's by my side within milliseconds, and Sarge has his arm wrapped around Sandy.

"Phoenix," Jaeger says as he shakes his head at me.

What, he expects me to shut up and not tell her what a huge idiot she is? Because that's exactly what she is, a stupid club whore. Why isn't she home looking after her daughter instead of here trying to screw them all?

"Phoenix," Jaeger now yells at me. "Get up," he orders me.

"I'm not one of your sluts," I angrily spit at him.

"Get your ass up, now!"

I want to grab Sandy, shake her by the shoulders and yell at her that her responsibility is her daughter and not this club.

"Now," he shouts at me again, breaking my wave of anger for a split second.

I stand and look down at the stupid, broken girl who, although she doesn't deserve for this to have happened to her–no one does–didn't do anything to safeguard herself against it.

"You got her?" Jaeger looks at Sarge and he nods once as he consoles a weeping Sandy.

"Phoenix." Jaeger links our hands together and pulls me outside. Without stopping he heads in the direction of a large shed.

The garage door is up and a couple of his crew, or gang, or whatever the hell they're called, are working on a big, black SUV.

"Out," Jaeger shouts at them.

The guys look at him, and then me, and leave within seconds. I turn to look at Jaeger and can see he's clearly pissed off.

Good, so he should be. Whoever that prick is that did this to Sandy deserves not only my fury, but the anger of the...

"What the fuck is wrong with you?"

What? Me?

I take a step back and can feel my eyebrows furrow together as my mouth falls open. "Me? *Me?* Seriously? You're yelling at *me*? Are you even listening to yourself?" I shake my head and eye Jaeger up then down. How is any of this my fault? I turn to leave. Screw all of this shit.

I take one step toward the garage door and Jaeger grabs my arm and tugs me back.

"Yes, you. Do you have any idea what's just happened in there?"

"Yeah I do. Do you? She's twenty-one and hanging around a place like this while her eighteen-month-old baby is being offloaded God knows where."

"Is that all you heard when she was talking to you?"

"That's all she said."

"Then you're naive."

"How so?" I put my hands on my hips and tilt my body slightly to the side, giving Jaeger the 'you're a prick' attitude.

"Because you jumped straight into a conclusion without even getting all the information. You're highly judgmental and clearly, you think like the rest of those narrow-minded fuckers out there." He throws his hand up indicating the general public.

"I think for myself," I say, agitated and angry at him.

"No you don't. You have a pre-conceived idea of what we are, and what she is. You know nothing, but you're quick to assume and then judge."

"Really?"

"You are certainly not what I expected you to be."

"So this is on me?"

"It's not on you, but you haven't asked anything. Do you know why she hangs around here and never leaves?"

"Yeah, to get you to marry her."

Jaeger chuckles and rolls his eyes, "You really have no fuckin' clue."

"Tell me then," I provoke him.

"It's not my story to tell, but seeing as your stubborn, pig-headed ways have likely convinced every guy in there to throw you out, I'll tell you."

"Whatever." A bunch of Neanderthals want me to leave, fine by me.

"She was one of the members' old lady."

"And?"

Jaeger flicks me a look, one telling me that he's not impressed with me.

"Shut your judgmental mouth for a minute and I'll tell you." He gives me a challenging look, but I remain quiet. "They were set to get married, but he died of a heart attack."

A heart attack?

"How old was he?" I ask and take a step closer to Jaeger.

"Twenty-seven. They'd been together since she was seventeen. He adored her and Destiny with everything he was. He didn't screw around on her. He absolutely loved her so deeply that it made us all sick to be around him. We were always giving him shit about it, but he didn't care what we thought. He just kept lovin' her."

"I don't get why she would stay here though, why she keeps coming back."

"Because although she'll suck us off and fuck us, she really is a good girl, and we're her family. We're all she's got. We'd never let anything happen to her."

"But she has a child. She has a responsibility to that baby and if you're as tight-knit as you say you are, then you guys have a responsibility to her too."

"The club provides for Destiny. We take care of Sandy's and Destiny's bills, whatever they are. But we don't judge Sandy for wanting to be here. That's her decision to make, no one else's."

"Where's the baby when Sandy is here servicing you all?" My distain is clear in my delivery.

"The club pays for a nurse to go stay with Destiny whenever Sandy needs the time away, because both Sandy's parents died when she was young."

"Why would the club do that?"

"Because Destiny has Down syndrome and Sandy can't always handle it on her own."

"And I bet you anything that you can't even remember her name most times."

His eyes dart away from me and he looks guilty.

"So I'm right. You can barely remember her name. But you're yelling at me and trying to make me feel bad because I believe she should be at home with her baby. Isn't that a little hypocritical?"

Jaeger turns away from me and takes a few steps, putting distance between us. Maybe I've pissed him off, or possibly I've hit on a raw nerve.

"You're entirely right, darlin', and do you know why you're right?" He leans against the SUV and crosses his ankles and his arms. Obviously he's defensive.

"Why?"

"Because I'm a bastard. I don't give a shit about anyone except my club and my brothers. I take care of her because Sax was part of my club, and we never let an old lady or their kids go without. But I don't care about anyone else, no one."

"I bet you let her suck on your cock though."

"Of course I do."

"And that there is not caring about her?"

"I don't force those sluts to come here. They all show up willing to screw, suck and do all sorts of things with one or a few of us. We don't force them to do anything. If they come here wearing those slutty short-shorts with their tits hangin' out and offer to suck me off, I'll take them up on the offer. But none of us will ever raise a hand to a woman or a child, no matter how much of a pain in the ass they are. Lucky for you."

I ball my hands into fists and the more he speaks the more I want to smack him on his pretty, perfect scarred chin.

"It's not up to us to judge them. They want to be here, then fine."

"What about Sandy? This guy she was with raped her, and by your own standards, she's someone you all should protect."

"That's a little more…"

"Bullshit," I say angrily, cutting off whatever crap excuse he's about to try to hand me. "I call you on it. He raped her. She's one of yours and you'll let him get away with it?"

Jaeger pushes off the SUV and takes a casual step toward me as he puts his hands in his jeans pockets.

"That's club business," he says as he looks down then immediately lifts his face giving me an intense dark gaze.

Yeah, he's warning me, telling me without saying a word to leave the rapist to him.

But I can't let this go.

"Just give me a gun. I'll take care of it."

"And what are you going to do? Shoot him?"

Is he mocking me?

"Did you forget I held a damn shotgun to you?"

Jaeger angrily walks over and grips my shoulders hard, his fingers digging into the skin. "You have no fuckin' idea who the hell you're dealing with. You won't turn vigilante and try to take this on. This. Is. Club. Business," he says clearly, slowly, and carefully, emphasizing the point.

"I'm not part of your club. You can't order me around. He deserves jail or death. I'm fine with either."

"You're with me, sugar, so you *are* very much part of this club."

My anger overtakes me, and I really can't help it. He's such a damned jerk.

I push my hand up under his and break contact. It's so fast that I think I've thrown him. I slap his face, hard.

"I won't prove you wrong," he says as he lets me go and steps backward to lean against the SUV again. "I'll never raise a hand to you."

"I'm not with you," I whisper, though I'm sure he doesn't believe what I'm saying. My own body betrays me. My blood races though my veins, my heartbeat is suddenly deafening as it pounds in my ears. My breathing intensifies and I feel a yearning toward him that's been bubbling under the surface from the moment I opened the door to him at the farm.

"You're with me now," he says again, so aggravatingly sure of himself. But I can't be with someone like him. He's no good for me; he'll ruin me.

"No I'm not," I murmur, the sound not even loud enough to travel to my ears.

He takes a predatory step toward me. If he touches me, I'm gone. I can't let him blindside me.

"You're with me," he asserts as he reaches to cup my cheeks with his big, warm, rough hands. "You're with me," he says in a low voice as he brings his face to mine, his lips ghosting over my own.

"No," I sigh as I lean into him and close my eyes.

"You belong with me." His warm, wet lips hover over mine. He's not being rough; he's being gentle, silently asking to be granted access to my mouth. Giving himself to me, while patiently waiting to consume all of me. "I want you." His hot breath touches my skin, sending sparks right through my body, stirring every nerve ending down to my very soul.

"I don't want you." My words hold no conviction, no value. They're meaningless, even to me.

"Then show me how much you don't want me. Kiss me." He waits without touching my mouth.

I lean into him, waiting for his lips to dance with mine, but he simply hovers, still not touching me. He's playing with me.

His pause gives me the break I need to keep my hormones from falling prey to this hunter.

I open my eyes and step away from Jaeger, regaining the control I carelessly let slip away.

"You may have my farm, but I'm not for sale." I turn on my heels and start to walk away from him.

"One day soon, Red, you'll realize that you and I will happen."

Like hell.

THIRTEEN

How is it possible that out of all the chicks in the world, the one that I want most is also the world's most annoying?

She's narrow-minded too, jumping to conclusions without stopping to consider all the facts.

But for now, I need to shift my focus away from my cock and Nix and bring it back into the club and dealing with Cain.

He may provide us with guns, but I sure as hell won't let him get away with almost killing one of our girls.

Walking back into the clubhouse behind Nix certainly has its advantages, like checking out how tight and luscious her ass actually is.

My eyes are drawn to the tops of her legs, where her ass cheeks jut out in perfect, round globes. Damn, I wonder if she's ever been fucked in the ass. If she hasn't, I'm glad I'll be her first. But if she has, then she'll know exactly what to expect.

I rub my hand down over the hard-on that I promised myself I wouldn't focus on. But I can't help getting a chubby with that delicious, tight ass swaying slightly from side to side as I keep my eyes on her.

"You're still a jerk and stop eye-fucking me," Nix yells over her shoulder as she reaches for the clubhouse door.

That girl, oops, I mean *woman* is gonna be the death of me.

Shaking my head, I try and dislodge those ass-fucking thoughts, but it's difficult when all I want to do is sink into her and screw her 'til she screams.

"Prez," Aaron yells from the bar.

I look at Sandy who's curled up at Lion's side and see that she's half asleep. His arms are wrapped around her and she has relaxed into his protection.

Sarge and Aaron are both at the bar with a bottle of Jack sitting between them as they both down a shot.

"Meeting," I say loudly, calling the members all at once.

I head into the meeting room and sit at the head of the table. One by one they all shuffle in and take their spots.

The door closes and they all look to me to start it off.

"J, what are you thinking?" Sarge says as he lights up a smoke.

"First, we don't run Cain's drugs, which means he'll cut off our gun supplies."

Murmurs come from all around the table.

"We need that money," Aaron argues, and everyone agrees with him.

"He doesn't own us," I add as I bring both my elbows up on the table and run my hands over my face and through my hair.

"Without that money, we're no longer a club," one of the members says.

Another adds, "There's always the tattoo shops and the brothels."

"We could get into a few strip joints, offer our protection," Sarge speaks. The entire table goes quiet and looks over at the heavily-tattooed, scary as fuck, Sarge.

"We need the guns," someone says. "Protection isn't gonna give us shit."

I sit back in my chair and listen to the points that everyone is making.

"Cain will get us killed. Any drug cartel can easily wipe us out,"
"Not if we play it smart."
"No drugs."
"It's the only way."
"Taking that shit is one thing, becoming mules and carting it around is something else."
"Cain will look after us."
"I'm not putting my hand up for it, I don't want it."

The table is divided, there's no way that we're all going to agree with what Cain wants.

"You let Cain in with drugs, he'll totally own us. We're Hunters not poodles."
"He'll look out for us."
"He'll look after himself."
"He's always looked after us."
"He doesn't give a fuck about this club, only his own pockets. Look what he did to Sandy."
"She shouldn't have gone with him."
"He fucked with one of our girls. That's a clear message he doesn't give a shit about us."

Anger is starting to creep into the meeting, but at this stage I'll let it go.

"If he did that to her, then what's he gonna do to us if we disagree with his plans."
"He's already said he won't supply guns if we don't haul his drugs around."

The table goes quiet. The only noise is the intake of breaths as a few club members drag in the smoke from their cigarettes.

"There's another way," I say as I get up and walk over to the door. When I open it, Jason is standing on the other side of the bar pouring himself a drink. "Bring us shot glasses and a couple of bottles," I tell him and go sit down again.

"What's that?" Sarge asks as I sit down and light up a smoke.
"The Pace family," I say.

GRIT

A collective groan is heard and I see a lot of rolling of eyes and hear a few mumbles of 'fuck'.

"I know they're looking to come into this side of the country and I think this is our chance to end it with Cain and start something else," I say as I take a drag of my smoke.

There's a knock on the door, and everyone shuts up. Jason walks in with two bottles of Jack and Nix saunters in behind him carrying the shot glasses on a tray.

She walks around to me and slams them on the table, obviously still pissed at me. My eyes wander over her body and notice she's still dressed in my clothes. Although she looks adorably fuckable in them, I don't want any of my brothers having fantasies about her. However, I'd be surprised if at least half of them haven't already jacked off to thoughts of those legs, or those tits. I know I have.

Several times.

"Take the truck and take her into town to buy her some clothes," I tell Jason as I point at Phoenix.

"On it, boss."

"I don't need your money," Nix automatically retaliates.

"Good, 'cause I wasn't offering. Spend your own money. But you can't be walking around here like that. Jason'll take you to town to get what you need."

Nix stands and puts a hand on her hip as she looks like she's just about to say something to defy me. Her lip snarls up and her eyes narrow as that smart-ass brain of hers thinks up something to say.

One of her eyebrows lifts and she turns to Jason, "Okay, fine, take me to town. I think I want another piercing." She turns on her heels and follows Jason out the meeting room, closing the door behind her.

"You're fucked with that one," Aaron says, smiling as he shakes his head.

Another piercing?

Christ, what's she getting pierced?

I shift in my seat. My cock has become rock hard again as my mind drifts to Phoenix getting those titties pierced, or maybe her belly button.

"She's right, you're definitely an ass," Aaron says as he throws the bottle cap at me and pours the shots.

"Yeah, yeah, whatever. Anyway, about the Pace family providing us with guns." I bring everyone's attention back to the meeting, but take one more look at the door, wishing she'd walked in here and got down on her knees to suck me.

"I hear they went up against Yakuza and came out on top," Sinner says from near the other end of the table.

"They did," I confirm, then down my shot. "And we've never heard of them running anything but guns."

"I don't think we should cross Cain," Aaron says as he pours another shot for himself.

Some at the table agree with him, and some don't. I look to Sarge who's sitting back with his arms crossed in front of his chest, remaining quiet.

"Where does it stop with Cain, though?" I get up from my seat and take the three steps over to the barred window. "What if he starts moving women and kids. We gonna do that too?" I lean up against the window frame and watch as Phoenix gets in the truck and waits for Jason to jump in the driver's side.

"That shit we won't touch," Aaron says, and all the members agree.

"If it's big money, then why not?"

"We don't touch cunts and kids like that."

"Then I think we should hear what the Pace family has to offer. See if there's a way around Cain."

"Second that motion," Sarge says immediately, initiating the vote without any more discussion.

"All in favor?"

"Aye," a group agreement from around the table. Just Dark and Sinner shake their heads.

The vote has to be unanimous, and only I can override it.

"Sinner, Dark, you're saying no?" I question.

"We shouldn't go against Cain," Sinner says.

"We haven't made any decisions yet, so what Cain doesn't know won't hurt us. Unless we have a mole at the table, and if we do, then we'll deal with them the way we always do."

Sinner turns his head and raises his hand, "Aye," he motions after a few moments of consideration.

Dark does the same thing.

"I'll talk to Pace. Meeting over."

I stand and walk out first, taking my phone out of my pocket to call Jason.

"Boss," he answers.

"Where is she?"

"In one of those clothes shops for chicks. She's trying on all sorts of shit."

"Make sure you don't leave her alone."

"I won't. I'm just outside the store," he stops talking, waiting for me to say something else to him.

"Um, just make sure she's safe."

"On it, boss."

I hang up and look around the place, walking back into the empty meeting room, I need to set the wheels in motion to get in contact with Pace.

Emily Pace approached me about thirteen months back and told me she'd be interested in doing business with me. At the time, I totally disregarded her.

She went on to say that a mutual friend, one of our tattooists would be able to get in contact with her when I changed my mind.

A phone call to Micko, our mutual friend, has me waiting for Emily to call me.

Twenty minutes later, my cell rings.

"Yeah," I answer.

"Northeast Sheds, off the interstate, in two days at high noon." The phone disconnects abruptly.

In two days, I'll have a meeting with Emily Pace.
And hopefully, I won't get the entire Hunters MC killed.

FOURTEEN

"Where's Sandy?" I ask Lion as I walk into the kitchen. "She's in the back room lying down. She wouldn't stop crying, so I gave her some sleeping pills to help her rest. She went and had a shower and I gave her clean clothes to change into."

"She alright?"

"Not really. But I think she will be. I gotta tell you, J, he fucked her up real bad. He ripped her up, and her jeans were covered in blood. I threw them out."

I slump in the chair opposite Lion and take in what he said. I saw for myself just how badly he'd beaten her, I can just imagine what else he did to her. From what I've heard, he's a sick motherfucker.

Leaning my elbows on the table, I bring my hands up and bury my face into my open palms.

"She'll be alright as long as her wounds close on their own," Lion continues to say.

"Yep," is my only response. What else can I say? Lion's just a prospect. He's not privy to club business yet. He just does what I say until he gets voted in.

I hear the roar of the V8 as it comes into the yard and I know that Nix is back. I don't want to look like a pussy-whipped motherfucker, so I wait 'til she comes to me. I don't chase chicks – well, unless they want me to, and even then it's only so I can fuck 'em. But I only chase the ones I know can suck like a vacuum or fuck like a whore.

Jason walks into the kitchen first and drops a handful of shopping bags. Nix follows quickly and drops even more bags on the floor.

"That's a lot of plastic there," I say as I move my head to indicate the bags.

"I didn't figure you were into 'save the environment' bags," Nix quips snidely.

Smart-ass.

I look down at the bags, then back at Nix. "You can have a drawer," I say as I stand and walk toward my room.

"I'm not staying long enough for a drawer. Aren't you going to help me?"

I turn to look at her, standing with her hip jutted out and a hand resting on it.

"You bought it. You have two hands. You can do it." I turn and head in the direction of my room again.

I kick my boots off and lay on the bed. I can hear her coming down the hallway as the plastic bags rub up against the walls.

"Jaeger, I need to go home," Nix says as she dumps the bags inside the room on the floor.

"Not gonna happen. You're staying here. The Crowes are most likely still at the farm and that means you'd be taken easily. You're staying here where I can keep an eye on that fine ass of yours."

I watch as she takes a deep breath in, her shoulders rise and her eyes turn to an angry, hardened dark blue. But I turn my head away before she can start in on me again.

"I can't stay here. This place isn't for me."

"What's that supposed to mean, Red?"

"It means that after I saw what happened to that girl, I don't feel safe here. I don't want that to happen to me, and hanging around here is a sure-fire way of guaranteeing I'll come to harm."

She's on her damn high-horse again. The 'I'm better than you are' bullshit.

She's only been here for two days and that condescending shit is getting old.

"Listen here, you spoiled fucking brat," I start as I stand from the bed. "I'm trying to save your God damned, highly judgmental ass. This looking down your nose at us is seriously grating on my last fuckin' nerve. If for one moment you stopped and thought about the bullshit that flies out of that snobbish fuckin' mouth of yours, you'd see that I'm trying to protect you."

"Why the hell would you do that?" she counters and takes a small step back.

"I ask myself the same damn question every time you open that fuckable mouth."

"That's why I act up. You say shit like that and think it's okay. It's not okay. You can't say things like 'fuckable mouth' to me."

Damn, that just made me hard. The way her pretty mouth curls around the 'F' and how her chin slightly protrudes with the 'uck'.

"I can say whatever the hell I want, and for some reason I need to make sure you're protected."

"You're an ass! I'm not a damned child," she screams at me as she throws her hands up in frustration.

My body's beginning to vibrate with an all-consuming, carnal desire to fuck that gorgeous mouth of hers. To drive into her mouth hard, while tears of elation run down her face from choking on my cock while she deeps throats me. I need to claim her.

"Then stop acting like one."

"Fuck you," she yells at me and turns to leave my room.

"No way are you leavin'." I lunge toward her and grab her by the hair, snapping her back to me.

"Fuck you," she says again, but this time her eyes focus on my lips and I notice her chest rapidly rising and falling in short bursts.

She's as turned on as I am.

She's clearly my target now. I'm the hunter desperate for a taste of my prey.

Her eyes soften, her breath hitches and I watch her nipples strain against the thin fabric of the t-shirt.

Stepping right into her personal space, I can feel my body on high alert as it anxiously looks forward to being buried deep inside her.

I take the edge of the t-shirt in my hands, and rip it over her head, looking down at a pretty–but in my way–red bra.

Her skin is perfectly pale. Her stomach is flat, and there's a damn piercing in her navel. I didn't feel anything there before while she slept and my hands were on her.

"Is this the piercing you got today?" I say as I move my hand to touch the small dumbbell that's sitting perfectly in her navel.

"Yeah, it's new," she says as she steps back further.

"Running isn't going to stop what's going to happen between us. You're body's craving me as much as I want you."

"No," she moans and closes her eyes.

"Don't fucking lie to me, Nix. Never lie to me. I won't put up with that."

She tilts her head to the side, her beautiful pale long neck begs me to kiss it, to mark her, to take her and screw her.

"I don't want you," she whispers, her body telling me there's no truth in her words.

"Don't fucking lie."

Her eyes open and she looks at me, her orbs tracing the ink down my arms, looking at all the designs and the intricate work. She reaches up and runs a finger from my elbow, all the way down to my wrist, outlining the stretch of the design.

Phoenix's mouth pops open and I take another step toward her. We're a mere hair's breadth apart. Her bra is touching my t-shirt.

"I don't want you," she says again, looking down to the floor then back up into my eyes. Her pupils are huge.

"Liar," I growl and smash my mouth to hers. My hands snake down to her ass and I tug her up, lifting her feet from the floor. Her legs wrap around my waist as I walk us over to the bed.

I break our kiss and throw her on the bed, and in one quick swoop I yank my t-shirt off and unbuckle my belt.

Her eyes are taking in my chest, all the ink, the scars and markings that cover my body.

I grab the new jeans she's wearing and wiggle them down her body.

Fuck me.

There's a small tattoo of a blue phoenix on her left hip, which surprises me. The ink's been there for a while, and it's blended nicely on her skin.

"Well, that's something I didn't expect to see on you."

"What?" she says as she furrows her brows together, looking pissed off at me.

What's new?

Without saying anything else, I fall to my knees beside the bed and start kissing the indigo blue ink that sits so brilliantly on her pale skin.

I run my tongue along the outline of the phoenix as I grab her hips and pull her closer to my mouth. I want to lick and taste her and feel her trembling around my tongue, knowing that she's getting what she needs from me.

Hooking my fingers into her cute, lacey red so-called panties, I rip at the thin strip of string that's holding it together.

"Jaeger," she whispers as her hand runs through my hair.

Holy shit, she's got a small silver barbell piercing her clit hood.

This girl is definitely not what I expected. She's a surprise package. And damn, am I a lucky son-of-a-bitch to be fucking her.

"Jaeger," she says again.

My eyes are glued to her piercing and the third time she says my name it breaks me out of the raging desire that's found its way to my balls and cock. "Yeah, babe." I lean in and skim my nose across her soaking wet cunt. God, she smells fantastic. And I'm so pleased that she waxes, not all of it, there's a thin landing strip of red hair on her otherwise bare pussy. It's enough to let me know she's a God damn beautiful woman.

"I don't want you," she says as she grips my hair hard and brings my face right against the trimmed hair.

"Keep saying that," I murmur. "I'm listenin' to your body, not your mouth."

Her legs open further and she grabs my head with both hands to try and force me to lick her tasty pussy.

Fuck that shit.

"Put your arms above your head, and heels up on the bed. Open this hot pussy for me. I want to see you open and ready."

"Shit," I hear her whimper as her arms go above her head to grip the pillows and her heels come up on the bed. Her ass is on the edge of the mattress. She's open and uncovered, all ready for me.

"Don't fuckin' move, you got me?"

She sighs a barely audible 'yes'.

Good, about time she damned well listens. It's a nice change from fighting with her.

She's totally opened and exposed for me; her cunt looks so appetizing with that cute clit ring, just waiting for my tongue to devour it. Phoenix is breathing hard, and her pussy is vibrating with that uncontrollable yearning to have a cock or tongue inside her.

I love it when I see a needy hole ready to be filled, ready to clamp onto whatever I want to put inside her. Be it my tongue, cock, or a vibrator.

"Greedy girl," I say as I spread her lips and lick that sweetness from her hole to her clit.

"Damn it," she moans and writhes on the bed. "More," she begs as I sit back on my haunches and just stare at her.

I say nothing. I remain quiet, letting her realize she's on display for me. Nix tries to close her legs. Maybe she's embarrassed. But she's absolutely beautiful. She's wet and I can see all of her.

"Don't you dare," I say in a low monotone.

Her knees go back to being spread wide open, and I watch as she battles her own insecurities.

Why is she like this? She's all mouthy with clothes on, but now, with just her bra on and her legs wide open, she's self-conscious. Doesn't she know how hot she is right now?

"Finger that pussy for me. Show me how you like to be touched," I say as I stand and slide my jeans down my legs.

"What?" she asks, breathlessly.

"Fuck your fingers, sugar. I want to see your cunt dripping with your own cum before I fill you with mine."

I stand over her and look at her face as it morphs from shyness into desire. Her eyes fill with a burning fire as her chest heaves with her labored breath.

She moves her hand and licks her first two fingers, slowly, teasing the hell out of me. Nix slides her hand down the column of her throat and squeezes her neck, telling me silently she likes to play hard while having sex.

I rub my cock through my boxers and feel the head straining against the material.

Nix keeps her hand moving down to her tits where she grabs the left one, squeezing the nipple and pulling at it through the sheer red material of her bra.

"Fuck," I say as I slide my boxers down my hips. But I keep my eyes on Nix's travelling hand.

With just her index finger, she traces the line of her stomach down to the start of that narrow strip of hair.

Nix sits up on the bed, her knees wide open, her heels still on the very edge of the mattress. With her left hand, she spreads her lips open and with her right hand she dips her two fingers straight into her pussy.

No stretching, no teasing, no working them in slowly.

Fuck me!

"You like that?" she asks as my eyes snap back to hers.

Her fingers move in and out, and her thumb goes directly to her clit that's just poking out from beneath its pierced hood. God I want her taste in my mouth again. The flavor of the one lick I gave her is quickly fading to nothing. And I want to savor her taste and smell. I want her to rub that pussy all over my face, coating me in her dripping wet arousal.

Her thumb applies pressure on her clit and the piercing, and the moment it does her eyes close and her head lolls all the way back as she moans sweetly.

I can feel myself being hypnotized, watching the way her fingers toy with her body, playfully enticing heavenly noises from the back of her throat.

My appetite for Nix has just grown greedier. My cock follows suit and is as hard as it's ever been.

There's a frenzy growing inside me, an intense, dire need to suck that fat clit into my mouth, flick the piercing and not let it go until she's quaking hard against my face, giving me all her cum as I lick her dry.

"Move," I growl as I plow my face into her pussy, mouth already salivating as I know I'm about to enjoy myself.

She barely has a chance to move her hands before I spread her open and suck on her clit. It's so plump, soft, and so full of blood as I consume it, licking, stroking, kissing and sucking. Her hands weave back into my hair.

I curl two fingers into her desperately ravenous hole to stroke the roof of her pussy. Her entire body tightens beneath me. Yeah, she loves this. I scissor my fingers as I keep licking her slit, drinking every drop of honey she produces. It's unbelievable; she's got the best tasting pussy I've ever had.

She clamps onto my fingers, as I play with the taut skin between her slit and her ass. Her hips keep rotating to get that friction against her pussy as I continue to rub the juiciest pussy I've ever tasted.

I let her clit go, but not before I brush the mouth-watering little nub and jewelry with the flat of my tongue, causing Nix to rasp a heavy intake of air.

Sitting back to look at her magnificently wet core, I can't help but want to ravish her with just my mouth.

"Fuck me," Nix says, giving me very clear directions.

"Not yet," I reply before burying my face back into her snatch.

My tongue delves straight into her mound, and her trembling, greedy hole is waiting to accept me. I spread her legs further and cup her ass in my hands, separating her ass cheeks with my fingers.

My thumb grazes her tight asshole, just working around the puckered rim.

"Hmmm," she mewls as her hips keep rotating. She's fucking my face.

Hell, I don't think I'm going to be able to hold on for too much longer if she's responding like this.

"Keep still," I grunt as I flex my arm around the top of her thighs as my other hand keeps playing with her asshole.

I push my thumb into her anus, just stretching her. She tries to push me out, but that's a natural reflex from women.

My tongue finds the piercing and flicks it as I suck her clit into my mouth and push my thumb in further.

"God yes," she whimpers brokenly. Her hips start to roll on their own accord again and I try to restrict her movement as I keep eating her pussy.

My tongue flicks her clit and then greedily fucks her hole, in and out.

Up then down.

She wiggles, trying to get the right angle.

Licking up through her pussy lips, enjoying the perfect nub with its silver bar, I push my thumb into her ass.

Nix's breathing is going crazy, sounds of pure ecstasy are coming from her and her hands go back into my hair as she pulls me closer to her soaking lips.

I feel her start to tremble. That sends me damned wild and I wanna stay here forever.

She explodes with a cry and tries to push me off her, but I brush her hands away and keep licking, my mouth sucking, my tongue hammering as far into her as I can get and my thumb fucking her ass.

Phoenix tries to close her legs around my head and push me away, so I lick faster and suck harder.

"Oh shit," she groans. "Jaeger, you have to stop." I love the sound of my name on her lips as she's coming. "Oh my God! Stop!" She tries again to push me away, weakly.

Like a thirsty man, I drink everything she's flooding me with.

"Holy shit," she says as her hips begin to slow.

But just because she's covered me with her cum, it doesn't mean I've had my fill of her.

I keep sucking on her clit and flicking the ball with my tongue as my thumb pushes all the way into her ass, then comes out to trace the rim.

"You have to stop," Nix tries to tell me. But I've never been real good at listening.

I press my tongue on the underside of her clit as my upper lip engulfs the top. Knowing she's super sensitive right now, I move my tongue down inside her pussy and carefully probe her as I continue to thumb-fuck her ass.

"Oh shit, no. I can't go again. Shit, shit, shit, shit."

I think she can.

I push my thumb into her, and pull out of her. I'm driving her wild, and she's sending me crazy.

My cock is hard, there's pre-cum dripping onto my thigh and I'm about to lose it.

Stopping my oral assault on Nix, I stand and wipe my mouth on the back of my hand.

Her eyes are dark with want, her tits are half out of the bra and her red hair is a mess, most likely from thrashing around on the bed.

I lift her legs so they're up around my shoulders and guide my cock toward her slit.

"Condom!" Nix yells.

What the hell's wrong with me? I was about to screw a chick without a condom. I've never done that before. *Ever.*

"Side table, top drawer," I tell Nix. She moves her upper body, opens the drawer and gets the pack of condoms out.

Her legs have only marginally slipped, I move them back up against my chest as she hands me a condom in the wrapper.

I tear that mother open and slide it onto my hard-on.

"Jaeger," she says as her eyes follow my hands while I put the condom on.

"Yeah, babe."

"Fuck me hard."

Hell yeah!

I line my cock up and push into her. Nix's hot wet core engulfs me. She clamps down on my shaft and moves her hips up, obviously positioning me exactly where she wants.

I start pumping in and out of her, holding her legs up off my chest and push them slightly back, giving me more depth and giving Nix a deeper thrust.

"Oh God," escapes her lips as her eyes close and she fists the bed covers trying to get more traction. She clenches as I slide into her, and releasing as I come out.

"Keep doing that, sugar" I tell her, because it feels fantastic.

Closing my eyes, I just want to concentrate on how good Nix feels around me. The way she's pulsating as I thrust deep inside her. Those sexy noises and cute little grunts every time I hit that sinfully luscious spot she's desperate for me to keep stroking my cock against.

My arms are wrapped around her thighs, pushing them that little bit further toward her head. Damn, she's flexible. The more I push, the deeper I can lunge into her, giving us both what we want.

Sweat starts rolling down my spine, my legs are feeling heavy and the tightness in my balls makes them heavy.

I start intensely thrusting into Nix. Her gorgeous cunt takes the pounding that I'm giving her. My balls are smacking against her ass and the sound of wet pussy swallowing my cock fills the room.

"Fuck!" Nix yells again as her body nearly flies off the mattress.

I splay my hand, open fingers, on her stomach and fuck her like she's never been fucked before.

My heartbeat achingly hammers with so much ferocity that I can't hear anything over its thumping in my ears.

My balls tighten, and I thrust into her hard. Nix's hand caresses the one I've laid on her stomach, and that one simple touch makes my eyes fly open and sends a tremor throughout my entire body.

I push into her with small jabs until I feel my body tighten. I come with a long groan and fill the condom.

I'm not sure how much longer I stand, but Nix's legs have slumped against my chest and I'm puffing heavily for air, trying to get oxygen into my lungs.

I pull out of her, letting her legs drop to the bed, and walk into the bathroom, wrap the condom and chuck it out.

When I walk back into my room, Phoenix is beneath the covers and has her back turned away from me.

I pull back my side of the covers and mold the front of my body to the back of hers. I get a face full of her hair, but I don't give a shit, I want her in my arms.

"Jaeger," she breathes softly.

"Yeah, babe."

"That will never happen again."

I smile against the rogue hair that's tickling my face.

"Yeah right," I say, though I know her words aren't real.

Because what we have together is something more than I've ever felt before.

And the damn stubborn-ass chick better figure it out, and soon, 'cause I'm going to fuck her every chance I get.

FIFTEEN

"Phoenix," I say, trying to wake Nix. One of her legs is sticking out from beneath the covers and her hair's a tangled mess all over the pillow. She's snoring softly and there's a bit of drool dripping down from the side of her mouth. "Phoenix," I say somewhat louder, hoping to rouse her before I have to resort to shaking her awake.

"Hmmm," she moans as she closes her mouth and turns on her side.

"For a cowgirl who's supposed to be up early, you're certainly fitting into the laid-back lifestyle easily enough."

She opens her eyes and turns her head to look at me.

She's a damn mess, but still sexy as fuck.

"What the hell are you talking about?" Red sits up in bed and drags the covers over her bare body, sheltering her gorgeous, bouncy tits from my view.

"You wet for me, Red?" I ask as I lean closer to her. "That's nice. But you'll have to brush your teeth and wipe the drool off your face if we're going to fuck."

She swipes at her mouth, and horror flashes across her face as her fingers touch the dampness that's starting to dry. "Go away. And

I told you last night we aren't having sex again," she growls at me.

"Yeah, right. That's why you slept bare last night so I could feel your skin against mine. Anyway, if you want to suck me off, then hurry up and do it, or get out of bed."

She stands and wraps the sheet around her, carefully not allowing me to see any part of her. When it's wrapped around her like a toga, she gives me a look of sheer disgust and walks into to the bathroom.

"You gonna suck me off in the shower?" I ask as I follow her to the bathroom. She slams the door, and I hear the click of the lock. *Well I guess not.*

"You're an arrogant asshole," she says from the other side of the door just before the shower starts.

I chuckle to myself and nod in agreement.

"We're having a barbecue today and you gotta make something. Hurry up so I can take you into town."

"What the hell do you mean I 'gotta make something'?"

"Not hard to understand. All the old ladies are making something and that means you have to too." What about this confuses her?

"I'm not part of this club."

"Yes, you are."

"Go away. Let me shower in peace."

Screw this. I try the handle, and it is indeed, locked.

I take a step back and put my boot to it. The door flings open and Phoenix lets out a high-pitched cry.

"I don't like talking through a door, Red."

"Stop calling me that and get out," she says as she tries to cover her body with her hands.

"I saw you naked when I fucked you last night. Why the hell are you covering up now?" I lean down, take my boots off and throw them out into the bedroom.

"What are you doing?" she asks.

"I need a shower, too. I'm coming in with you." I yank the t-shirt I'm wearing over my head and unbuckle my belt and take off my jeans.

"Like hell you are. Get out and give me some damn privacy."

I open the shower door and step inside. Phoenix backs up into the corner, still trying to cover herself up, though the arm covering her tits drops.

"After I've fucked you in here, then we're going to get dressed and I'm taking you into town to buy whatever you need to make something for the cookout tonight." I take a step closer to her and cage her in the corner of the shower with my arms, which are propped against the tiles on either side of her body.

"You can't do this," she whispers as her gaze drops to my stomach, then further down to my stiff cock.

"Why?" I lean in and skim the column of her throat with my nose. The water is hammering at us hard, the heat playing havoc with our already blazing bodies.

Nix arches her back, her nipples taut as they brush up against my chest. Her breath is coming out in short, rapid bursts.

"Because I told you, I won't have sex with you again."

"Fine. Suck me off then." I suck her earlobe into my mouth, pulling it between my teeth before tracing the shell of her ear with my tongue.

Phoenix gasps as her hands come up to my chest, she starts rubbing my nipples with her thumbs as she moves her body to close the gap between us.

"You're a pig," she groans as she tilts her head, letting me devour the sexy skin on her throat.

"But I bet you're wet."

"God, no."

I trail my hand down her heated body and she involuntarily pushes her core into it, silently telling me to keep doing what I'm doing. I spread her pussy lips open and dip a finger inside, testing exactly how wet she is.

Nix grinds against my hand, her hips moving in small circular movements as I insert a second finger and really start to finger-fuck her.

"Stop," she moans as she holds onto my shoulders and pushes down on my hand, making my fingers go further into her.

"Do you really want me to stop, Red?" I lean down and flick her nipple with my tongue, then engulf the nub in my mouth as I suck and pull on it between my teeth.

Phoenix's hands grip my hair on a sharp inhale. She pulls on my head to bury it further into her boobs.

"Yes, stop." She lifts her left leg around my waist and rubs her ripe body all over my hand and my groin. We're a mess–a luscious, ravenous, fevered, tangled mess.

"Turn around and put your hands on the wall," I say as I remove my hand from her pussy and take a small step back from her.

Phoenix's cheeks are red, and there's a fine pink color stretching from her face down her throat to the top of tits. She's so fuckin' beautiful right now. She looks at me from beneath those long eyelashes and a small, dangerous smile plays on her fuckable mouth.

She turns and puts her hands on the wall as she sticks her butt out, ready for me to do what I want with it.

I grab one of her ass cheeks and squeeze it forcefully. She mewls and pushes back a little more.

God, she loves it rough, and I want to give it to her as rough as she can take it.

I smack her once, hard.

She groans and wiggles further back.

My hand print looks great against her alabaster skin. It suits her, and God knows, I want to do it again.

My cock is straining, desperate to be buried deep inside Phoenix. I can't wait 'til I fuck her ass, or even her mouth.

"You're a dirty little bitch that loves a hard fuckin', aren't you, Phoenix?" I smack her again.

But this time, she pulls away and straightens her back. Phoenix swings around and the look she's giving me is anything but aroused. What the hell happened?

"You're an idiot, now leave me alone and get out." She points toward the door.

"What the hell's your problem, Red?"

"You are. You talk to me like I'm a slut. Dirty talk is fine, but calling me a bitch is not. And for the love of God, stop calling me Red. I hate that name. Either Phoenix or Nix, but if you keep calling me Red I'll make you call me Miss Ward. Now get out before I smack you one in that pretty boy face of yours."

I take a step back and open the shower door, "My cock's hard so you better suck it tonight, Red." I add the name she hates and step out of the shower, wrap a towel around me and leave the bathroom.

"Asshole!" she yells at me.

I chuckle and shake my head. Damn, she's a whole lotta fun.

Dressing in jeans and a green t-shirt, I lie on the bed and wait for Her Majesty, Queen of Stubbornness, to come out of the shower. She takes her damned sweet time, so I sit and wait patiently.

Red comes out with a towel around her hair, and another around her body.

"What the hell took you so long?" I ask, though I have a fair idea what she's going to say.

"I had to get myself off when you decided to be a prick."

"I could've done that for you." I smirk and know her hot-headed temper is bound to goad her into saying something to me.

She takes the towel off her body and throws it at me. *Damned tease.* She prances around the bedroom naked, looking for clothes.

Phoenix goes over to the bags that are still lying on the floor where she dumped them yesterday. She bends at the waist, ass in the air and legs slightly spread, showing off her asshole and pussy.

"Hmmm, what should I wear?" she asks herself as I see her hand start to travel up the apex of her thighs.

Damn her, there's only so much self-control I can muster if she starts playing with herself.

"Can you not do that?" I ask as I sit up in bed.

"Do what?" she says, all false innocence, as she reaches around to her ass.

Holy shit, if she fingers her ass, I'm gonna lose it and fuck her right now.

"Please, Red, if you know what's good for you, you won't touch yourself like that."

"What are you talking about?" She peers around at me from beneath her straightened legs, moves her hand to her mouth and sucks on her pointer finger.

Fuck me. She's going to, isn't she?

"Don't finger yourself, please," I beg her, not really wanting her to stop, but I know she won't let me touch her either, and that will make my already blue balls unbearable.

Her hand goes around to her ass again, and she rims her puckered hole with her finger. I stand and take a step toward her, my cock still hard from the shower. But now, I'm only holdin' onto the smallest thread of control with my fingernails.

Phoenix's finger slips into her ass, and her eyes close as a moan slides past her lips.

Fuck!

"Can I touch you?" I ask as I take another step closer.

"Are you going to keep calling me Red?"

What the hell? This is all 'cause of *that*?

Damn, I wanna fuck her though.

"No," I say as I gulp down the giant golf ball of arousal sitting in my throat.

"Sorry?" she says as her finger begins to slowly thrust in and out of her ass while she's bent over, exposing every succulent part of herself.

"No, I won't call you Red ever again." I sound like a pussy-whipped, spineless cock.

"Good," she says as she takes her finger out of her ass and straightens up.

What. The. Hell?

She grabs a pair of panties from a bag and slides them up over her hips, which is quickly followed by a bra, a t-shirt, then jeans, and a pair of flip-flops.

She strolls past me into the bathroom and washes her hands.

"What just happened?" I ask her when she comes out of the bathroom.

"I might give you a blow job after the barbecue tonight, but until then, every time you want to call me Red, think of what you'll be missing. Now, are you going to take me to town so I can get shit for this cook-out?"

She waltzes past me to the door of the bedroom, opens it and turns down the hall.

Well played, Red, well fucking played.

SIXTEEN

"SO WHY IS THE CLUB HAVING THIS BARBECUE THING?" PHOENIX ASKS me as she makes me push a shopping cart around the grocery store.

"What the hell are you buying here, Nix? The whole fucking store? You just gotta make a salad or some shit like that." I look down at the cart and there's all sorts of crap in here, toilet paper, deodorant, razors and more.

"Are you going to tell me or do I buy a package of crackers and some cheese and call it good?"

"The old ladies heard what happened to Sandy, so they wanna get together and show her their support. They talked us into havin' a cookout tonight. They thought it might help Sandy to relax or some shit, I don't know."

"What exactly do you guys mean by a cookout?" Red, I mean, Nix asks as she goes down the candy aisle and picks up a chocolate bar, putting it in the cart.

"You'll end up fat if you eat stuff like that," I say as I point to the candy bar.

"And you'll end with no damned teeth if you keep talking shit."

"What are the 'old ladies' bringing?" she asks as she air quotes and makes a stupid face.

"Fucked if I know. Call 'em and ask 'em."

"First, you won't let me near a phone, although I have to say you don't keep a very good on eye on me 'cause I called Milina when Lion took me into town yesterday. And second, why would I call them?"

"'Cause that's what you're supposed to do, talk with the other old ladies and get to know them. And who the hell is Milina?" I stop pushing the cart and can feel my eyebrows furrowing together in the first waves of anger.

"Why would I do that?"

"That's what you're supposed to do, now that you're with me. Now who's Milina?"

"I'm not an old lady."

"You're my old lady. Who the hell is Milina?"

"I'm not your anything."

"I've claimed you, and you're not going anywhere. Now, for fuck's sake, who the hell is this Milina?"

"You've *claimed* me? Are you serious? What am I, a piece of meat?"

"Hi, Jaeger," says some girl in pig-tails, tight little short-shorts, and a tube top thing that just barely covers her nipples. She walks past Phoenix and me in the candy aisle. Looking straight at me, she licks her lips and then bites on the bottom one.

Who the hell is she?

"Oh I see. I'm supposed to be claimed like you claimed her?" Phoenix says as she points to Miss Pig-tails who's standing a few feet away, smiling at me.

"I don't even know who the hell she is."

"You don't remember me?" Miss Pig-tails asks, pouting. "You said I gave you the best head you've ever had," the chick says in a shaky and distraught voice.

"No offense, darlin'. But I tell everyone who blows me that."

"I thought you liked me," she says as she starts to sob.

Fuck, not another one bringing on the waterworks.

"Nah, not really, now do you mind? We're talking here," I say to Miss Pig-tails as I shoo her away with a flick of my wrist.

"You really are something else, Jaeger," Phoenix states, putting her hands on her hips.

"Thanks. Who's this Milina chick?" I watch Miss Pig-tails turn and leave down the aisle, still crying. *Whatever.*

Phoenix's jaw is clenched together and her lips are in a thin line. If she was a dragon she'd be breathing fire right about now.

"My best friend," she finally replies.

"Great. I wanna meet her, make sure she's good for you. Invite her around tonight." I hand Nix my phone and she looks down at my outstretched hand with a perplexed look. "What's the problem? Call her."

"Fine, but I leave with her when she goes."

"Nope. That ain't gonna happen."

"What goes on in that pea-sized brain of yours?"

"I think about fuckin' you, and you suckin' me until you cry 'cause you can't take any more of my cock in your mouth. I think about driving my cock into your ass, and I definitely wouldn't mind a vibrator in your pussy while I hammer into that tight little ass of yours."

"For God's sake, Jaeger, keep your voice down." She trails a hand through her long red hair and looks over her shoulder to see if anyone's listening.

"It's not a crime for me to tell my woman what I want to do to her."

"I'm *not* your damn woman. You have to stop this, Jaeger. We had sex. It was pretty good sex, but that's it. There's nothing else between the two of us."

Like hell. I duck around the shopping cart and grab her wrist tightly. There's an undefinable look on her face, a cross between shock and arousal.

"Stop. The sex was awesome, not just pretty good. And you and I are more than just fuck buddies. You belong with me, not to me, but with me. Get that through that damned thick stubborn brain of yours. You're my old lady, period. So stop fightin' it."

"Let go of me."

"No, not until you tell me you understand me." I lean into her and my mouth swoops down on hers. I don't wait for her stupid brain to catch up to her body. I just take what I want and give her what she hasn't yet realized she needs.

"Let me go," she mumbles against my lips, though her body defies her. Her nipples poke out from beneath her t-shirt to rub against my chest, her mouth dances with mine, and sexy little noises come from her throat as I passionately kiss her and continue to claim her right here in the candy aisle.

"Tell me you understand." I slightly pull back to look into her liquefied blue orbs.

"I get you."

"Say it, so I know you get it."

"I belong to you," she sighs

"See?" I ask as I take a step back. "That red hair matches your temper, but I'm not going to let it get between us. You don't listen to anything I say, but your body knows the score. Like I said, sugar, you belong with me."

"Fine," she says with resignation in her voice. "I belong with you."

"Great, now let's get what my old lady needs and get out of here. She owes me a blow job."

Phoenix turns on her heels and walks away from me.

Now we're even.

··✤··

"What's the deal between you and her? Can I try for her, or what?" Aaron asks as we sit by the fire outside, drinking beers and watching the old ladies fuss over Sandy.

Sandy looks like shit. Her face is showing pretty bad bruising, her left eye is still almost swollen shut and she's walking with difficulty. All the club's old ladies are helping her out, offering whatever it is she needs to get her through.

Phoenix looks a little lost surrounded by a sea of inked men and women. Everyone in the club looks like they belong here, all inked and pierced. Phoenix's piercings are beneath her clothes, and although she has a small tattoo of a phoenix on her hip, she still sticks out.

The other old ladies look her over, though like the stubborn person she is, she continues to stand outside the circle as she lets them all know she's not going to put up with their crap.

"You try and we'll have to settle it on the pavement, old school," I say to Aaron as I swig from my beer then light up a smoke.

"She's got you by the balls."

"That she does," I say as I laugh and take a deep drag. But I keep my eyes on Phoenix.

Phoenix turns her head and looks over at me, catching sight of how I'm eye-fuckin' her and she smiles. She takes the few steps over to where Aaron and I are sitting.

"Milina will be here shortly; she said about eight," Phoenix says with excitement in her voice.

I stub the smoke out and reach out to grab Phoenix and kiss her. She backs away from me and knits her eyebrows together and looks at Aaron.

"No secrets in this club," Aaron says with a laugh, and drinks from his beer.

Phoenix shrugs her shoulders and walks away, going toward the gate to wait for her friend.

"Stay inside, don't leave the property."

She shoots me a 'go jump' look and keeps walking.

"You, my best friend, are truly screwed with that one." Aaron chuckles and goes back to his beer.

"Lion," I call to him from across the pit fire.

Lion jogs around to me and stands in front of me. "Yeah, boss," he says.

"Shadow her. Make sure she stays inside the gates."

"No worries, boss."

Lion walks away to find Phoenix and Aaron chuckles again.

"What the hell is going on with you? She's got your balls and it looks like she's got you by the short 'n' curlies, too. Is there anything left of you? 'Cause you're really pussy-whipped."

"Piss off, VP. I just wanna make sure she's alright."

"Why wouldn't she be?"

"The Crowes want her as payment for what Ward owed them, and Cain was asking about her, too. I'm not sure how he knew about her, but he did."

"What did he say?" Aaron sits back in his chair and crosses one leg over the knee.

"Just that she's someone that can be useful to him."

"How so?"

"He wouldn't say exactly, just that she'd be useful."

"Who's going to the meet tomorrow? You taking Sarge?"

"Yeah, you stay here and hold down the fort. Sarge can come with me. I'll bring the offer back to the table."

"Hmmm," Aaron says as he brings the bottle to his mouth again. "She staying here?"

"Yeah." Before I get a chance to saying anything, Phoenix walks back, giggling and laughing with her friend Milina.

Milina is shorter than Nix, dark hair loosely falling over her shoulders. Damn, she's a hottie too. She's wearing jeans and a sweater with flat shoes. I can't help but look her up and down. Maybe Nix wouldn't mind a threesome with her.

"Hey, is this Milina?" I ask as I feel myself cock an eye brow, getting a serious hard-on at the thought of Milina eating Nix's pussy as I sit back and watch them.

"Yeah. Jaeger this is Milina; Milina this is Jaeger and Aaron," Nix says as she points me out then Aaron.

"Hi there," Milina says, voice full of confidence. But the way she's slightly turned to her side, I can tell she's intimidated by us.

"Red–shit, I mean Nix, come here," I catch myself, I think, before she hears me. But her eyebrows shoot up and she tilts her head to the side. "I meant to say Nix. It was a slip of the tongue."

Milina laughs and Phoenix shakes her head.

"Well, hopefully I can slip my tongue into your cunt later," I say as I wink at Phoenix.

"You're an ass," Phoenix snaps and grabs Milina by the upper arm, dragging her away.

I look over at Aaron and shrug. What's wrong with her now?

Aaron's laughing hard. "What?" I ask and light up another smoke.

"Do you even *have* a filter? You can't say shit like that to regular girls."

"Why?"

"'Cause they don't like it. It pisses them off."

"You kidding? She's probably already wet, and will most likely ride me hard later on when her friend leaves. So what's the issue?"

Seriously? What the hell is the problem?

Open communication, isn't that what chicks want? Touchy-feely shit? Don't they love being cuddled and held and told how much we want them? That's sort of what I'm doing here and she just keeps pushing me away.

"If it's just a chick you're banging, then say whatever the hell you want to them, 'cause they most likely love that crap. But saying it to a chick you actually care about? That's suicide, my friend. Even I know that."

"Says the self-confessed manwhore," I say and chuckle.

"Man, do what you want. Just saying, she ain't gonna put up with that from you for too much longer."

"Whatever. I'm getting in touch with my feminine side, or whatever the girls say, 'cause I like that pussy and wanna keep her around. I think she gets turned on every time I open my mouth."

Aaron laughs again, shaking his head, and I keep an eye on my girl as she walks down the food table with Milina. Milina's laughing at something that Nix has said, and it's obvious they're long-time friends.

"Who's the chick?" Sarge's voice snaps me out of the eye-fuckin' I was giving Nix.

"Milina, Phoenix's best friend," I answer as he takes the empty seat on the other side of Aaron.

"Hmmm," Sarge says and looks over at Milina.

The girls come back carrying a plate of food each. There's a spare chair near the fire pit and Sarge drags it over beside him.

Phoenix looks around for another chair, but there isn't a spare one anywhere. "Here," I say as I grab her hips and guide toward my knees.

"What are you doing?" Nix asks.

"If you wanna sit on the ground you can." I let go of her hips, letting her make her own mind up.

She reluctantly sits on my lap and Milina sits beside Sarge. He turns his back to us and starts talking to Milina.

And by talking, I mean I can hear more than just the usual grunts coming from him.

"I'm outta here. Let me know about tomorrow," Aaron stands and takes a step away.

"What's happening tomorrow?" Nix asks as she forks some pasta salad and pops it into her mouth.

"Club business," both Aaron and I say in unison.

Nix starts to stand from sitting on my lap, and my arms tighten around her hips.

"Where are you going?" I whisper in her ear as I cement her to me.

"Moving seats now that Aaron's going." She scoops up some more food on the fork and eats it.

"I like to watch your mouth, so stay here."

She looks down at me and smiles. Her eyes have darkened and her lips curl up at the edges.

See, I was right. She loves it when I talk dirty to her.

"What about my mouth do you like to look at?" She takes another bite of her food, slower, more sexy.

"I can't wait until you wrap it around my cock. The way you pop your tongue out and lick your lips is driving me crazy."

"Is that all you want me to do? Get down on my knees and suck your dick?" My cock is flaring up as she teases me with her words and body.

"You really want to hear what I want you to do?"

"Only if it's something sweet," she says as she lowers her gaze to look at the food on her plate.

"Sweet is me lyin' on my back on a bed, naked, with you sitting between my wide spread legs, using both hands to cover my cock and balls with baby oil. Your warm hands slowly strokin' my cock and rollin' my balls with the tightest of grips. And, just as my balls start to rise, you use your finger and thumb in an old hog-tie, wrapping them around my balls as you stretch them and pull them away from my body, stopping my cum from spurting out onto those fuckin' hot titties of yours.

"My cock bouncing, begging and craving to unload, but you don't fuckin' stop. You bring me to the brink and you do it all over again, and again, and again. And just when my balls are red from the pulling and tugging and deprivation, you fuckin' wrap those plump candy lips around me and suck me 'til you drink every last drop of my cum. That's what sweet is to me, Nix. An hour of pain, followed by a moment of pleasure."

"Shit," Phoenix says as she stops eating and looks at the plate, too scared to lift her gaze to me.

"What?" Don't tell me I said something that's pissed her off again.

She puts the plate on the chair next to us, wraps her arms around my neck and closes her mouth over mine. Her mouth dominates mine. She's licking and sucking at me, while hungrily drowning us both in an intoxicating, heated kiss.

She pulls away only to lean into me and start kissing and sucking up my jaw toward my ear. "God, Jaeger, you're such an ass. But I want you so badly."

I stand at the speed of light, half pushing Nix off me, half dragging her with me. "Take care of her," I say to Sarge as I point to Milina. Grabbing Nix by the hand I head straight for my room.

"What are you doing? Milina will be on her own. You can wait," Nix says as she tries to break the tight hold I have on her.

"Sarge will look after her. You need to give me a blow job, right now." I push her into my room, closing and locking the door behind me.

"I'm not going down on you, knowing my friend is out there alone." She points past the door toward the back of the clubhouse.

"You want me; I want you. It's simple math. If you're not going to suck me, then bend over and let me fuck you."

"You are a jerk." She sidesteps me and moves toward the door.

"What the hell is your problem?" I ask as I pull her back into the room before she can leave.

"It's the way you say things, like I'm expected to just be here for your cock." She indicates toward my groin

I run a frustrated hand through my hair and tug on the ends.

"I'm trying this open communication bullshit you chicks seem to always go on about. You know the whole 'let's tell each other how we feel' thing. I'm telling you how I feel, and you get pissed. What the hell do you want from me?"

"I just don't want you to act like such a caveman," she retorts angrily. "There's more to me than just my mouth or my ass or my pussy."

"I can't do nice, Nix. I can only do truth with you. Not the whole flowers and candy crap. I'm not that type. But I'm also not the type that'll ever lie to you either."

"What's that supposed to mean?"

"It means I might tell you I want those lips around my cock, and how I want to watch your tits bounce up and down as you ride me. But I won't lie to you about anything. Isn't it better to have me tell you those things, then not say anythin' and go get them from someone else?"

"Well..."

"I'd rather fuck you in the ass than go to anyone else and stick my cock in them."

"How damn romantic." She rolls her eyes and takes a deep breath.

I take a step closer to her, and lower my agitated tone, "I don't do romance, Nix. I don't do pretty and soft. I'll tell you what I want, how I want it and although you may not like how I say it, it'll always be the truth."

The longest moment passes between us.

Nix looks away from me, as she considers what I have to say.

"Do you know what this feels like?" She gestures between us.

"What?" God help me. I hope she doesn't say something like what comes out of those those instant love, happily ever after bullshit books that horny women read these days.

"To me it feels like we're magnets, pulling together, but rejecting each other every time we get close."

"Sugar, the only one pushing away is you."

She looks at me and frowns, thinking about what I've said.

Another moment of silence turns into several.

The heat in the air is cooling, Nix's shoulders slump and finally, I think she gets it.

"I'll try a bit harder not to lose it with you. But can you please tone it down?" she asks.

"Don't like your chances," I answer honestly.

"Didn't think so."

My balls are still blue. I'm desperate to unload inside her mouth, but I gotta go with what I've got.

"C'mon, Nix, let's go talk with your friend." I sigh and take Phoenix's hand in mine, tighten my fingers around hers and lead her outside toward Sarge and Milina.

"Okay," she replies as her fingers hold onto mine.

"Nix?"

"Yeah."

"I *really* want you to give me a blow job tonight." See? I can tame it down.

I hear her let out a huge sigh, followed by a small laugh.

"We'll see," she says, resigned to my more subtle ways.

I chuckle at her, and lead her outside.

SEVENTEEN

SARGE AND I HAVE AN EASY RIDE OUT TO NORTHEAST Sheds. When we arrive, there are two black SUVs already parked, telling me that Emily and company are already here.

"You ready?" I ask Sarge as he takes his helmet off and slings it over the handlebar.

"Hmmm," he answers his usual way.

"Let's hope I don't get us killed."

"Better not, I got me a girl I like," Sarge says, surprising me with his honesty.

"Nix's friend made an impression, did she?"

"Somethin' like that." A smile creeps across his face, which makes him look like a scarier fucker than he does when he looks normal.

"Alright, let's get this show started," I say, walking toward the shed's entry.

The door's open and Sarge steps through the threshold first. He holds onto his gun, ready for anything that may come to us.

"Gentleman," Emily says as she stands from the chair she was sitting on. Sarge drops his gun to his side. Beside her is a tall guy whose eyes say not to fuck with any of them, and standing behind both of them is a chick dressed all in black. She's got a shoulder holster on with two guns hanging from it near her tits, and one strapped around her thigh. Her hair's pulled back into a severe ponytail, and she's wearing dark glasses, which to me is dangerous 'cause I'm not sure where the hell she's looking.

Out of the three of 'em, the chick standing in the back feels the most menacing.

"Emily," I hold my hand out to shake hers. "This is Sarge," I say introducing him to her.

Emily takes my hand in hers and shakes it, then Sarge's.

"This is my partner, Ben," she says as she gestures over to the tall guy. He reaches out his hand to shake mine, then Sarge's.

My eyes automatically go over to the chick standing in the shadows. Silently, I ask who the hell she is.

I can't help but check her out either. She doesn't look like she'd be able to handle the three semi-automatics she has strapped to her body. She's curvy. She's got hips and tits, but the way she stands, with her back straight and her chest out, tells me I should be scared of her.

"She won't bother you, unless you bother us," Ben says, answering my question.

I look at Ben, then back to Emily. My eyes wander over to the hot chick in the back again.

"Look at me like that again, and I'll take your eyes out with the knife you're carrying in your left pocket," she says coolly, not raising her voice at all.

How the fuck does she know I have a knife in my left pocket?

Who the hell is this chick?

"15," Emily says over her shoulder.

Fuck!

Now I know who she is. She's a damn legend. I heard about that one hit she did that took a guy out from two miles away.

And I know she's beyond ruthless, a cold-hearted killer. Rumors about what she does are always floating around. I take the warning she gave me; I don't look at her again.

"Why did you call?" Emily asks as she sits in the folding chair, crossing her arms in front of her chest.

"We're looking for a new supplier," I answer and mimic her pose, while Sarge sits on the chair beside me.

Ben sits too, and leans his elbows on the table in front of him. His look is hardened, deadly. I've seen that look in men's eyes before, just before they take a swing, usually at a death match.

"We don't get involved in feuding. We won't be played off against anyone," Ben states as he looks over his shoulder to 15, essentially warning us.

My eyes travel over to the ghost standing in the back. Her posture hasn't faltered; her presence alone is intimidating.

I sit back in my seat and take a deep breath, "We just want the guns."

Sarge grunts, and nods his head in agreement.

Emily rubs her chin, and Ben's gaze holds mine.

The sheds are quiet, not a sound can be heard. The air is filled with ice. Negotiations have begun.

"90/10 split our way," Emily begins the process.

"Hmmm," Sarge counters with a roll of his eyes and a shake of his head.

"We can move a good quantity every week, for 60/40 your way."

"Bullshit," Ben says, smirking as he laces his fingers together and puts them behind his head.

"85/15, our best offer," Emily responds.

"Not gonna happen," I say as I stand and take a few steps away to light up a smoke.

"Then it looks like this meeting is over. Nice talking to you, Jaeger. When you're ready to get serious, you know how to contact me," Emily says, as I hear her chair scrape against the concrete floor.

Shit, we need the guns in order to keep going. But I don't want my club going in the direction of drugs too, and I know that the Pace family won't run drugs.

"What if..." I start saying, stopping only to take a drag on my smoke, "What if we run for a two-week trial at 85/15, and if you're happy with our work, then agree to 70/30?"

I turn to see Emily sit down on the folding chair and turn to her partner.

Nothing's said between the two of them, which gives me a moment to look at Sarge, who hasn't changed his laid-back position.

"Run a month at 85/15, and we'll meet back here in exactly thirty days. If we're happy, we'll agree to 70/30. If not..." She turns to look pointedly at 15.

I've got a feeling that if they're unhappy with us, we won't even make it the month.

At this moment, I'm not sure who exactly is more dangerous– Cain or the Pace family and 15.

I look over to Sarge. His eyes are following me as I take another deep inhale of my smoke before dropping it to the ground and stubbing it out below my boot.

"A pleasure doing business with you." I walk over to Emily and Ben as they both stand from behind the folding table.

The four of us shake hands and Emily gives me a phone.

"Keep it on you. It's our only means of communications for now. Make no mistake though, if we're brought into a dispute, we'll settle it our own way."

"Understood."

Sarge flanks me, behind and to the left, in my peripheral vision.

Emily walks out first, followed by Ben.

15 stands in the same spot, not moving, not following, just rooted in the same position. If she didn't speak earlier I'd be convinced she's a damn robot.

Sarge and I walk out and leave her, not knowing what the hell she's doing.

Ben and Emily get in the back of one of the black SUVs and I notice there's a driver in that one because the car takes off.

15 comes out of the shed, ignoring us. She gets in the other SUV

and she leaves, too.

Sarge and I are standing near our bikes, looking at the cars flying down the dirt road at high speed. Dust is flying up and soon the SUVs have disappeared into the brown cloud.

"Let's take it back to the table," I say as I get on my bike.

"Yeah," Sarge answers as he puts his helmet on and starts his bike.

I pull my phone out of my pocket and send Aaron a message, 'Table. Three hours.'

I start the bike, slipping the phone back into my pocket, and Sarge and I leave.

Riding back to the clubhouse, the quiet of the smooth road below the tires of the bike allows me to think about what might happen once we tell Cain to fuck his offer to run drugs.

When Cain initially came to me, ready to fund the club so we could run the weapons for him, Aaron and I were all for it.

The Hunters quickly developed, becoming one of the fastest growing outlaw clubs this side of the Mississippi. I run things precisely, and if a member's suspected of being a snitch, they're never seen again.

The ride is filled with my thoughts about Cain, and what the aftermath may turn out to be.

This is going to end up in a huge clusterfuck, I can just feel it in my bones. Something big is gonna happen, and I know that shit's gonna hit the fan. I just need to make sure me and my club ain't standing in front of it when it happens.

EIGHTEEN

Phoenix

WHAT THE HELL IS WRONG WITH ME?
I'm damned smart, I'm cluey, and switched on. So why the hell am I as attracted to Jaeger as I am? It doesn't make sense; we're obviously not compatible.

He's the President of a motorcycle club, which I highly doubt is a by-the-book, strait-laced club.

I'm...well, I'm me.

I don't get involved with tattooed, foul-mouthed bad boys with shaggy hair and scars on their chins.

I don't get involved with anyone. Sure I'll screw a guy I like, but after a few dates I always end up bored with them, so I break it off.

I'm far from a goody-two-shoes. I enjoy sex; I enjoy a guy paying attention to me. I don't like that whole alpha-male crap, though. Who does?

Why am I lying on Jaeger's bed, waiting, eager for him to come back from his 'club business' bullshit?

Maybe it's just the sex. It was pretty good. Ah, who am I kidding? The way that man licked my pussy and fucked me was seriously right up there with the best sex I've ever had.

I turn on my side and look at the door, hoping he'll open it, waltz in, and demand that we have sex again.

Every time he opens his mouth and says something crude, I should be angry and pissed off, but I'm not. Instead I get wet and turned on. What is up with that?

The jerk turns me on like crazy and he can certainly pin me with just the hot way he looks at me. But I can't help but think about my farm.

I want it back. I want to be living on it, without the worry of having some ass come and try to take it away from me again. Or worse, according to Jaeger, take me.

There's a heaviness in the air around the clubhouse. It's been here for a few days now, like everyone's waiting for something to happen.

Since Sandy came into the clubhouse all beaten and bruised, the dynamic in the club has changed. Not that I know what it's like ordinarily, but I felt a clear shift in the way everyone's been interacting, almost like they're waiting for some huge event to happen.

As I lie on the bed, I can hear a few of the guys in the bar area laughing and carrying on about something.

Screw staying in here. Seeing as I can't get in contact with Milina, I may as well go see what's going on out there.

I walk out to the bar area and Aaron's standing behind the bar, his arms propped against the bartop in front of him, his body leaning at a slant while his head hangs down.

Jason's playing pool with Lion and one of the other fully-bearded guys, and Sandy's sitting on a bar stool drinking something.

I round the bar to pour myself a drink, and stop myself as my eyes see the top of a bleached blonde head bobbing up and down, giving Aaron a blow job.

The moment I see her and freeze, Aaron opens his eyes and turns to look at me.

I can just imagine the look on my face. Really, she's just going down on him out here, in front of everyone.

"Sorry," I mumble and try to get out of there before I interrupt their, well...um, time together.

"You wanna taste, Nixy?" Aaron says as he smirks and weaves his fingers through the bleached blonde bunny's hair and starts thrusting his hips.

"Um, no, and it's Phoenix," I answer as I turn to leave them to it.

"If you want to suck my cock, just let me know," he says through tight grunts. "Yeah, baby, keep sucking me off," I hear him say in a lower tone as I walk away.

Pig.

Disgusting and perverted pig.

As I quickly get out of that whole strange 'let's give a guy a BJ while everyone's standing around' environment, I hear the front door open and Sarge asks for a Jack.

If Sarge is here, that means Mr. Arrogant Ass will be in here soon.

A small smile dances around my lips. I'm damn excited that he's here, but I certainly won't let on when I see him.

I'll make him work for it, bastard that he is.

I open the fridge and see a tub of potato salad on the bottom shelf that was left over from the cookout yesterday.

Bending at the waist, I lean in to get the bowl, when I see his legs behind me. Jaeger runs his hands along my hips and brings his pelvis flush with mine.

"Hmmm, I'd like to fuck you like this," he says as he thrusts once against me, emphasizing exactly what he wants to do to me.

I straighten and close the fridge door.

"Really? I thought you were supposed to be trying to calm it down." I take a step away from him and lean up against the kitchen counter, crossing my arms in front of me, in defiance of his statement.

"C'mon, sugar. This is me being subtle." He gives me a cheeky grin, the little scar on his chin making him look sexier.

"How was whatever it is you did?"

Jaeger's face falters, his cute smile drops and his eyes lower.

"Good, but I don't wanna talk about that, I just want to kiss my girl."

My girl, hmmm, caveman.

Jaeger stalks toward me, slowly. His heated gaze burns straight through me with the same intense, dark orbs that always make me melt inside.

"Nix," he says in a low voice before his mouth descends on mine. The kiss is anything but gentle. Jaeger is pushing his body into mine, his obvious hard-on pressing into the lower part of my stomach.

He's got a gentle smell of smoke clinging to his mouth; the taste travels into all my senses as my tongue and his tango together.

Jaeger's hand moves slowly from my hip, up past my ribs to tighten at the nape of my neck.

Holy shit. His fingers apply pressure as he devours my mouth. Claiming me, owning me, consuming every part of me.

Jaeger's other hand moves up to my breast as he starts to roughly grope me, kneading my breast between his fingers. He pinches my nipple through my clothes and growls into my mouth at the same time.

Why do I want this? Why am I so turned on when he's so rough with me? Is this really what I want?

"Unless you want me to fuck you here in the kitchen, get your ass into our bedroom," Jaeger whispers as he nips on my ear and pushes his body further into mine.

Damn it, why do I want to run as fast as my legs will take me into the bedroom? This isn't me. I don't do bad boys like him.

I like gentle and sweet, not rough and sweaty, all-consuming alpha men.

I turn to slowly walk toward Jaeger's room and he swats me on the ass, hard.

My body shudders as a bolt of ice rips straight up my spine. The blood pumping through my veins quickens, heating every part of my body.

"I love the way your ass moves when you walk away from me. It's got the perfect amount of bounce to it," he says from behind me.

Why not tease him? I add swagger to my hips as I walk in front of him.

The door to his room is closed and when I reach to open it, he stops me by pulling both my wrists behind my back, capturing them in his one big, warm, calloused hand and pushing me face first into the door.

His entire body is on mine as he holds me against the cool of the wood door.

Jaeger moves his hand into my jeans and straight to my pussy, I open my legs to allow his hand room to stroke me.

But he pushes a finger into me and I can't help but intake a huge breath followed by a small groan.

Christ, he feels so good as he proceeds to finger me.

"You're fucking beautiful, and so damn turned on. If I pull your jeans down right now, you'd probably let me fuck this hot ass of yours, wouldn't you, sugar?" Jaeger licks my neck and sucks the exposed sensitive skin into his mouth.

"Hmmm," is all I can say or think as he keeps fingering me right here in the hallway outside his bedroom.

He's everywhere, beautifully overtaking me, all parts of his body touching every part of mine.

"Do you want me to fuck this ass?" he asks as he drives his clothed body and erect cock against me, continuing to finger my sex.

"God, yes," I moan as I push back, trying to get that burning hot friction between us.

"Only I'm to touch your cunt or any other part of your body," he hungrily growls as he licks my jaw.

Shit!

Why does he turn me on so much?

His finger is soon joined by a second; I let out a small sigh of satisfaction as I grind down on his attacking digits. He feels so good as his assault on me begins to intensify. He adds his thumb to my clit in slow meticulous circles as he continues to finger-fuck me out here in the open.

"J, man," Aaron, or someone calls from somewhere. What am I even thinking?

"Fuck off," he spits over his shoulder, but keeps his fierce hold on my wrists while his hand down my pants gives me what I'm craving.

"I'm the only man who'll ever touch you again."

With my arms restrained behind my back, and all the sensations coursing through my body, I can't help but to simply submit to the intense ecstasy that Jaeger gives me.

"Say it. Tell me you understand," he says, claiming me.

"I understand," I cry between short bursts of air.

"I want to hear you say it." He lets my wrists go, weaves his fingers into my hair and tugs it to the side, exposing my neck to him. "I need to hear you say the words, Nix." Jaeger licks the column of my throat before sucking on my earlobe. "You're so fucking wet, so ready for me to screw you. Tell me what I want to hear so I can bend you over the bed and ram my cock into your needy cunt."

"Stop talking, just fuck me," I barely manage to say.

"Hands flat on the door, either side of your head," he demands. And I obey.

My blood is violently pounding through me, I can feel the powerful rush as it speeds along my veins, heating me with a heavenly desire.

"Tell me, or I stop and won't give you that release you're chasin'."

Damn him, he's reading every frenzied sign my body is giving him, but I don't want to tell him that only *his* hands will ever touch me again. I don't want to admit to him that only *his* mouth will lick my sex, only *his* tongue will lap at my nipples.

No, I don't want to say those words. Because once I do, then I'll have to acknowledge that I actually like the dumb-ass, macho-man crap he does.

"You don't want to come, sugar? That's fine by me." He lets go of my hair, pulls his other hand out of my jeans, and before I even have a chance to miss his warmth and his contact, I grab onto his hand that was deep inside me.

"Don't go," I say as I turn my head, resigned to the fact that I enjoy him and his stupid ways.

Jaeger steps back, his arousal so obvious, his deep brown eyes are famished, and the only food that will satisfy his craving is me.

"Only you," I mumble, hoping that's enough to keep him happy.

He takes that one step toward me, and pushes me against the door. His entire body blankets my own, covering me in a hot, protective way.

"I'm good enough to fuck you, but not good enough for you to say the words I want to hear?"

What?

"No!" I cry, "that's not it."

"Tell me why I should give you my cock if you don't want the man attached?"

"I..." What do I say? What can I say?

"You what?" he licks my neck again, teasing me with the pleasure that waits if I just tell him that I won't let another man ever touch me again.

"I'm the flavor of month. I'm the thirty-three percent that normally says no, I'm nothing more than a challenge to you. When a sixty-six percent girl walks through those doors, you'll forget about me and go to her."

"Is that what you think to protect yourself?"

"It's true, Jaeger. I've seen the women that hang around here, the way they hang off your every word, giggle at you like a school girl when we go to supermarket. And you want me to believe that I'm anything more than a lay? A screw? I'm just fresh meat that's a challenge because I fight you every time you open your mouth."

Jaeger steps away, leaving me to peel myself off the door and turn to face him.

"Tell me it's not true, tell me all the crap you say to me, you've never said before," I challenge him, straightening my shoulders as I'm zipping my jeans.

He snorts and rolls his eyes at me. "It's the furthest thing from the truth," he says as he crosses his arms in front of his tight strong chest. "I told you I'd never lie to you."

"Whatever." Liar, how dare he tell me he hasn't used that dirty mouth to seduce other women.

I turn the door handle to his room, enter, and try to shut it behind me. I just need to clear my head, away from Jaeger.

"You don't get to run in here and close the door on me. We're doing the whole bullshit girly thing of 'talking'." He air quotes and screws his nose up.

"If it's so painful to do it, leave." I sit on the bed.

"I've screwed girls, and I don't give a shit about them. But I've wanted you from the first moment I saw you. I've wanted to get my mouth on your pussy and stay there for life. The first night I saw you, I just wanted to fuck you, and I've often thought of you while I'm screwing other chicks."

The first time he saw me?

What the hell!?

I turn to look at Jaeger who's sitting on the arm chair in his room. I feel my brows knit together and my lips purse into a thin line.

"What are you talking about?" I ask.

"You really have no idea, do you?" he asks.

No idea about what?

NINETEEN

PAIN IN THE **G**OD DAMN ASS.

That's what Phoenix is, and what she'll always be—a damned pain in the ass.

"Yeah. I saw you years ago, and I've wanted you ever since."

I watch her reaction, and it's one of pure confusion. Her eyebrows are drawn down together and she's biting on her lip as she just stares at me, almost blankly.

"What?" she finally asks after a long minute of silence.

"Years ago, I saw you and I wanted you."

"Yeah, I get that, but where did you see me?" She draws her legs up and hugs her knees, obviously protecting herself from what she thinks I may say.

"It was a fight. You were with some older guy, clinging to him, and looking frightened as hell. The fear you had, the way you were looking so innocent and scared, it turned me on. The other guy got a punch in, which is the only way I dragged my eyes away from you."

Phoenix's mouth falls open, and I see a shiver rip through her as her shoulders begin to shake. Emotions flash across her face in quick succession. Horror, surprise, then understanding, but the one emotion I didn't want her to feel is the final one I see. Fear.

She scoots back on the bed until her back is at the headboard and she's as far away from me as she can possibly be.

"I remember. I freaked out and made my uncle take me home." She pauses, her face tellin' me she's thinkin' about it. "You killed him," she says in a tiny whisper. She looks shocked and clearly disturbed.

"Yeah, sugar, I did," I say softly.

Phoenix looks away from me, not wanting, or maybe not willing to meet my eyes any longer.

"You killed him," she repeats in an even smaller voice.

"Yeah."

"You killed him."

"Yeah."

"You've killed a person."

"People," I correct her.

"*People*?" Her eyes slowly find mine. She's shaking all over now, and retreating further into herself.

I stand from the chair, and take a step toward her. Phoenix's eyes go straight to my feet and with the next step, she tries to melt into the headboard of the bed.

"I'll never hurt you, Nix." I hold my hands up, showing her that I'm not the monster she saw that night.

"You're a murderer," she sighs as I watch her beautiful face pale with tears spilling from her eyes.

"I am," I admit.

I take another careful step toward her, and she cringes and pulls in a sharp breath.

"I won't hurt you, but you have to let me near you."

She's shaking her head, not believing a word I'm saying.

Like a wounded, frightened kitten, she balls into herself further, refusing to believe in me, in us.

"Nix, all I want to do is protect you. I'll kill any motherfucker who puts their hands on you. But I'll never lay an unwanted finger on you."

GRIT

Her eyes are red and tears fall, clinging to her cheeks.

Her vulnerability and fear are so beautiful and sexy. She's everything I've never thought I deserved and every time she's near me, I just want her.

I have an insatiable need to be inside her, to be with her and to protect her.

It's crazy and stupid. I shouldn't want her like I do. She's right about one thing. She's way too good for me and for this life.

But I'm far from selfless and noble. I'm an egocentric, narcissistic, self-centered prick, and I want her all for myself. I'm not sharing her, ever, with anyone. And if she thinks she has a choice in the matter, she has another thing coming. I'll keep her here until she finally realizes that we're meant to be in this fucked up thing called life together.

With me at the helm, always protecting the only good thing that's ever happened to me–her.

"Nix," I say as I take another step toward her. She whimpers and shakes her head at me to stop my progression toward her. "Phoenix, if I wanted to hurt you, I already would have, so stop this immature, bullshit behavior and look at me."

"Immature," she shrieks and jumps off the bed.

There she is. My wild tiger is back.

"Yeah, immature. You're acting like me killin' somebody is the worst thing you've ever heard."

"Do you even hear yourself? You've killed before!" she says, angry.

"Yeah I have, and I'd do it again. I'd do almost anything to protect you."

Her look changes from angry to questioning as she put her hands on her hips. "Why?"

"I don't know. But I'll do anything for you. You're…" I try and find the right word, any word that I can use to describe what's going on inside my fucked-up, deviant, black mind.

"What am I?" she asks, less angry but still confused.

"I don't know. I just have a need to protect you from anythin' or anyone that can hurt you."

"You can hurt me," she drops her chin to chest and starts crying again.

"Never," I say with authority and force. "I'll never hurt you. I'd cut off my own arm before I'll raise it in anger to you."

I close the distance between us, and pull her into a hug.

She's rigid and cold, I'm pretty sure she doesn't believe anything I'm saying.

"I don't know how to feel about you," she quietly admits.

I wrap my body tighter around hers, not giving her a chance to escape. Slowly, I feel the rigidity leaving her.

"What do you mean?"

"You're not what I ever thought I wanted. You're arrogant, an asshole, an alpha male, and I don't go for those types."

A chuckle reverberates through my body. An alpha male. What a stupid-ass description. Alpha males don't exist. There are only men with balls and men that are pussies.

"Then you've been going for the wrong sort of man, because obviously, I'm the right one for you."

"But you've killed," she says, holding onto whatever she can so she can justify to herself why she shouldn't be here.

"Yeah, and I've never claimed to be a good man. But I'll be the best I can for you."

"Can you promise me not to kill anyone?"

"No can do, sugar. I can only promise you that I'll never cause you any pain."

She melts into me, and her hands go to my hips. It's like she's still unsure of me. I suppose if the guy you've been sleeping with tells you he's killed before and will kill again, it's a pretty big thing for a woman to wrap her mind around.

"Nix, this is who I am. It's who I've always been, and who I always will be. I haven't lied to you or told you something just to shut you up. There are things I can't tell you, but only because I don't want you in danger."

"But I'm in danger being here with you," she says as she moves closer into my chest.

"You'll always be safe when you're close to me, and any of these guys," I say as I point out toward the bar, "they'll protect you too." Nix's nose screws up, but her eyes have cleared of the tears that were falling.

"I don't know, Jaeger. It's tearing me apart. I just need some time to think about all of this."

She's right. This lifestyle is a bit hard to handle, especially if you've never been around it before.

"What's happening with my farm?" she asks, hopeful that I have good news.

"I was supposed to go to the bank and pay out what your dad owed, but I had to push it back 'cause of some other things. The bank manager is coming out here in two days with the paperwork."

"So that's it? It's gone, just like that?" She lays her head on my chest again and I can feel the vibration of quiet sobs as she tries to come to terms with it.

"Yeah, that's it. It's going to be mine by the end of the week."

More silence passes between us. Nothing is said and nothing needs to be said.

Phoenix breaks the quiet, "I need to find a job and somewhere to stay."

"You're not going anywhere. But you can get a job."

Her back straightens and I feel an impending argument.

"You'll let me have a job?" Yep, she's pissed.

"Yeah, you can get a job, I'm cool with that."

Nix steps away from me. And so it starts again. Oddly, I'm relieved.

"*Let* me? Seriously, you think you can stop me?"

"Uhhh, yeah."

"You're a dick!" she yells and takes another step away.

"Why are you moving away from me? I wanna fuck you."

"Go away!" she shouts again. "You're an arrogant ass."

"I already told you I was."

She rubs her hands over her face, then trails them through her red mane.

"Seriously, Jaeger, you said you'd tone it down."

Tone what down? What the hell's the problem this time?

"You don't need to work. I'll support you."

Shit, I think that was the wrong thing for me to say. Phoenix's face changes into a demonic, angry scowl. She grinds her teeth together, her hands ball up into fists, and her entire body is shaking as her eyes widen with red-hot fury burning in them.

"Give me your damn phone so I can call Milina to come get me, you selfish..." She's trembling with rage, and she's trying to spit something out, but she looks like she's struggling.

"Arrogant asshole? Dickhead? Cocky bastard? Smug prick? Controlling idiot? Which one of those do you wanna call me, sugar?" I help her along, in case she's truly stuck.

Her mouth opens, closes, opens again, then closes.

"Fuuuuuuck!" she yells. "I hate you!" she screams.

"No you don't."

"I do. How dare you!"

"Whatever. Anyway, if you want to get a job I'm alright with that, but you're not leaving. Here," I take my phone out of my pocket and throw it on the bed, "call Milina and plan a trip into town tomorrow. Go get that shit done that girls get, you know that feet and hand crap and whatever else you want. I'll pay for you two to go do girly stuff. I'm going to get you a phone of your own, but when I come back, I want you naked so I can fuck you."

I turn to walk out of the room and Phoenix snorts, I'm pretty sure, sarcastically.

"So romantic," she says as I open the door and walk down the hallway.

"I never said I was," I say loud enough for her to hear me.

TWENTY

Phoenix

"Here," Jaeger says as he throws a box on the bed. I look at it and it's a cell phone. "Number's on the side of the box. It's charged and ready to go. Why are you still dressed?"

I look down at the box, then back at Jaeger who's already got his t-shirt off. The ink all over his body is intricate and woven all together, though they're still all separate pieces.

"That really got me in the mood," I say as I pick the box up and open it, taking out the cell phone.

"You were in the mood and ready to let me fuck you against the door outside an hour ago. Now the door's shut and I wanna screw you in here."

He's so damn frustrating, so confusing, so annoying...just so.....grrrr.

"What's the problem? You're not wet?" He toes off his boots then unbuckles his belt, getting ready to have sex with me...or probably, without me.

"You aren't doing anything for me just standing there." I wave my hand from his head down to his feet, "And really, after your little revelation, I don't think I'm in the mood for sex."

"What, that I've killed people?"

I take a deep breath and feel myself sigh.

Yeah, about that…how do I handle the responsibility of knowing that the man that I'm with has murdered people, and has admitted that he's capable of doing it again.

"Nix, it's something you'll have to learn to live with. It is what it is. The people I've killed were there knowing that the fight could go either way."

I lower my gaze, not really knowing where to look or how to react. A normal woman wouldn't even be in this position to start with.

But who am I kidding? Normal isn't something I've ever grown up with.

My mother died in a carjacking gone wrong, which left my father to look after me. He never wanted a girl to begin with. He only wanted a boy, which is where my name, Dillon, comes from.

From a young age, I fell in love with the concept and the look of the phoenix, and refused to answer unless I was addressed as Phoenix or Nix.

After Mom died, Dad turned to drinking, which soon turned to drinking and gambling. Then he dropped the drinking and went harder with the gambling. He neglected the farm, which was passed down from his grandfather to Granddad to Dad, to, well…it should've been mine.

But Dad gambled it away, as he did my mother's jewelry, the cattle we had, his car, and everything else of value that wasn't bolted to the ground.

"Nix," Jaeger says, bringing me out of the heavy headspace I just travelled to.

"Yeah."

"Let's go take a shower. There's some club business I gotta get to in about an hour, but for now I just want to have a shower with you. You can wash me, 'cause I want your hands all over me. I'll settle for you to jack me off, sugar."

"Is there any chance at all you can curb your desire?"

GRIT

"I bet you're getting wet again, so why would I stop?" He shrugs his shoulders while taking off the rest of his clothes.

"A losing war," I mumble as I walk toward the bathroom and start to take my clothes off. Truth is, he's sexy as anything and when he does say those things, they mostly do turn me on.

Which brings me back to the question, *why*?

I'm pretty sure that I've known all along what kind of person Jaeger really is, but I had pushed it down to a place that's so far buried it would never see the light of day again.

But after being here only a handful of days, a spotlight has been shined on it. Every bulb lit to its fullest wattage, burning with such heat and intensity that I can't look away from it now.

Jaeger is, and will always be, someone scary. He's someone I should heed my mind's warnings about–warnings as clear as those in every horror movie, every book with a villain–and just run.

But also in these few days, something else has happened, and I sort of like him. My body enjoys him while my mind scrambles to make sense of the situation I'm in and fight this growing attraction.

His alpha male ways make me crazy. I fight with myself every time he opens his mouth. My brain tells me to be disgusted. But my body becomes highly charged, craving his words, and worse still, needing his touch.

"You don't get that ass in here in the next five seconds; I'm going to bend you over the vanity and fuck you hard."

I hear the sound of the running water pelting on the tiled floor in the shower, and know that Jaeger will already have his cock in hand, waiting for me.

Stepping into the shower, I'm greeted with a very excited Jaeger, washing his hard, toned, and quite delicious body.

"Wash my back," Jaeger says as he thrusts a cake of soap into my hands.

He turns his back and leans his arms up on the wall as the hot water cascades down his body. His head is lowered and I catch a glimpse of his face. His eyes are closed and his mouth is open.

"Just touch me, Nix," he says, his voice low, almost like he's on edge, begging.

I run the soap over his shoulders and instantly Jaeger relaxes into my touch, his head falling forward.

Although the water is pounding down on our bodies, I see the scars on his back, neck and shoulders. They're small, light in color. Older wounds.

Fascinated by his marked body, I temporarily stop washing him, tracing a finger along the longest scar that runs from his shoulder blade down to his mid-ribs. The tattoos on his body cover a lot of his wounds, but seeing him in the shower, completely relaxed gives me the chance to study them and see just how many he has.

"How did you get this one?" I ask as I run my finger from tip to tip.

Jaeger shudders, though he keeps his head down while he answers, "Fight. The guy had a knife. I thought he was down, so I walked away. When I heard him grunting, I turned to look over my shoulder, and I caught the tail end of the knife. I was lucky though, 'cause he would've punctured a lung if I hadn't turned."

Softly I kiss the scar, just touching the angry line.

"That feels nice."

Nice? Did Jaeger just say a word that normal men would use?

"How about this one?" I ask as I kiss his neck and start to soap his back again.

"Aaron," he says through a small moan.

"Aaron did it?"

"Yeah, we were fuckin' around, had a fight to let off some steam and he cracked a beer bottle. Thought he could cut me with it."

I move my hands down to his tight ass, soaping up his muscly, hard butt.

"Do you do shit like that often?" I ask as I flatten my body against his back. My breasts are pushing into him and my sex is rubbing on him.

Jaeger's left arm reaches behind him to clasp my ass, and he squeezes me closer to him, holding me flat against his body.

"Whenever we need to get shit out of our systems. It's what we do."

"Is that right?" I ask, nipping his earlobe into my mouth, slowly sucking, then flicking it with my tongue.

"God yes, keep your mouth on me."

I put the soap back on the soap holder and move my arms to hug him from behind.

With my front flush against Jaeger's back, I move my hands to his rigid, firm chest. My thumbs find his nipples, starting to tease them. I duck down and lick up his spine, from mid-back all the way up to his neck.

"You feel fantastic on me, Nix."

"I'm not on you, but I can be if you want me to be," I whisper in his ear, as my fingers continue to play and torment his nipples.

"I want you every way I can have you. But right now, I want you on your knees, I'm close to coming, and I want my cum in your mouth." Jaeger hasn't turned around. He's still facing the wall with his head down.

"Is that all you want from me? Just to fuck my mouth?" With soapy hands, I reach down to his firm, stiff cock, taking it in my hand and squeezing, applying pressure to it.

With deep, slow, tight movements, I stroke from tip to base.

"What are your doing to me?" he moans with desire and want.

I grip harder, as I keep my hands sliding along the length of his cock.

"Making you want me," I answer.

Jaeger's moaning, his breath coming in short, rapid bursts as he thrusts his hips into my hand.

"Tsk, tsk, tsk, no you don't," I say leaning further into his body.

"On your knees, now," he almost hollers at me.

"No," I reply, cockily.

My fingers tighten around his shaft, and I pull with force then slide my hand back down.

The heat in the shower is stifling. Jaeger's control is almost gone, and I love dominating this moment.

Jaeger abruptly turns, his hands on my shoulders as he pushes me down to my knees.

"That mouth has done too much talking. Time I fill it with my cock. Open up and take everything I give you."

Holy shit, the dirty, arrogant ass has just turned the heat up to scorching. The water has rinsed the soap away and his wet cock glistens in front of me.

I purse my lips together and give him an 'eat shit' cheeky smile.

"Open that argumentative mouth," he demands. "I'll fucking drag you out of here, blindfold you, and tie you to my god damn bed if you don't open that mouth of yours right now."

Christ, can I get any wetter?

I open my mouth and wait for his rock-hard cock to slide into my mouth.

He slips his hard-on deep past my lips. I keep my mouth open, not moving, not sucking or licking.

"Fuck me with your mouth, Nix. And make it a blow job I'll never forget."

Yes, sir!

He pushes in as far as he can go, and my gag reflex overtakes my throat. The head of his cock is touching the back of my throat; I try to pull away but Jaeger laces his fingers through my drenched hair and holds my head in place.

"I said for you to fuck me, not make love to my cock."

Screw you, idiot!

I suck on his knob, just teasing the head with my tongue, dipping into his slit, then trace the knob. Grazing the tip with my teeth, I bite down with just enough pressure to be on the painful side.

"Yeah, that's it."

I look up through the falling water and Jaeger has his head slightly back and his eyes closed, while his hands are tangled in my hair and his hips are moving in small thrusts toward my face.

GRIT

Knowing that sucking on a guy's balls drives them crazy, I move my head and lick the underside of his ball sac, my nose buried deep between his balls as my mouth licks the sensitive skin that's desperate for my touch.

"Hmmm," Jaeger moans and pushes my head further into his sac. I smile because he can't hide what he wants me to do to him.

Sucking his balls into my mouth, I keep alternating between flicking and licking with my tongue. My hands go to Jaeger's ass and pull him closer to me, getting more of him in my mouth.

"Get my cock in your mouth," he groans as his fingers loosen his grip so I can move to fully envelop him.

Greedily, I taste the pre-cum that's only just clinging to his slit before the spray of the shower can wash it away.

Salty, thick cum. He coats my tongue with the small drops I taste.

"Don't you dare waste a drop. I want you to drink every last bit I give you."

God damn it, stop talking and fuck my mouth.

I grab onto his ass and drive him further into my mouth, he hits the back of my throat and although I feel like I'm going to vomit, I hold it together. How women relax their throats, I have no idea.

Jaeger thrusts further into my mouth. The feeling is horrible because I'm gagging, yet it's strangely erotic and a total turn-on.

He pulls out and greedily plunges back in, pulling my head further down onto his cock. Impaling me, fucking my face, using me.

Tears are spilling from the corners of my eyes with every lunge as he forcefully drives himself into my mouth.

I love it, yet I hate it. The gagging is almost too much; his cock is touching every part of my throat. My lips are stretched to their limit as my tongue tries to keep up with the huge foreign object assaulting my mouth.

"Hmmm," I moan, totally turned on. I drop my right hand from Jaeger's ass and snake it down to my pussy, spreading my lips to find my needy clit, ready to be touched.

With two fingers I apply hard pressure to it, rubbing it in circles, just the way I like it.

"Don't you fuckin' touch yourself, Nix. Make sure I get off, then I'll look after you. I'm so close, keep fuckin' me."

I remove my hand as quick as I can, putting it back to Jaeger's ass.

My tongue twirls around Jaeger's cock, as I hungrily suck. Jaeger pushes harder into me.

This feels all sorts of wrong, but so illicitly right too.

I ravish his cock with my mouth; teasing, capturing, biting. Jaeger's hips speed up, his long shaft thumping as he keeps pushing and burying it further into me.

"Hmmm," I moan again.

"I'm coming," Jaeger lets out a strangled moan, while his hips go full speed.

His cum spurts down my throat, thick and salty. I almost lose it, but manage to swallow it all down in one huge gulp.

"Sugar," he says, smiling as he pulls out of my mouth and lifts me from my knees. "That mouth of yours is gonna be kept real busy."

I smile at his 'subtle' ways, and feel my lips tingling, almost numb from his treatment of them. My knees ache from kneeling on the tiled shower floor, but I feel damn sexy knowing that I just brought Jaeger to climax with a blow job.

Jaeger turns the water off and gets out, grabs a large red towel, and holds it out for me.

"What are you doing? I can dry myself," I say as I step into the towel.

Jaeger doesn't say anything. Instead he goes about drying my body. Carefully, he starts with my shoulders, then down my arm. The towel is soaking up the water, absorbing it as Jaeger keeps toweling my upper body.

He gets to my breasts and when the softness of the towel touches my nipples, I almost moan aloud. As he rubs the material over my right breast, he scratches at the nipple and pinches it through the fabric.

He repeats it, harder and his head lowers and takes my left breast in his lips.

"Oh shit," I say as I arch my chest and push my breast further in his eager, warm mouth.

Jaeger moves the towel down to my pussy and begins to rub the edge of the towel over my sensitive outer lips.

"Let it go, I've got you," he says as he straightens his back and holds me in his arms.

He opens my lips and finds my sensitive, desperate clit, aching to be fondled by him...or the towel.

My hips begin to move back and forth as the cotton of the towel grazes me with increasing pressure.

Being depraved of an orgasm in the shower has heightened all my senses as Jaeger rubs the towel over my wanton sex.

"Do you like this?" he whispers in my ear.

I can't answer; I can't think. I just moan.

Heat is pounding through my veins, my heart's hammering inside my chest and a fountain of emotions is bubbling deep inside my stomach.

"Yeah, babe. Fuck my hand. I love how you move."

My eyes are closed, and all I'm hearing is my labored breath and Jaeger's sexy words.

"Kiss me," he says.

Before I have a chance to open my eyes, his mouth is on mine. His kiss is drowning me, and overtaking everything I'm holding on to.

Jaeger's hand speeds up, his mouth consumes me, his body is grinding up against mine.

He's everywhere, all over me, inside me, taking what he wants.

Giving me everything I need.

My emotions are just on the brink of rapture, my senses on overload as I become hypersensitive to everything close to me.

Jaeger's subtle tobacco scent forces its way into my nose, mixing with his natural aroma.

The sexy groans coming from both of us tease my sense of hearing, making me crave him more.

Jaeger's touch is blistering hot. My skin becomes a raging inferno as his body devours mine.

"I'm so close," I sigh in the smallest of voices, barely loud enough to reach my own ears.

"That's it, keep rubbing this beautiful cunt on me." Suddenly, Jaeger lets the towel go and drops to his knees. His mouth violently attacks my sex. He doesn't stop, frantically curling his tongue to reach inside my core.

"Ohhh!" I yell as I grind my sex onto his mouth, my release so powerful that my legs shake and I start to collapse to the floor.

Jaeger's arms dart out and catch me before I can fall. He swoops me up into a tight embrace and walks us out to his bed.

He pulls the covers back and sits me on the edge of the mattress.

"Hang on," he says as he ducks back into the bathroom.

He comes back with a different color towel and begins to run it through my hair, taking the moisture out of it.

"What are you doing?" I ask as I reach up to dry my own hair.

"I told you, I'll take care of you." He smacks my hands away.

I close my eyes and let him towel dry my hair, relaxing into this sense of comfort.

"Why are you doing this?" I ask, almost frightened to hear the answer.

"Because I'm not just a monster, I'm also a man."

Jaeger has never given me the impression that he's the sweet, caring type. But right now he's looking after me and treating me with the utmost respect.

Can Jaeger be the man I need?

TWENTY-ONE

TODAY'S GONNA BE A FUCKED-UP DAY. I NEED TO CALL CAIN AND LET HIM know the decision that the table made late last night.

What a clusterfuck that was. Four of the members didn't want to go against Cain, and we spent hours at the table hashing it all out. By the end of the night, we'd all agreed that we needed to cut the connection with Cain.

My major issue with him is the way he's strong-arming us and dictating what the club should do. He wants us to help him with drugs, but who says he'll stop there? He could take us into human trafficking, people smuggling, or kiddie porn. The underworld is huge. Once they experience the taste of money, the greed becomes overwhelming. And such an intense desire usually ends in carnage.

We've managed to remain off the radars of most law enforcement agencies, and that's exactly how I want to keep it.

Phoenix moves back, wiggling her ass against my morning wood.

God, she feels so good against me. Her body is so warm and soft, and I like the fact that she goes to sleep with me each night and wakes up in my bed every morning.

"Hey," she says without turning.

"Hey," I reply and thrust my hips against her ass, silently telling her that I'm going to screw her before she even thinks about starting her day.

"Hmmm," she moans. I move my hand up to her tit and pull on her nipple. She's so responsive, I know she fights this attraction we have, but her body never lies.

Every time I finger her pussy, she's drenched before I even start doing anything. And when I go down on her, damn, her taste, her smell, and her moves drive me crazy.

Speaking of going down on her, I'd love to tongue her wet pussy right this minute. She's got the sweetest tasting cum I've ever had.

"Babe," I say as I move to kiss her shoulder.

"No," she answers flatly.

Yeah, right, I'm not buying it. Especially seeing as she's trying to conceal those sexy little noises she makes when I pull on her nipples.

"Babe," I say again and lick from her shoulder down to her elbow.

"No." I can hear defiance in her voice now.

Moving my hand slowly away from her tits, I casually snake my fingers toward her pussy.

"God, no," she groans. She's gotta be fighting with that stubborn-ass brain of hers again.

My fingers feel the small amount of hair covering her pussy and I part her lips and go straight for her clit.

"Hmmm, oh, um."

"You've lost this battle, babe. Open your legs and let me lick your pretty little cunt."

Nix turns on her back and I automatically maneuver so I'm hovering over her.

"No, Jaeger." She pushes me off her and slips out of bed and into the bathroom.

She closes the door, but since I kicked it in the other night, the thing doesn't latch shut properly.

"Hey, what the hell's going on?" I ask as I stand and follow her to the bathroom.

"Nothing," she answers, though she sounds like she's crying. What's wrong with women? They freaking cry and then go all silent on us. What am I supposed to think? She said nothing's wrong with her, well, then I guess there's nothing wrong with her.

I put on a t-shirt and jeans and leave her and her 'nothing' alone.

Screw getting into the minds of chicks. They're seriously fucked up.

Throw a punch, for Christ's sake. They'd feel better if they just pounded someone. Then they could walk away and forget about it.

That's what men do.

When I walk into the kitchen, Sarge is sitting at the table and Aaron's opposite him. Both are having coffee, not saying a word to each other.

A normal morning.

I flick my head back at them, and they repeat the gesture.

I pour a cup of coffee for myself and get a mug for Nix too. Pouring one for her, I walk it into our room and see she's still in the bathroom.

"Coffee," I yell through the door that's pushed shut, but not latched.

"Thanks," I hear Nix faintly say.

Turning, I leave and go to find the boys.

"Where's Jason?" I ask, looking between Aaron and Sarge.

"Don't know," Aaron replies.

"Nix is going into town with Milina and I want him with them."

"I'll go," Sarge says, a little too eager.

"Babysitting a couple of women now, eh?" I say as I sit at one of the spare chairs and look at Sarge.

"Going to get new ink anyway. I can take 'em." He stands and walks away.

"What's that about?" Aaron asks me.

I shrug my shoulders, "Ask him."

"Thanks for the coffee, I'm just going to call Milina and see how far away she is," Phoenix says as she puts her coffee cup in the sink and turns to walk out of the kitchen.

I catch her by the wrist and bring her back to sit on my lap.

"What the hell's going on?" I ask as I smooth her hair away from her face.

Nix lifts her eyes to quickly look at Aaron then to me. "Nothing. Can I call Milina now?"

"Sure thing." I release her from my knee and she walks away looking like shit.

"What's going on there?" Aaron asks as he moves his head to indicate Nix.

I shrug my shoulders again; "Ask her," I say as I chuckle.

Aaron lets out a laugh and stands, "I think Sarge should stay here in case Cain comes out."

He's got a point, but at this stage I doubt Cain will want that, I think once I tell him, he'll send his men around to take us out. Or at the very least, hurt us by taking only one or two out.

"Just leave him," I say as I flick my wrist at him in a dismissive manner.

"Your call." Aaron leaves the kitchen, and seconds later Nix walks in with half a smile on her face.

"Milina will be here soon, I don't know what time I'll be back."

"Sarge is coming with you." Nix rolls her eyes and her shoulders slump when I tell her. "He's getting ink so he won't hang around with you, but make sure you take your phone."

"Yeah, fine." Her attitude turns icy again and she moves to step away.

"Phoenix," I say, but she continues to ignore me. "Nix," I say a little louder, because she's now left the kitchen and has walked away from me. Damn, she's fucking annoying. "RED!" I bellow, knowing this'll piss her off.

It works like a charm. She comes charging in, her face ashen with anger, her eyes wild with the need to smack me one.

"I told you I don't like that."

"Act like a spoiled bitch and that's what you'll get called. Sit your ass down and tell me what the hell is wrong with you this morning."

"Nothing."

"'Nothin', my ass."

"It's just..." She sits in the chair opposite me and slumps against the back. Her resolve evaporates.

"What? And don't give me bullshit. I fucking hate liars."

Her eyes look up from the gaze she had focused on the floor, her blue orbs are full of tears and her mouth is turned down at the corners. She looks so sad.

"I miss my farm."

I fold my arms across my chest and lean back in the chair.

"Is that it?" I ask, almost dismissing her mood for what it really is, nothing.

"Is that it?" she repeats my words back to me.

I can see a tiny bit of spark coming back into her, like the temper she displayed when I called her Red.

"Yeah, is that it?"

"You don't get it, do you?"

Get what? I don't think I'll ever understand women, even if I live to be a hundred years old.

"Explain it to me." Not that I really wanna hear it, but if it's enough to upset my girl, then I probably should pretend to care.

"I miss *home*," she says as she brings her hands up to her face to hide behind them.

"Are you kidding me? I thought something serious was going on."

"You're a jerk," she says as I watch her shoulders shudder and her body vibrate. Obviously she's crying.

"So you keep telling me. But seriously, Nix, is that it?"

She looks up at me, and I think I said something wrong 'cause she looks M.A.D. Incredibly angry.

"You're a dick," she yells and stands to her feet with her hands on her hips, trying to intimidate me.

"Whatever, but if that's the only issue you have, then you really don't have any problems."

"I miss my home, and I want my farm. I want to leave here and go back," she says as she sweeps her right hand, indicating the clubhouse.

"It's too dangerous. Not gonna happen."

"Just let me go back."

"Nope," I say, picking my coffee up and drinking some.

She swipes the mug out of my hand and the hot coffee spills out of the mug as the cup smashes against the fridge, breaking on impact.

"I want to go home."

"Nope," I say again, looking at the coffee cup that's been smashed into pieces.

"I hate you!" she yells as she storms out of the kitchen, like a teenager having a temper tantrum.

"No you don't," I say loud enough for her, though with a lot of humor to my voice.

Sarge walks into the kitchen and looks between the coffee all over the fridge door, the smashed porcelain on the ground and me, chuckling.

"That went well," he says and lets his own laughter rip from his lips. "Heard her shrieking like a banshee out in the yard."

"She wants to go home." I rub my hands over my eyes and try to relax, but knowing she's pissed isn't great for me.

"Women are different," Sarge says with a shrug.

"Tell me about it."

"Sometimes it's best to shut the fuck up and not fight 'em." Sarge sits in the chair that Nix was sitting in.

"You pussy-whipped?" I ask as I feel my eyebrows draw together in question.

"Hmmm." He reverts back to normal Sarge. "Women wanna be told what to do, but you need to make it look like it's their idea."

"That's fucked. She should just do what I say and be happy with it."

Sarge shakes his head. "She's right, you're a dick."

I look at Sarge and he shrugs his shoulders, nonchalantly.

"C'mon wise man, share your many years of wisdom with me," I taunt him in a fake voice.

"Make her think it's a bad idea to go back there. Don't tell her, just fucking drop hints and shit like that."

Huh, drop hints. Sure I can do that. Although it's easier for me to just tell her she's not going and for her to listen without throwing a tantrum.

"We're ready," Nix says as she and Milina step into the kitchen.

Milina's looking very cute. I'd definitely like to see her and Nix go down on each other while I watch. These two would be hot as hell in a 69 position. Nix on top, sitting on Milina's face, driving her hips into her face. I wonder if Milina waxes.

I go to open my mouth to ask her, but for some reason I think that may piss Nix off even more. But hey, doesn't every chick want to please her man? And watching Nix lick Milina's cunt would definitely make me happy.

"Hmmm," Sarge murmurs, but this time the sound's more strangled then it has ever been.

Damn, Sarge has it bad for Milina. Maybe he's thinking the same thing I am. He better not be thinking of my girl like that, I'll fucking smash his face in.

"I can drive us. You don't have to waste your day with us," Milina says to Sarge.

His eyes pop open wide, and I notice right then how bad he has it. Pussy-whipped wimp. I chuckle at him and shake my head.

"You're no fucking better," he quips and stands to take the girls into town. "I'm taking you," he says to Milina.

She turns to leave and I notice he puts his hand to the small of her back, guiding her out of the room.

There's an age difference between them, but hey, who am I to judge? If they like each other and she can get him hard, then I'm all for it.

Mind you, a little taste of her and Nix together...

"Hey, Dark's not answering. I'm gonna take off and see where the fucker is," Aaron says, interrupting my Nix/Milina fantasy.

"Yeah, whatever," I reply and go right back to thinking about a spread-legged Nix, with Milina eagerly licking her as she fingers her own pussy.

··✥··

"I hear there's trouble brewing down your end," Emily says into the phone.

"Not to my knowledge." I look at the phone to see what time it is, and notice that the girls have been gone for two and a half hours. Aaron hasn't returned either, and I haven't heard from Dark all morning.

"If we step in, you're not going to like the consequences," she says, her tone one of warning.

"No need. There's no trouble here." I tap my finger on the wooden meeting table and swivel my chair around to look out to the compound.

"Supplies are coming your way."

"Understood."

"Good." She disconnects the call, leaving me looking out at the yard.

I get up and leave the meeting room to check on the boys and see what's happening. Emily's phone call has put me on edge.

"Hey," I say as I watch Jackson, one of the prospects, working on his bike. "Whatcha' doin'?"

"Didn't get pussy last night, so I'm polishing my knobs," he says with that stupid humor.

"Was gonna ask if you wanted a hand, but I'll leave you and your knobs alone." I take a step back and chuckle at him.

His bike's pulled apart and he's sitting on the ground polishing all the chrome and steel.

"How 'bout I don't pull my knob out and you give me a hand?"

Funny, asshole.

"Nah, don't wanna touch your knob. And really, it's probably small and you'd be done in less than five minutes."

Jackson laughs and shakes his head. "What you're saying is you'd touch my knob if it was big?"

"I'd fucking shoot it."

I hear Jackson laughing as I walk back inside to call Sarge and see where the girls are.

Going over to the bar, I pour myself a Jack and drink it down. Pulling the cell out of my pocket, I dial Nix's number. The phone rings until it goes to voice mail. Maybe the girls are doing something that prevents Nix from answering.

I dial Sarge's phone next, and his goes straight to voicemail. It doesn't even ring. I put the phone back in my pocket and pick up the bottle.

Pouring another drink, I lift the tumbler to my lips, but before I even have a chance to drink the whiskey, all hell breaks loose.

TWENTY-TWO

Phoenix

It's so cold. My body's shivering, trying to generate some heat. Jesus, it's cold. Where am I? Where's Milina? What's happening?

I can smell the cold. It's crisp and frosty and the cold clings to the inside of my nose.

My head hurts. Why does it hurt? *And why am I so cold?*

I blink and try to focus on where I am, but I can't see anything.

I wiggle my toes. Everything feels strange, wrong.

"Help," I say, though my voice is weak. I attempt to sit up, but my legs are bound together at the ankles and my arms are tied behind my back.

What is going on?

I move my head back and can start making out blurry objects. I blink with heavy eyelids and try to focus again.

"Jaeger," I try to talk. My throat hurts; it's scratchy and dry.

My eyes gradually focus, and I see that I'm in a room with floor to ceiling silver shelves with tons of frozen food on them.

The floor I'm lying on is freezing and the cold is cutting straight through to the core of my body. The fine white mist that fills the air tells me I'm in a freezer.

A walk-in freezer, industrial, exactly like one a restaurant would have. I try to turn my head to see if I can see Milina. She's tied up and knocked out close to me.

"Milina," I say in a hushed voice as I try maneuvering my body toward hers.

Her eyes are closed and she's laid out on the floor, as I imagine I was a few moments ago.

"Milina," I say again, hoping she hears me and wakes.

Still, I get nothing from her. She's silent and still. But her chest is rising and falling, and her eyes are moving frantically behind her eyelids. A bluish bruise is forming under her left eye and her lip has a split in it.

What the hell happened?

"Milina," I say again, louder, but not loud enough to raise suspicion if anyone is outside the freezer, because I have no idea who's there and what they want with us.

"Mmm," she whimpers and tries to move.

"Shhhh."

"Mmm."

"Shhhh, Milina, you've got to be quiet."

I watch as her eyelids flutter open, then close again. She tries to move her arms, but they're restrained like mine. With clear agitation, she wiggles pointlessly, trying to free herself.

"Milina, open your eyes," I say as quietly as I can.

"What's happening?" she questions me, though her voice is high and becoming hysterical and panicky.

"Shhhh, open your eyes, but you have to be quiet."

I watch as she continues to futilely tug and move around, trying whatever she can to get loose of the binds.

"What's happening, Nix?" she asks as the determination leaves her body and her movements become less intense. "Your forehead is bleeding, Nix. What happened?"

I can't move my hand to wipe at the blood, but I can feel the throbbing pain from the exact spot that Milina just pointed out. "I don't know." I look around the freezer as best as I can, and don't see anyone else in here. "What's the last thing you remember?" I ask her, trying to jog my own memory.

"Um." She squints her eyes and her eyes roam the room, while she must be trying to remember what happened too.

"We were getting a pedicure, and we were sitting next to each other talking about Jaeger and Sarge."

"Yeah, that's right. We heard gunshots," I say, still trying to piece the disjointed puzzle together.

"Then that guy ran in," Milina says, creasing her eyebrows together.

"Yeah," I agree. I look away for a moment trying to remember past the haze.

A quiet moment passes between us. Time stretches as an image starts to form.

"Shit," I whisper and look over at Milina.

"I thought he was with Sarge, but he punched me in the eye."

"And he hit me with the butt of the gun," I say remembering what happened.

"Who are they, Nix?"

"I don't know." I answer honestly.

"Are they with Jaeger and Sarge?"

"I haven't seen them before. I don't know who they are."

"What do they want with us?" Milina asks. She's starting to lose it again, her chest is heaving heavily and tears fill her eyes as she starts trying to pull against the ropes again.

"Milina, you need to calm down. Fighting the ropes isn't going to help. We need to keep a level head until we know what's going on."

Her tears begin to roll down her cheeks and her crying is reaching a fever pitch of frantic. "How can you be so calm?" she asks me.

"I don't know. But we can't lose it and get ourselves killed in here. We just have to be quiet and figure out what's happening."

Milina's sobbing and the sound of the compressor motor kicking on are the only sounds in the freezer for the longest time. It feels like we've been in here for days, and every second that ticks by is

GRIT

elongated by the uncertainty of what horror awaits us.

"Nix?"

"Yeah."

"Are we going to die in here?"

"I hope not."

"It's so cold. I can't get warm."

"I know. I'm cold too. And really tired."

"I'm going to try and sleep; maybe it's just a nightmare."

My mind slows as the icy air touches every part of me, my nose is dripping from the glacial draft that's being pushed around by the loud wheezing motor. My eyelids get heavier, and I can feel my body beginning to lose its battle to stay alert.

"Nix," Milina's voice is now soft, whispering, airy.

"Yeah." My tone's so low that I'm not sure she can hear me.

"You're my best friend. I love you."

"I love..."

··✦··

"What the hell happened?" A deep, booming voice startles me.

"We sort of left them in there."

"You're a fucking idiot! You could've killed her. Leave before I put a bullet between your fucking eyes," he hollers angrily.

"Where am I?" I try and say. My head's throbbing with a deep, painful rhythm.

"Dillon, can you hear me?" the voice asks me.

"Yeah," I reply as I try and force my eyes open to see where I am. "Milina," I call for my best friend, but hear nothing.

"Wake up, Dillon."

My eyes flicker open, and my sight adjusts to the light in the room. It's not cold in here and I'm lying on a soft surface. I can't hear the whir of the freezer motor and I can move my hand to touch my aching head.

It takes me a few seconds to realize that my hands aren't bound together anymore. I lie on my side, and see a man in a suit sitting in a corner chair. One leg is crossed over the other and he's nursing a tumbler of dark, amber liquid, carefully watching me.

"Where am I? And where's Milina?"

A small smirk appears on his face, and he lifts the tumbler to his lips and takes a sip.

He's got neat, short brown hair. His dark eyes haven't left mine.

"Where am I?" I ask again as I try to sit up on the bed.

"Tsk, tsk, tsk," he says as he raises his finger and wiggles it at me.

An uncomfortable silence envelops the room. I have no idea who he is or why he's just watching me and not saying a word.

The man takes another sip of his drink and lowers it to rest on his knee. He raises an eyebrow as his eyes travel down the length of my body and back to my face.

"You're beautiful," he says as he lifts the tumbler and finishes its contents.

I look past him and take in the room. There's a huge window to his left, and outside the window, I can see that a giant tree is shadowing any scenery that might be visible.

"I said, you're beautiful," he asserts, his voice louder and testy now.

"Thank you," I answer, hoping that's the right thing to say.

He puts the glass on the small wooden table beside the chair and casually leans back; his eyes bore into me intensely as he brings his fingers up to his mouth and runs them along his bottom lip.

His eyes narrow, and he keeps his predatory, scary stare on me. There's a shift of energy in the room, and it feels crowded with the sharp, twisted desire that's suddenly coming from the man in the suit.

"Very beautiful," he almost whispers as he keeps his hard eyes on me.

Tick, tock, tick, tock.

My heart's hammering in my ears, warning me of the deadly hazard in this room.

"Do you know who I am?" he asks as he abruptly stands.

I shake my head, not confident enough to actually open my mouth and say anything in case it's the wrong answer.

In two large strides he's beside the bed, looking down at me.

"I'll give you today to rest. There's a bathroom behind that door. You may take a shower. Tomorrow we'll start your training."

"My training for what?" I ask in a small voice.

He flares his suit jacket out and places his hands on his hips. He's holding my gaze, though his eyes are wild and angry.

"Stand," he barks at me. Fury rolls off his body.

Momentarily I'm stuck in a daze of 'what the hell' and don't move.

"Stand," he screams at me as he leans down and grabs my arms, pulling me off the bed.

I tumble into him and he pushes me back. I'm unsteady on my feet and fall to the gray carpet on my hands and knees.

"What did I do?" I ask as I look up at him. My body's trembling and my heart is straining as it pumps trying to keep a steady beat.

"Shut up," he yells. I feel it before I have time to brace myself. A backhand so powerful and sharp that my head snaps to the side.

"I'm sorry," I whimper, still not sure what's going on.

"I said, shut up." This time I see it and cringe away, but the muscle behind the smack twists my neck a little too far and I fall flat against the floor.

"You're damn lucky your training isn't starting until tomorrow, or I'd be beating the shit out of you today. I'm a man of my word; I won't go back on it. Now…" he pauses and takes several deep breaths.

I don't know what to do, should I lay still or get up?

"Up on your knees, head down. Don't look at me."

Slowly I move my body to do as he says, still not sure what's happening.

"Faster," he says, and although his voice is calm, gentle, and quiet, it makes me shiver in fear.

"I'll have food sent in here for you soon. As I said before, you're allowed to use the bathroom, and you're free to walk around in here. Don't make a sound though, not a single fucking peep. I want to be able to see you but not hear you. Do you understand?"

Should I answer or will I get another smack if I do? I'm torn and freaking the hell out, because I just don't know what's happening.

"When I ask a question, I expect a response," he says, again with a tightly controlled coolness.

"Yes," I whisper, too frightened to say anything else.

"You will address me as Master," he says.

I'm still on my knees, and the confusion hasn't lifted. If anything, that last sentence has sent me further into a spiral of confusion.

"I'm going to have so much fun breaking you," he utters, sensually.

He runs his hand down my hair, in a caressing and soothing manner. But I make no mistake; he's a crazy.

Psychotic crazy.

"If you try to break the window to get out, you'll earn a beating. You'll also fail, because the glass is bulletproof and shatterproof."

I hear him walk away, then I hear the bedroom door open and close.

I close my eyes and slowly count to twenty in my head. When I'm sure that there's no sound in the room other than my own erratic breathing, I look up to see I'm on my own.

I collapse to the floor in a mess, crying and curling into myself.

I'm frightened, unsure and absolutely terrified about where Milina is and what's happening to her.

Please God, let Milina be quickly saved by her family.

If only I had someone who cared enough about me to save me. I wish my mom was still alive. She would've fought to find me.

I lie on the floor, and pray that Milina is safe.

My mind screams at me to fight. But my body is too frightened to do anything other than lie on the floor and wait for my death to come.

GRIT

My head keeps up its angry assault on me, warning me not to just give in.

As I pray for Milina's safety, I also pray for someone to notice that I'm gone and look for me, too.

There's a small spark of will that's burning brighter by the second.

He may want to train me. He might break my body; He may even crush my bones. But my mind will remain my own–he'll never have that. I'll protect it with every barrier I can build to keep him out.

Whoever *he* is.

TWENTY-THREE

THE RINGING IN MY EARS IS STARTING TO QUIET, AND MY BLURRY EYES are beginning to regain full vision.

The bar collapsed on top of me when the assault on the clubhouse began.

Pushing the heavy wood off, I get to my feet and stumble, disoriented. My head's pounding and there's thick, red blood dripping into my eye.

Slowly I lift my hand and swipe at my bloodied eyebrow. The instant my fingers make contact I know that my forehead is spilt and I'll need stitches.

"Jackson!" I yell, but I don't hear a response.

Looking around the clubhouse, it's a disaster zone. There's rubble strewn across the entire bar area. The sofa is upturned, and on the opposite side of the room from its usual spot, the pool table has been completely destroyed. There's a massive hole in the wall where there should be a door.

Shit, Phoenix, where is she?

I take my phone out of my pocket, but it's been destroyed too, shattered beyond usable.

Dragging my heavy feet into the meeting room, I go to the small cupboard and get another phone out. The first thing I do is try calling Phoenix again.

Her phone goes straight through to voicemail.

Shit.

I dial Sarge's number. It rings three times and he answers, sounding groggy. "They took the girls," he manages to say, although it sounds like he's slurring.

The only person that I can think of who would want revenge on us is Cain. But Cain doesn't know yet that we've made the decision to cut all ties with him.

Unless...

There's a mole at the table.

Shit.

"You alright?" I ask, knowing the answer's not going to be a good one.

"Fuckers shot up the tattoo shop. Mindy the receptionist is dead. I caught a stray through the arm. But I saw two of 'em with the girls over their shoulders. Must have knocked 'em out. I tried getting to 'em but they turned and kept shootin' up the shop."

"Can you drive back?"

"Yeah. Nothing serious. I'll be back in fifteen."

Sarge hangs up and my next call is to Aaron.

"Yeah," he says, answering the phone immediately.

"Clubhouse. Now."

My tone tells him that I'm serious, "Shit, what's happened?" he asks as I hear him start his bike.

"Did you find Dark?"

"Nope. Looked for him, but his old lady has no idea where he is either. I'll be there in a few."

Hanging up, I go back out to the yard to see what the hell's happening out there.

Jackson's dead, motionless, lying on the cold cement beside his bike parts.

Christ!

Jason rides in and I watch him slow as he comes through where the gates usually stand.

He rides up beside me, takes his helmet off and looks around.

"What the hell happened?" he asks. His eyes take in the clubhouse that lays broken and in rubble.

"We got hit. I need you to call all the members."

Jason gets off his bike, and takes a step away from it. His eyes are jumping from area to area, trying to understand what's happened.

"The members. Tell 'em to get their families into lockdown," I say, angrily.

"Yeah, right. On it." He takes his phone out and starts making calls.

I pick Jackson up, carry him inside the clubhouse and lay him on an untouched spot near the kitchen. I go back outside and find that Lion's buried under the collapsed side wall of the clubhouse. I can hear him calling for help, and trying to maneuver himself out from under it.

The wall has him pinned from his hips down, making it hard for him to move.

"Wait, don't move," I say as I try and shift the debris on my own.

"Jason," I yell for him to come and help.

"Shit!" I hear him say as he runs over to me. Jason starts helping me move the collapsed wall off Lion. Within a few minutes, we've heaved it off him and I see that Lion's leg is pretty ripped up, right down the bone near his knee.

Jason automatically leans down. Lion puts his arm around Jason's neck and Jason lifts him up.

I walk around the rest of the yard while Jason helps Lion inside.

A few stray bricks fall from the clubhouse. Dust particles fly through the air and the sound of sirens can be heard coming toward us.

Running inside, I need to hide any weapons before the cops get here. "Who's packing?" I ask Lion and Jason. They both shake their heads and I bolt into the meeting room, open the cabinet, and grab what we have there. A quick mental inventory reminds me of the guns in my room.

I grab them and a duffel bag from my room, return to the meeting room and pack them all in there. There isn't much on the premises because we haven't had a run for Cain for a few days, and the guns from the Pace family haven't arrived yet.

"Jason?" I yell.

"What do ya need?"

I motion to the bag in my hand. "Take it and go to the safe house. Now."

He grabs the duffel bag and is gone within seconds.

"J," I hear Sarge yell.

I find him in the kitchen, holding his arm.

"Fuck, man," I say as I rub my hand over my eyes then through my hair. "How bad?" I ask as I jerk my chin out toward his arm.

"Had worse. Just need a bandage."

There's still blood dripping from the wound. It doesn't look life-threatening, but it's bleeding pretty steadily.

"What the hell?" Aaron says as he walks in and assesses the damage to our brothers and the clubhouse.

He lights up a smoke and takes a few deep breaths, trying to calm down.

"Cops will be here soon."

"Yeah they were coming up behind me," Aaron says.

I go and stand outside and wait for them all to get out of their cars, weapons drawn, looking at us like we're the criminals.

Which we are, but not in this clusterfuck.

They come screaming into the driveway, lights flashing, sirens blaring, drawing attention to themselves and to us.

"Jaeger," the Police Chief, Brian Michaels, says as he walks over to me and shakes my hand. He's on our take, and has always looked after us here.

"Brian," I say as I extend my hand and lead him away from anyone listening.

"What the hell's going on? Blasts were heard a county away. I can't keep the others out of here. Not with all this damage." He sweeps a look at the huge hole at the clubhouse.

"I know. Just keep 'em busy outside."

"Who did it?" he asks.

"Club business," I answer, not letting him know anything that's happening.

Sarge walks over, clinging to his injured arm and stands by us. "What the hell happened to you?" Brian asks as he points to Sarge's arm.

"Flesh wound," Sarge answers, nonchalantly.

"Anyone hurt bad?"

"Lion, he's inside, and Jackson, he didn't make it."

Brian rakes a hand through his hair and looks over at the other cops raking around the yard.

"Where is he?" Brian asks.

"Taken care of," Sarge answers, as he gives me a look, telling me they're good to go inside.

"Jaeger, you gotta clean this shit up. I can't have crap like this happening around here."

"Give me two days."

"I don't think I can. The anti-terrorist unit will want to come and investigate this." He swings his hands around the yard.

"Hold 'em off as long as you can."

"Not sure I'll be able to. Can I let paramedics in to look at Lion?"

I look at Sarge and he nods, telling me that they won't encounter Jackson. "Yeah, send 'em in and do what you can with keepin' it quiet." I clap my left hand on his back and extend my right, shaking his, essentially ending this conversation.

Brian walks away, still assessing the damage to the club house.

"Jackson?" I ask Sarge as we begin to walk inside.

"In your room."

"Great, thanks."

"Either there or the meeting room."

The paramedics walk past us and go inside, looking for Lion.

"Where's Aaron?" I ask Sarge.

"Inside."

Sarge and I both walk in to see the paramedics looking at Lion's leg, "We'll need to take you to the hospital," one says to Lion.

"Not gonna' happen. Stitch me up here."

"We don't have the equipment, and we can't. You may need to have it operated on, so we need to take you to the hospital," the persistent EMT tells Lion.

"No, stitch me up or leave me alone and I'll do it myself." Damn, he's got balls to stitch that shit up here.

"Lion," I say, my tone holding authority.

"Not going," he declares, his eyebrows knit tightly together.

"Lion," I say once more, my voice quiet, though I'm fucking seething that he's defying me.

"Fine, take me to the damn hospital."

They get a stretcher out and lift him, Lion crosses his arms in front of his chest, signaling that he's pissed off.

"No club emblems allowed in the hospital," one of the paramedics says pointing to Lion's plain black leather cut with the small patch stitched on the front that says 'Prospect'.

But the back of the cut has the crest of the MC, our intensely burning red scull, with flaming red 'Hunters' curved above it. It's the same as on our bikes and clubhouse.

"Lion," I say and hold my hand out for it.

"This is bullshit, man," Lion growls with a sneer at the guy about to wheel him out. He takes off his cut and gives it to me. He makes it clear he's not too pleased about it.

After the paramedics leave, the cops hang around for a while. Brian walks over to me; I'm standing looking at all the shit and debris lying around the place.

"I can get them out of here for now, but once first light comes, they'll be back. And the FBI's coming too. They've already been deployed."

"Fuck. When?" I ask, running a hand through my hair.

"Before first light. You have maybe a few hours."

"Thanks, Brian." I hold my hand out to him to shake.

"Clean up whatever it is you need to get done before they get here."

I nod and take a deep breath, letting it out slowly.

Within half an hour, all the strangers are gone, leaving just the members, minus Dark, waiting around in the meeting room.

"Jason, keep look out. You." I point to Shark, another prospect, "help him."

He nods, and both Jason and Shark walk outside, keeping an eye on the yard, watching for the assholes who wanna try and take my club down.

I close the meeting room's doors and go to the head of the table, sitting in my chair.

"What the fuck?" Aaron asks. It's the first time since this afternoon that we can talk openly.

The entire table erupts in excited talking. Questions are being asked and no one really has any answers.

I bash the gavel down once, and a blanket of quiet fills the room.

"This is what we know. Dark's gone. Aaron went around to his place and his old lady said she hadn't seen him. Sarge was getting inked when the shop got shot up, and he saw two of 'em carrying the girls out of the fucking beauty salon they were in."

A collective 'fuck' is heard around the table.

"I'm thinking Dark's a mole for Cain. And Cain did this," I say, addressing the table.

"Or," Aaron says and sits forward in his seat.

"Or what?" I ask.

"The Crowes."

Shit, yeah. *Crowes.*

I lean back in my seat, resting my left ankle on my right knee.

"I'll set a meet with Skinny," I say, thinking out loud.

"We take the fucker out, screw the sit down," Aaron says, chest sticking out, anger rolling off him in waves.

"We take the Crowes down, we're in for a shitstorm. 'Cause we know the Crowes are hooked up with the Excalibur cartel," I say and watch the reactions of the entire club.

"We need to take Cain's offer, keep us in his good books," Aaron says, and the table murmurs, half nodding their heads.

"Then we may as well hand the club to him, 'cause if we take his offer, he'll own us."

"Not unless we have a meeting with him and tell him what the score is," Cruise, one of the members says.

"Tell him what the score is? Insist he runs it our way? How do you think that's gonna play out for us, either way? We're on board with the Pace family now. We screw with them, then we deal with their people who, incidentally, is 15."

"I heard she was working for them," Wake, another one of the members, says.

"Shit," a few of the members moan, defeated.

"For now, we're in lockdown. The old ladies and kids are at the safe house, I'll arrange a meet with Skinny. The girls are gone, and we need to get them back," I say as I stand and stretch my back.

"Fuck 'em, J, they're just cunts. You can find others," Wake says, clearly not giving a shit about the girls.

From the corner of my eye I see Sarge's face harden. He's getting pissed off fast, 'cause his girl is gone along with mine.

"That's not how we work," I state, walking toward Wake, acting as a barrier between Sarge and him.

No use in the club fightin' among ourselves. We can let off steam later, when the girls are back and we've sorted this clusterfuck out.

"They're just dead wood," Wake keeps going. He's bound and determined to cop a round with Sarge.

Sarge's anger is starting to show. He's shaking his head and holding on to the meeting table, knuckles going white.

"That's not how we work," I say once more as I put my hand on Wake's shoulder and dig my fingers into him.

"They old ladies?" Shit, Wake's a dumb motherfucker, not

knowing when to keep his mouth shut.

"Yeah," Sarge answers.

"That's not how we work," I emphasize the words, making it clear by my tone that I'm pissed.

"Whatever." Wake slumps back in his chair, the rest of the members avoid my eyes.

I'm going to find Nix, and get her back. If anyone's laid one finger on her, I'll kill 'em.

Simple as that.

She's my woman. No fucker has a right to touch her.

TWENTY-FOUR

Phoenix

IT'S BEEN A FULL DAY SINCE I'VE BEEN IN THIS ROOM. THE DOOR OPENED late yesterday, just when the sun was setting on the horizon, and a huge, burly, heavily-armed man walked in with a tray of food.

He looked at me, his eyes starting at the top of my body and slowly moving down. His face morphed from indifference to sheer lust. I could tell that he was fighting his desire for me. But he must've remembered something, possibly orders from the guy who hit me yesterday. He just shook his head and left.

An hour later the same guy walked back in, deadpan and emotionless. He took the tray of uneaten food and left.

I wasn't going to eat anything. I had no idea what it had been contaminated with. What if they had put some type of sedative in it, or poison? I wasn't going to risk it. So instead, while I was in the shower, I gulped water from the tap.

I was permitted to shower, and walk around in here, per the instructions of Mr. Psycho.

Now, I'm standing at the foot of the bed, not sure when or who will be coming through the door. Just a few seconds ago I heard the click of a lock, but no one has come in yet.

My pulse is pounding in my ears. I'm shaking from fear and nerves, and my body is cloaked with cold sweat. The anticipation of the person about to enter gives me hope that someone might be looking for me.

The door swings open, and Mr. Psycho steps through.

His back is straight, his chest out. His presence commands my attention. But screw him if he thinks he's going to get it.

I roll my eyes, slump my shoulders and look out the window to the right of the room, where the old tree gently swings in the light breeze.

"Kneel," he commands. I refuse. "I said, kneel." His voice hardens.

I know this is going to earn me a beating. I already have one large bruise under my eye where he backhanded me twice yesterday.

I continue to look outside. I won't be his pawn; I won't let him break me.

I greeted Jaeger with a double-barrel when he showed up to my home. I'm certainly not going to roll over now. Although the odds are stacked against me, I'm still going to fight. I have no weapon and I'm stuck who knows where, but he's not going to take my will away without a fight.

"Kneel before your Master," he growls, anger and spite quite clear in his delivery.

I swallow the huge lump in my throat, close my eyes and hope to God he doesn't kill me. But maybe death will be better than what he wants to do to me.

I hear the scuff of his shoes against the soft carpet and he's charging toward me, waves of fury rolling off his body.

I brace myself, instinctively knowing that I'm about to get backhanded again. I wince and close my eyes, waiting for the moment of impact.

Rough hands grip my throat. He applies pressure with his thumbs, and I struggle to pull his strong hands away, trying to get them to relax their hold. But it's futile. He's too strong.

I feel myself starting to slip. A brilliant, bright blackness begins to overtake me.

But it's so peaceful, so beautiful, *so quiet.*

"You fucking slut," I hear a jumble of drawn out words and that's what makes it to my ears.

The black is so beautiful, and it's pulling me toward it, like a high-intensity magnet, reeling me in.

Stunning and beautifully isolated. I love this feeling. *I'm so free.*

"No you don't."

The tightness around my neck eases and I feel my body collapse from under me. My legs are gelatinous and I know I can't support myself. The safest place for me to be is here on the floor, as I float up and away from this shell called a body.

I hover above me, looking at the man. He rakes his hand through his hair, stabbing at it, angry.

He drives a boot into the torso of the slumped being on the ground. Am I dreaming? Did he just kick that person?

He lowers himself carefully and places an ear to the mouth of the woman beneath him. He gently sweeps her fiery red hair away from her face, as he cradles her head and brings his mouth down on hers.

I close my eyes, not wanting to see this intimate exchange. Why is she lying there? What's happening to her? I need to wake from this dream.

I feel my lungs fill with air and I instantly begin to cough, trying to open my eyes. The light in the room is so bright, but he's here, the man I saw in my dream. He's holding my head and looking down at me.

"I'm glad you didn't die," he says as he bends closer and takes my mouth with his.

The kiss is soft and gentle and such a contrast to the hardness and intensity that he's shown me so far. But he isn't Jaeger, and his breath is laced with scotch as he grips my hair and holds my face to his.

His tongue keeps delving into my mouth, but I don't respond. I don't want any part of him in any part of me.

I try to pull away but his clutch is controlling, hazardous, and severe.

"Don't," I say against his lips. "I don't want you."

He pulls back and looks into my eyes. His own fevered gaze is spine-chillingly cold. There's a darkness so deep inside him that his entire body seems consumed with it. The shadows that veil his eyes are plagued with sin, damned by malice, and pure evil courses through his body.

My own breath leaves me as the realization of my immediate future catapults into me, holding me tight. I'm going to die by the hand of the man who's taken me.

"I said for you to kneel before your Master," he says in a low, steady tone. He lays my head down on the carpet, stands and takes a step back. "You've made me repeat myself too many times. I don't take well to my slaves being brats."

The word 'slave' sends an icy chill down my spine. I know what he wants. I've read enough to know what BDSM is. Though I believe he's certainly not a Master, but more of a controlling, deranged psychopath. Because my understanding of BDSM is that it's all safe, sane and consensual, at least that's what I've read.

"No," I whisper with as much authority as I can muster.

Without a second's hesitation, he hurls himself at me, grabbing me by the shoulders and putting me on my knees in front of him. The moment he steps back, I lift my face to look at him, challenging him with just my eyes.

"Lower your gaze, slave."

"No," I fight him.

"Lower your fucking eyes!" he yells.

"No," I push further.

He won't break me, he won't take my mind.

"Lower your eyes," he screams as he steps up to me, closing a fist and drawing it back.

"Fuck you!" I holler and stand from the kneeling position I was in.

I haven't even fully straightened before his fist connects with my face. The first blow shocks me, although I was expecting it. The second punch knocks me to the ground. With the third punch I feel the skin on my face split and warm liquid begins to drip to the floor.

"Kneel!" he yells again.

"No," I say even more determined than I was only seconds earlier.

His foot connects to my stomach, and a stabbing pain causes all the air to leave my body. I double over in pain and clutch my stomach, while thick red blood drips into my eye, clouding my vision.

"Kneel or I'll sell you or use you in my brothel."

I lie on the floor, trying to catch my breath, not able to get air into my body quick enough. My pants are shallow and labored as I try and recover from the beating he's just given me.

"It's your choice. You kneel before your Master or I'll sell you to the worst possible person I can find."

He steps back and lets the words hit me with the full effect he intended.

When I catch my breath, and finally am able to move, I kneel before him.

I'd never survive a brothel, or wherever else he would sell me.

Moments tick by, my head's spinning as I'm getting light-headed. He walks around me, slowly examining me like a race horse he's considering buying.

"You'll address me as Master."

I remain quiet, I don't say a word. I don't think I've got any fight left in me today. If he hits me once more, I may lose consciousness again.

"You're so beautiful, Dillon." He squats in front of me and lifts my chin with one finger. "So very sexy, I'm proud of you for realizing that I'm your Master."

I close my eyes so I can't see the beast in front of me. He's truly demonic and scares the shit out of me.

"When I leave, I'll send in a first aid kit. Tomorrow when I come back, I want you naked and on your knees waiting for me."

He softly squeezes my chin and lifts my head. His mouth descends onto mine, as he begins to kiss me with vigor and excitement.

"Hmmm," he mumbles against my lips. "I can't wait 'til I taste your cunt." He waits for a reaction, but I don't give him one.

Inside though, every part of me is screaming at him, with everything that I am. I want to lunge at him and fucking kill him.

But my body is broken. It's bruised and battered and I can barely stay upright even in this kneeling pose.

"Answer me," he says, quietly.

"You didn't ask me a question." I brace myself again.

Instead of the thwack of a fist, I hear laughter. Deep rumbling as he chuckles with passion.

"You're quite right, my beautiful slave. I didn't, and for that I apologize. Tomorrow, will you please be waiting for me, kneeling and naked?"

This guy is truly a brute with deep-seated psychological issues. He goes from devil to caring in the same sentence, but I'm under no misapprehension. He can easily kill me and he wouldn't think twice about doing it.

"Yes, Master," I say in a tiny voice through clenched teeth.

"Good. And please eat. It upsets me to think that you're going without. Until tomorrow, my sexy slut."

He steps out of the room, closes and locks the door behind him.

I collapse back on the ground, exactly like yesterday, but this time I sob uncontrollably.

I cry because I still have no idea where Milina is.

Or what's happening.

Or why Jaeger hasn't found me.

But mostly I cry because for the first time in my life, I feel alone and frightened.

TWENTY-FIVE

"**S**KINNY," I SAY AS I HOLD MY HAND OUT TO HIM, TRYING NOT TO START a war with him, or the Excalibur cartel.

"Jaeger, what's happening, man?" he asks as he claps a strong hand to my back, trying to show dominance in our exchange.

"Clubhouse got shot up."

"Heard. That's seriously fucked-up shit. You pissed anyone off?"

"Who don't we piss off?" I light up a smoke and turn my body so that he and I are talking without any of our crew listening.

He lets out a humorless chuckle and nods. "What do you need?" he asks as he leans against his bike.

"We don't need anything, just seeing if we can help you at all?"

He brings his eyebrows together, causing a deep crease in the center.

"Whatcha' fuckin' playin' at?" His voice gets angry as he reaches inside his cut and pulls out a Glock.

"Hunters got no beef with the Crowes," I say as I catch sight of Sarge beginning to hover, tense. I shake my head, discreetly, telling Sarge to stay where he is.

Skinny's crew sees that he's holding a gun to my head and start walking up to see what's happening.

"You took the house and the girl. We're not happy," he says as he lowers the gun, still kept in his hand, ready to kill me.

"The girl's mine."

"I hear old man Ward sold the girl," he says, emotionless.

What the hell?! He sold his *daughter*? What kind of fuckin' sick, perverted ass sells his kid?

"Who to?" I ask, trying to hide my anger.

"Heard it was your boss." Skinny shrugs as he puts his gun away and takes out a packet of smokes.

Fucking Cain.

"If the red-headed one is yours, I'll take the other one," he says.

How does he know about Milina?

I step back and turn my head to Sarge, who would've caught what Skinny said about his woman.

"Yeah, about that." I shake my head, indicating he ain't gonna take her either.

"Club needs a new whore."

"She's his." I jut my chin toward Sarge.

"Pussy-whipped," Skinny chuckles.

The tension seems to have lessened though I'm still concerned about how he knows about Milina.

I turn and walk to Sarge who meets me in a few steps. "We got a mole."

"Dark?"

"Seems the most obvious candidate, seeing as he's gone AWOL."

"Where's Aaron?" Sarge asks.

"Had to take care of some shit, said he'll meet us back at the clubhouse."

"What about the Crowes?"

"Leave 'em, no issue to us. Except they want our girls, and the farm."

"And that's not an issue?" Sarge lets out a humorless chuckle, and raises his eyebrows.

"Not now. Our first concern is getting the girls back. Fuck what they want."

Sarge nods then steps away without turning his back.

I walk back to Skinny who's still smoking and hold my hand out to him again. "Thanks, man."

"Heard you were in the transport business now."

"Nah, the club's not up for that."

He shakes my hand, and nods, understanding that we're not gonna undercut whatever the fuck they and the cartel do.

His club, his business.

"I'd be watching my members if I were you," he says, and his tone holds a warning.

I nod my head once and walk away.

He clearly knows somethin' that he's not saying.

I know now that the war between the Hunters and the Crowes hasn't started yet. They want the girls or the farm, and I'm not willing to give them either. But there's still time to come to a peaceful agreement.

I flick my head at Sarge, he and the other four club members that came to the meet all get on their bikes.

We leave in formation to go back to the clubhouse. When we pull up in front I motion for Sarge, who rolls his bike over to me.

"How's the arm?" I ask.

"Hmmm," standard Sarge answer.

"I'm gonna go around to Dark's place and talk to his old lady, see if there's something she remembers."

"Aaron talked to her."

"She may've remembered somethin'."

"When we gettin' first shipment from Pace?"

"Next day or two."

"I'll ride with ya'," Sarge says.

"Right."

Sarge and I leave and head down to Dark's place.

When we get there, we knock on the door and Dark's missus, Tabatha, looks through the glass door to see who it is.

The skin under her eyes is black and puffy, though there are definite tear stains down her cheeks. She opens the door for us and steps aside.

"Why aren't you in lockdown with the rest of the women and the kids?" I ask as she shuffles toward the small kitchen.

"No one told me I need to go," she says as she picks up a small silver hip flask and drinks from it.

"Can you tell me what you and Aaron talked about when he came here yesterday to see where Dark was?"

Tabatha stops drinking and puts the hip flask down.

"Aaron?" she asks as she furrows her eyebrows together, giving me a questioning look.

"Yeah, yesterday, before the explosion, he came to see ya'."

"I haven't seen Aaron in weeks, since the last time I came to the clubhouse for a cookout. What explosion?" she questions me.

What the fuck?

I look at Sarge and I see him straighten his back and stick his chin out. He's fucking pissed off.

"He said he came yesterday to ask you about Dark," I say again, in case the alcohol has gone to her head and she's simply too wiped out to understand. But she doesn't look stoned or drunk to me.

"Dark said he had a job with Aaron two nights ago, never came home. I tried calling the clubhouse, and got no answer." She leans against the kitchen counter, putting the hip flask down. Her hands are shaking and tears are now rolling down her cheeks.

"Dark said he had a job to do with Aaron?"

"Yeah." She nods, but she's barely holding on. "What's happened to my husband?" she asks, her body trembling with terror.

I look over at Sarge, and back at Tabatha.

"We'll find out, Tab. Pack a bag, and get to the safe house."

She drags her tiny, five-foot body down the hall, I assume into her room to pack.

I stand for a moment, thinking about what she's said.

If Aaron didn't show up here to ask Dark's old lady about where he could be...and Dark had a job to do with Aaron two nights ago and hasn't been seen since...then I can only come up to one fuckin' conclusion.

Aaron's the God damned mole at the table.

I turn to look at Sarge, who's obviously come to the same conclusion as me.

"I'm gonna kill him," Sarge says, with a fury I've never before seen rolling off him.

"Not yet," I answer as run my hand through my hair. "He'd know where the girls are."

"He's made his choice."

"Agreed. We'll take it back to the table and we'll decide what to do. Call the members; tell them to be at the clubhouse."

Tabatha walks out wheeling a small suitcase behind her. Her chest is heaving and she looks like she's about to lose it.

"Can you get to the safe house on your own?" I ask her.

She nods her head and swipes at the tears clinging to her red, sunken cheeks. "I'll be alright," she says in a tiny voice.

She really won't be, but the other women will help her when she gets to the safe house.

"Go straight there. Don't stop for gas or anything else."

"Alright, J."

She rolls her small suitcase behind her and heads out to the garage. Sarge and I leave the house, get on our bikes and wait for her start down the road before Sarge turns to me.

"A brother who's fucked us over," he says, calm, yet highly pissed off.

In silence, we start our bikes and leave Dark's house, heading back to the clubhouse. When we arrive, the boys have managed to put up a temporary fence, closing off any unwelcome visitors.

"Get the prospects to stay outside, and let us know if Aaron shows up," I instruct Sarge.

He walks away and he does what he has to as I go inside, grab a bottle of Jack and head into the meeting room. All the members are waiting inside and they're getting loud and anxious. I walk in, close the meeting room doors, and put the bottle of Jack down on the table.

"We'll probably need at least three more bottles to get through today," I say as I sit in my seat.

"What's going on?" Wake asks as he puts his elbows on the table and leans in.

"Sarge and me met up with Skinny. He told us that it looks like old man Ward sold Phoenix to Cain," I say as I look around the table.

"That's fucked," a few mumble together.

"Skinny also said to watch our crew."

"What the fuck, man?" Half the table stands in an uproar, ready to start punching.

"Settle," I say. But the anger and boom of the guys in the room drowns out my words.

I pick the gavel up and smash it on the table once, stilling everyone into quiet.

"If we're a club divided, we may as well not be a fucking club. You were all sworn in, and each of you has been vouched for. Skinny could be causin' problems, which is why I don't fucking want to believe him. But..." I trail off for a second as I reorder my thoughts.

"But what?" Hash, a member, asks.

"Sarge and I went to see Dark's old lady to see if she remembered anything she'd forgotten to tell Aaron when he went to see her."

"What happened?" Wake sits back in his seat and brings the bottle of Jack up to his lips as he swigs directly from the bottle.

"Aaron never went to see her."

"What the hell's goin' on?" Hash asks. The rest of the members look at me, stunned.

"Skinny knew that Sarge's old lady is with Phoenix, which told me we have a leak. And when Sarge and I went to see Dark's old lady, she told us that Aaron was never there, it confirmed it. Just gotta figure out why. I think Cain's got the girls."

A collective 'fuck' is heard through the room.

"Cain's fucked up," Wake says.

"Yeah," I confirm. "He is. But first it's gotta be unanimous," I say. They all know I'm talking about Aaron.

"In the ground," Matt, one of members says, without hesitation.

"In the ground," Hash repeats.

"Dirt," Wake says, agreeing with the other two members.

My eyes go to every man at the table, each of them voices a variation of wanting Aaron dead.

The final vote rests with me.

Aaron once showed me a way off the streets, got me earning decent coin, and helped me start the Hunters. I have fierce loyalty to the man that helped me drag my beaten and broken body off the streets into this life, and everyone around this table knows that.

But you choose to die by the life you lead.

He's chosen to betray his brothers and for that, he'll die by his brothers.

And it won't be a quick, easy death.

It'll be a fight to the very last breath.

"Ground," I say with certainty, sealing the fate of the one man I never thought would betray me.

TWENTY-SIX
Phoenix

I HEAR THE RATTLE OF A KEY GOING INTO THE LOCK AND KNOW I ONLY have seconds before he's inside the door.

He wants me stripped and on my knees, waiting for him to do whatever he wants with me.

Or I suffer the alternative; I get sold to someone who'll make me use my body to pleasure strangers time and time again.

I don't want to submit, but I'm also smart enough to know that at this stage, I have to. I strip, right down to nothing, and kneel at the foot of the bed. My hands are on my knees and my head is lowered.

The cold in the room turns icy and every part of me feels exposed, on display for the sick prick about to walk in the door.

My body is already heavily bruised and every time I take a nervous breath in, there's an ache in my side.

I can feel the tears starting behind my eyelids. They're threatening to break free, but I have to push on and keep going.

Until...

Until I can find a way to finally get away from here. If I gain his trust, then maybe one day he'll leave the door unlocked and I'll be able to make a run for it.

"You're such a sexy little slut," his smooth, terrifying voice booms with excitement. I don't say anything, I'm still hurting from the beating he gave me yesterday, and I don't want another one today.

He walks over to me, circling me slowly. A hunter ready to strike against his helpless prey.

"Stand," he commands.

I stand and keep my head lowered. The tears are falling now, and I'm trying to be silent. I don't want him to know that I hate him, that he's gotten to me.

"That small patch of hair has to go," he says as he runs just his warm fingertips over my shoulder, down my spine to the top of my bottom.

A shiver of cold bursts through me, despite his warm hands. His malice sends ice through my veins.

"Open your legs," he says as he slowly circles to stand in front of me.

I wipe the tears away from my eyes and my cheeks, and take a deep breath as he waits for me. I step out, spreading my legs.

He automatically goes for my sex, inserting a finger inside me, slowly trying to coax arousal from me.

My body sparks awake, though my mind hates him and what he's doing to me. I straighten my back and look up at him, giving him no emotion whatsoever. He can finger me, or even fuck me, but I'll hold back what he wants–to see me explode with joy around him.

"You're wet," he says, his voice dangerously low and husky.

I don't say a thing to him; I keep that mask of indifference on and look him dead in the eye.

"You're wet and your nipples are erect."

I don't look down to see if his words are right. I can feel the way my body enjoys this. *Traitor.*

"Does my slut want me to eat her pussy?" he leans in and whispers into my ear. The scruff of his beard is gliding across the sensitive skin of my face that's still raw from the bruising.

"No," I whisper, though I know it's going to earn me another beating.

He lifts his free hand to entwine his fingers in the back of my hair. With a hard yank, he pulls my head back, totally exposing my throat to him.

"Do you want me to hurt you?" he asks, his voice now cold and brutal.

"No."

"Then answer me with the truth, your body is loving me fucking you with my hand. Grind those hips on me and tell me you want your Master's tongue deep inside you." He flicks my clit piercing; to emphasize the ultimate betrayal my body is showing.

"Yes, Master," I answer, though my mind is screaming at me to stand up to him, tell him he's a motherfucker and run.

I don't want him, or this. I can't do this.

I can't have him do this to me, to tease my body and to keep my mind enslaved with fear.

"On the bed, slave. Open these beautiful legs and let me eat your pussy."

Standing still I fight with every ounce of me, I won't move until I absolutely have to. I refuse to give in to him and let him rule me.

I lift my chin and stand tall and proud. Although I'm completely exposed to him, I hold on to my dignity and my mind and will not give him that.

"On the bed, now," he says. His tone is vicious and angry now.

Fuck you! I want to scream it, but I can't be hurt anymore. I'm still in too much pain from yesterday.

He grips my upper arms, digging his nails into me and pushes me toward the bed.

"If I have to ask you once more, if you fail to comply with your Master's wishes just one more time, I'll let my entire security team fuck you." I take in a huge gasp of breath as my body begins to shudder from the magnitude of the terror he's wakened inside me. "Together," he adds with a snarl.

I step back, and go to the bed.

I can't control the tears, they're streaming down my cheeks, and it feels like there's an endless supply of them.

I slowly sit on the bed, and look over at him. He takes his suit jacket off, and unbuttons the wrists of his long-sleeved shirt. He rolls the sleeves up and walks over to stand in front of me. Pushing my legs apart he stands between them, discreetly thrusting his hips toward me, showing me the hard-on inside his pants.

I swallow the huge lump of shame in my throat and lean back on the bed.

"Open these legs so I can taste my property," he says as I feel him move closer to me on his knees.

Sobbing, I part my legs and take another huge breath. I feel his hand on my thigh, as he starts to kiss my sex.

My tears are hot and constant now. I close my eyes and pray.

Pray that he'll take what he wants quickly and then leave me alone.

And I pray that if Jaeger doesn't find me soon, that somehow I find a knife so I can kill the deranged Devil lapping at me with such greedy intensity.

TWENTY-SEVEN

"**W**HAT'S HAPPENING?" AARON SAYS AS HE WALKS INTO THE MEETING ROOM.

We finished the meeting hours ago, but I've been waiting for Aaron to show up from wherever he was.

"Pace family's sent out the first shipment. We've gotta go inventory it."

"When do you wanna do that?" Aaron sits down in his VP chair, his knee bouncing as he looks around the room.

"We'll leave in a few."

"Where is everyone?"

"Gone to check on the women and kids."

"Just you and me then," he says as his knee stops bouncing.

He's up to something.

But, so am I.

"Yep, just us."

"I'll just go take a piss and I'll meet up with you outside."

I nod my head and sit back in my seat, just looking out at all the devastation he's caused.

The fucker's tried ripping the MC apart. Worse still, he's done something to one of his own brothers. And now, he's probably making a call to take me out.

But I still have no fuckin' idea *why* he's done it.

I stab out my smoke and stand from the chair. Stretching my back, trying to look normal and calm, I walk out of the meeting room.

When I get to my bike, I see that Aaron's on his, sitting in idle, waiting for me so we can leave.

"Ready?" he asks. His tone has some underlying bullshit message he's trying to tell me.

"Yeah I am," I reply, knowing that tonight one or both of us will die.

I head us out of here toward the shed on the Interstate where we store our guns, but the guns won't arrive 'til tomorrow.

We head up to a set of traffic lights and Aaron rolls up beside me. I've already deviated from the usual route to the shed.

"Where we going?" he asks over the roar of our idling Harley engines.

"Gotta go to the warehouse first, fast stop."

He nods once and looks ahead, straight into the darkness of the night. No emotion, *nothing.*

When we get to the warehouse, everything's dark and appears deserted.

We turn off the bikes, get off 'em, and walk over to the side door.

I unlock the door and step aside so Aaron can go in first. Aaron switches the light on and he's faced with all the club members, including the prospects.

They all stand, watching his face as it morphs from surprise, to a question, and finally into a serious understanding of what's about to happen.

"I see," Aaron says as he steps further into the warehouse and the members surround him.

The prospects take position by the doors, locking them and standing guard.

I take my cut off, and whip my t-shirt over my head.

"What do you see?" I ask as I bounce up and down on the spot, warming my body for the upcoming onslaught.

"You know." He throws a look over his shoulder to all the members then back to me.

"We all know," I answer.

I put my left hand under my chin, and my right over my forehead and force my neck to its furthest point, cracking it one side then to the other.

"Tell me why, brother."

Aaron prepares his own body, by cracking his neck then rolling his shoulders. He lifts his t-shirt over his head and throws it to the side.

"Tell me," I say as I step into the makeshift boxing ring, outlined by all the members.

"'Cause you wouldn't just accept the fuckin' drugs."

"What?" Wake asks as he crosses his arms in front of his body.

"Cain offered us a ton of money, and you were dead set against it right from the start. Who the hell cares if he wants to start moving whores and kids? Not our issue."

He throws the first punch, I duck left and he misses.

"What, you think you could kill off the entire club?" I left jab twice, step back then land a short right straight into his gut.

"The plan was to get you to wipe the Crowes out, causing a war with their cartel. They'd wipe the Hunters out, and I'd start up a new chapter under Cain."

He knocks me one on the right side of my face. It makes me stumble back, but I quickly regain my footing.

"Where are the girls?"

Right jab, left uppercut, right hook.

"Fuck you," he says as he steps back and spits out some blood.

I watch his chest and he turns his shoulders toward me, telling me he's just about to throw a jab. I turn my shoulder and dip, slipping that left jab as I bring my right hand up in defense in case he makes contact.

Immediately, like any other fighter would do, he brings his right hand up, which I slip past by moving the other side. He throws a left hook. I slip and roll to the left, coming back with a right hand against his chin, knocking him back for a split second.

"You haven't lost your touch," he says as he swipes at the blood from his split chin.

He sticks his left jab, trying for a KO, but I wait 'til his hand is close to me and I parry the punch with my right hand, following it up with a left hook then a quick left elbow into his chest.

He responds by throwing a right hand. I drop my hips and pivot out to the left, coming back with my own right hand and a left hook.

My knuckles have split, and they're protesting in agonizing pain.

"Where are the girls?" I ask as I rock back away from the punch.

I don't roll my shoulder from his right hand, and he comes back with a short, straight punch.

I feel it land, and know that the stiches have split completely open on my eyebrow.

Keeping my stance straight, I plant my feet and bend my front leg, staying flexible at the knees, and rotate my hips. I drive a right hand straight, bringing my hips around and throwing a power left hook.

I step closer and move diagonally, making it harder for Aaron to hit me.

"Fuck you," he says as he comes back with anger.

He comes straight in with a basic one-two. One punch catches me, and I stagger back, almost causing me to lose my balance again. He follows with an uppercut and steps back diagonally.

I come back aggressively with a left uppercut, followed by a straight right hand, following that with a long-range left hook and then another straight right hand.

Pushing him back, he falls into Hash. Hash pushes him back into the ring.

I deploy a screw shot and move diagonally around his body, putting me in line for a perfect straight shot into his ribs, dropping him to the ground.

He falls to his knees and looks spent.

"Where are the girls?" I yell as I lay two swift kicks into his ribs, making him topple over and grab onto his stomach. "The fuckin' girls, where are they?" I stand, slightly off to the side, swaying from exhaustion.

He laughs and looks up at me. His eyes are all puffy and split, his lip is ballooning up and he spits some blood out of his mouth. A couple of teeth join the crimson that lands on the cold concrete floor.

Suddenly, I can hear all the sounds that are coming from all the members. "Kill him," they all chant, almost together though definitely individually.

"Probably frozen by now, or in the ground next to Dark," he moans as he tries to laugh.

Leaning down, I hold his head up by scrunching my hand in his hair and lifting it. I rabbit-punch his neck three times, killing him on the third strike.

"The girls," Sarge says as Aaron's lifeless body slumps to the ground.

"I know where they are," I respond as I fall on my ass besides Aaron.

"Where?" Sarge asks, eager to take off and go get his woman.

"Cain's restaurant has a walk-in freezer."

"Shit, that place is a guarded fuckin' fortress," Sarge says.

"There's also the house that's attached behind it."

I let the words take full effect on Sarge.

"It's a pussy shop," he says, realizing the full extent of what's happening to the girls.

"Yeah," I answer.

"Shit."

TWENTY-EIGHT
Phoenix

THE DOOR.

I hear the key turning and know I have only a matter of a few seconds to strip and be on my knees.

Although it'd be easier to remain naked, I won't do it. I'm not his when he's not in the room. And when he makes his presence known, I'm still not his, only my body is.

I kneel by the bed, head down and wait for whatever he wants to do to me. Yesterday he went down on me, and while my body enjoyed it, my mind fought it and I didn't orgasm. He got so pissed off that he couldn't make me writhe with pleasure, that when I began drying out, he stopped, got up, punched the wall and left.

Thank God he didn't punch me, or worse still, make me fellate him. It was bad enough that I had his tongue in me. I certainly didn't want his penis inside any part of me.

"There's my beautiful cunt. How are you today?" he says as he leans down and gently caresses my hair.

"Fine," I say, though I can't help the word be filled with venom.

"Fine, what?"

I take a deep breath, fighting with the title he wants me to call him. It feels like an hour passes but I know that it's only been less than a few seconds. "Fine, Master." I soften my tone and let him believe that I've accepted him.

"Is my slave going to allow me to fuck her today, or should I ask Mario and Felix to come in here and fuck you instead? Or possibly, you could go the way your friend is going just down the hall. She's going to make for an awesome money earner."

Every hair follicle stands to attention, tormented by his words and completely terrified for what's happening to Milina.

"Wh-what do you mean?" I stutter, but I quickly try to regain my composure and not show him how frightened I am.

"My boys are training her. Oh, she's definitely a pain whore, and soon she'll be just a whore. Although I do have to say…" He stops talking to chuckle, leaving me hanging for his next words, praying that Milina is safe. "I have a rather interested Sheik who's expressed an interest in adding to his collection. One of his regulars is no longer with him." He chuckles again, with so little emotion. "Some cunts just can't take a good beating." I flinch at his disgusting words. I know exactly what he means by that cold statement.

"Please," I beg. I want him to keep her safe and not drag her into this. He only took her 'cause she was with me at the salon when this all happened. If I was there on my own, she'd be safe.

"Please, what?" he says, his tone short and clipped. Angry, though he knows he holds power over me.

"Please don't do that to her, let her go and use me to do what you like." I hesitate for just a few seconds before I add the word he wants to hear, "Master."

He doesn't say anything. The silence is long and drawn out. The chill in the room grows icy as I feel my body begin to shudder with angst. I just want him to call off whatever his men are doing to Milina.

Tick.

Tock.

Tick.

Tock.

Minutes pass and I'm about to jump out of my skin.

The only sound in the room is my ragged breath, eagerly hopeful that he'll let her go and just keep me. Sell me, fuck me, keep me chained, break me...

"Please let me be your slave, Master," I plead with everything that I have in me.

"Hmmm," he murmurs. I can feel him close to me, if I tilt my head, I can see the tips of his shiny, black patent leather shoes.

"How much do you want to save your friend?" he asks, his tone lower. Strangely, more seductive.

"I'll do whatever it is you want, Master." I hate giving in to him, but I can't let him do this to Milina. She won't survive.

I'll fight every damn day. I'll battle to stay sane, to not break and to remain as emotionless as I can. I'll do it, for Milina. She has family that loves her, people that care for her. She can't wind up a statistic because of me.

"Whatever I want?" he asks, but his voice is oily and has an underlying tinge of mirth to it.

He's chosen his words to tear me to the very core. Because he knows that I'll do anything for Milina and her safety.

"Yes, Master," I say, a sob escaping.

My life as a whore, signed, sealed, and delivered. Instead of it being forced, I'll comply with it.

Because I have to save Milina.

"What else can you give me?"

For a moment I forget the rules, and my head snaps up to look at him.

"I have nothing but my body, and I'm prepared to freely give that to you, Master."

"Lower your gaze," he says.

My chin instantly falls to my chest and I begin to panic, because other than small amount of cash I have in the bank, I have nothing else to offer.

"How about this? I have a dinner meeting with some, ummm, very important people. I'd like you to join me for it, and if you can prove to me that you're a fantastic hostess, then I'll think about letting your cute little friend go."

I'm nodding furiously before he even finishes his sentence.

"But..." He weaves his fingers in my hair and jerks my head up so I'm looking into his malicious, hardened brown eyes. "But, if you fuck with me, I'll torture her and make you watch. I'll have all my men fuck her, rip her to shreds before I let them use their knife skills to carve her into tiny pieces. And just when you think you can't take watching her any longer, I'll throw her in a pit of snakes."

Fear is embossed so heavily in my bones, not for me, but for Milina, that all I do is nod and silently agree to his terms.

"Good. We have an understanding." He lets go of my hair and I instantly lower my head again, trying to be the good slave he wants.

I tremble with fear for what lays beyond today, for what might happen next.

"I'll send in some of that make-up you girls like to use to cover those marks, along with what I want you to wear. You have two hours to get ready. I know you don't have a clock in here, so I'll get one of my *boys* to knock on the door to let you know an hour beforehand." The way he says 'boys' scares the crap out of me.

My fate is sealed. I'm going to become something I've never wanted to be. Someone's possession, nothing more than a mere collection of holes for him to fuck whenever he wants.

"Yes, Master," I answer, knowing that he'll love my willingness and complete acceptance of his conditions.

"Now give me a kiss, and make it count, slut."

He jerks my head in a callous way and delves his tongue into my mouth.

I could bite down and try and run, but I know he'll take his wrath out on Milina.

I do the only thing I can. I kiss him with such intensity and desire that he has no reason to doubt my submission to him.

TWENTY-NINE

"Twice in two days. People are gonna start talkin'," Skinny chuckles as I reach out for his hand to shake it.

"The club needs a favor," I begin to say.

"We're not into helping our enemies."

"I'll make it worthwhile."

Skinny looks over at Black and shakes his head, telling him to back off. "What do you need?"

"Your club."

"Keep talkin'." He crosses his arms in front of his chest and stands with his feet apart.

"Cain's got our girls down at his pussy shop. I want 'em out, but he outnumbers us and I need backing power." I lean back on my Harley and adjust my sunglasses.

"You got anti-terrorism breathin' down your club's neck. Can't help ya'."

"Local cops are in our pocket. They say the Feds have been delayed, some bullshit happening over in the Middle East takin' pole to our small time. Got a few days before they come knockin', and I want my girls out before then."

Skinny lights up a smoke, drags in a huge breath and lets out a huge exhale of air.

"Cartel may be able to step in, wipe him out completely." He shrugs, indifferent.

"Don't wanna be involved with Excalibur, though you may wanna talk to them about the plans that Cain has."

"Really? What's the word?"

"Seems that Cain wants us to wipe out the Crowes."

"Why?"

"I wouldn't cave to muling his shit. After we'd take you out, he figured Excalibur would punch our tickets. Wanted to start his own charter, headed by his own man, for transporting, trafficking, whatever he wants to do." I look over my shoulder at Sarge, who's standing still, arms in front of him.

"Your info good?"

"Came from a member who's now one with the earth." I chuckle and look over at his men.

"Noticed your VP isn't here."

"Don't know what you're saying." I take my smokes out and offer one to Skinny. He looks at the pack, throws his stub to the dirt, toes it out, and grabs a new smoke from my pack.

"What offer do you have for us?"

"I know you want the farm. The banker wanker is coming out so I can sign the papers and pay off the mortgage. I'll hand it to you once it's done, clear, no debt. But the girls are mine."

"That red-headed one I can use."

"The girls are mine," I say again, shaking my head to reinforce that I won't budge on that.

A stifling silence passes between us. I can tell he's considering my offer.

"The farm becomes ours free and clear?"

"Absolutely. I just need the manpower of your club."

Again it's quiet. A bird flies over head, squawking as it approaches a nearby tree. A small gust of dry wind swirls past us and picks up the loose leaves from the ground before they fall back to their rightful place.

GRIT

"When do you wanna go in?" he asks, agreeing to my offer.

"Tonight."

"Where are the girls?" he queries.

"Cain has a restaurant, high class, though not for general public. Behind it, he has a whore house he takes his 'clients' to. I have a feelin' the girls are in there."

"A feeling? We doing this on the fly? You shittin' me?"

"It's all I got."

Skinny walks away from me to Spit, they both turn their backs and talk.

Sarge strides over to me, his menacing 'don't fuck with me' look as clear as day. "Hmmm," he mumbles.

"Yeah I know." If the Crowes don't help us, we're still goin' in. We'll lose half the club in the process, but we're not gonna let Cain fuck us over. And we still owe him for Sandy.

Skinny walks back, a hand in his jeans pocket and pulls me up with a jut of his chin.

"We won't help again if they're not in there, and we take the farm regardless of whether you get the pussies out. Dead or alive, or not even there, not our problem. Farm's ours and we'll leave you the girls."

"Understood."

Skinny reaches his hand out to shake on it, I extend mine and we both confirm our mutual understanding.

He's taking my farm, and I'm getting the girls back.

"Seeing as heat's on your club, we'll meet up at the old roadie farm. That's a couple of miles off from his restaurant and the whore house."

I'm not surprised that he knows where Cain's place is. It's Excalibur's business to know all the players. They could easily come in and wipe us all out, but we obviously aren't a threat to them.

We deal in arms. They mostly deal with drugs and skin trade, mixed with arms, but they have their business and Cain had his. Essentially everything was working 'til Cain wanted to become a bigger player. Now the club's just trying to dig out of the shit he buried us in.

"We'll be there at nine," I say as I start to walk back to my Harley.

Skinny nods, and in less than a minute his club is already kicking up the dust as they rumble down the track.

··✥··

"You think Skinny's gonna show?" Wake asks me as he checks his guns.

"Got no reason not to," I answer as I light up another smoke, trying to lead my club.

"They may bring Excalibur to wipe us all out."

Something I've been considering myself. But if they do, then there's nothin' we can do about it. Cartel rolls in here, everything gets flattened.

The cartel has loyalty to their own. That's how they work. They discreetly advertise, giving small-timers an opportunity to join them or fuck off before they steamroll their way in, destroying all the uncooperative players left.

"They may, and really, there's nothin' stopping them. We're all in the same spot, easy annihilation, if that's what they wanna do."

Wake takes a deep breath and looks over at Sarge, who's checking his machete's edge.

"All for two chicks." Wake's half-pissed, but we'd do it for his old lady.

"You can walk away any time you want, you know that. We voted you in, we can vote you out or you can leave. Black out our emblem and you get a free pass, but don't think about joining nowhere else." It's his one-time, get-out-of-jail-free card.

"Not what I'm saying. I'm a Hunter and fuckin' proud of it. Just sayin', a lot of fuss for two chicks."

"Hunters would do it for any other old lady in the club."

He slaps a hand to my shoulder and nods. "I hear ya, brother."

Wake walks away, leaving me a minute of peace.

We hear the Crowes as they come down the trail toward us.

Skinny's first, flanked by two of his guys. The rest of the club glides on in behind him.

I walk over to Skinny, who's still sittin' on his bike, waiting for me to reach him.

"How do you wanna do this?" he asks me.

"We go in quick, hard, and fast."

"What's the setup?"

"Restaurant at the front, house joined at the back. Three entrances. Front door, back door, and one down the side for deliveries."

He looks at my brothers, eyes the number of men here and then turns and looks at his. They've got an extra five or so to us.

"You split half, side access and half back, we'll take the front and set up a perimeter," I advise.

"That's fine. Tomorrow you'll come to our house, papers in hand, regardless how this works out."

"I'll make sure they're signed over to you."

Skinny looks back at his crew, gives them a wave of the hand and they all leave.

"We'll wait 'til you're in place, give you ten seconds, then we're in," he says.

I go back to my bike, and get ready for battle.

I'm not sure what we'll find when we get there. But either way, Cain's gotta die and I've got to get my girl back.

THIRTY

Phoenix

"**G**ENTLEMEN, IT'S A PLEASURE TO HAVE YOU HERE," *HE* SAYS AS I CRAWL behind him. The only thing covering me is tit tassels and a G-string. I feel like a cheap hooker on display for everyone else's pleasure.

"Well, well. What have we got here?" a deep, Southern voice asks.

"My new slave. I've just acquired her," *he* responds to the question and tugs on the leash that's attached to a thick, black leather collar around my neck.

"Is she for us to share?" another voice asks.

I try and keep as calm as I possibly can, but being totally exposed and exhibited is humiliating to my very core.

"Stand," he commands me.

I stand slowly and slump my shoulders down, trying to hide as much of me as possible with my loose curls hanging over my breasts.

"I want to see all of her," the Southern guy says, his voice slightly rough this time.

"Hair back," *he* says.

I look up to see there are three other men in the room. All three are looking at me with such ravenous, intense looks that I imagine they all want to rip me to shreds and abuse me.

Moving my hair to hang down my back, I quickly avert my eyes again. I don't want to see how they look at me any longer. I can barely listen to them talk about me like I'm nothing more than a rag doll with holes.

"Hmmm, she certainly looks pretty standing there. Can she suck cock?"

"I've been breaking her in. Tonight is her initiation. You can't fuck her pussy or her ass, but please feel free to enjoy her mouth."

Tears spring to my eyes, knowing that in a few moments, those filthy animals will have their penises in my mouth.

"Can I eat her pussy and lick that gorgeous rim?" the Southern beast asks.

"As much as you like…" He stops talking for a moment and I hear him chuckle. "Her body enjoys being teased, though she fights it with everything that she has."

"This is going to be so much fun," another man says, his grammar is so articulate and his pronunciation is so clear, that he sounds like an upper-class, wealthy man, not a beast. But his words expose exactly the sort of man he is.

He's just as satanic as the beast that has me chained. And they're the ones I'm mostly frightened of.

"Up on the table, beautiful," *he* says as he links our fingers and urges me toward the table.

The hesitation in my step is enough for him to do something that will drive me to the edge of my own sanity.

"Bring in the girl," *he* says over his shoulder to someone standing behind me. Most likely one of his men.

The room fills with silence, and my body begins to tremble with what I'm going to see. I know he's talking about Milina. He wants to use her to punish me for hesitating in doing what he wants.

My fingertips turn icy, my head begins to spin and suddenly I can't breathe. There's a huge knot in my chest, and it hurts so badly that I don't think I can see what he's going to show me.

With my head still lowered, all my other senses are hyper-aware of everything happening in this room. My skin prickles as I feel the leers and evil eyes of every monster in this room.

If my eyes were looking at them, I'd be able to see them licking their lips as their gazes take in every inch of my body, focusing on my sex and breasts. If I lifted my head, I might even see them rubbing their disgusting hard-ons through their tailored trousers as they imagine debasing me and sacrificing me to whatever sick desire may be playing around in their evil minds.

The door squeaks as it opens, and I hear a soft panting followed by pained moans.

"Here, Boss," says whoever was sent to get Milina.

I still don't look up, but I feel him pushing her into the room. Out of the corner of my eye I see a bloodied and bruised body fall to the floor, discarded like a heap of dirty undergarments.

"Nix," she pleads with me.

I can't help but turn my head to look at the girl whose body is slumped, and broken.

"Milina," I cry as I hurl myself at her, wrapping her body in my arms, trying to protect her against whatever else they plan to do to her.

The moment my skin comes in contact with her raw, battered body, she yelps in pain. The sound rips straight through me. My heart breaks with sadness, knowing that I could've prevented it all if only I hadn't taken her to the salon for those stupid pedicures and manicures.

"I'm so sorry, Milina. So sorry, so sorry." I kiss her head, but try not to apply too much pressure on her as I keep contact with her bruised and bloody skin.

"It's not your fault, Nix," she says between moans of pain.

"Get up," *he* instructs me.

"Don't look, keep your eyes closed," I whisper to Milina, I don't want her mind filled with any more horror than she's already seen.

"I love you," we murmur together, just loud enough for the other to hear.

The words are personal and shouldn't be shared with these monsters. They're only for Milina and me. They don't deserve love. They deserve to be fucking gutted, slowly.

I stand at the command and wipe the fat tears clinging to my cheek away with the back of my hand.

"Table."

I walk over to the table, head held high, shoulders straight and back, chin up. Fuck them. They will not break me. I'll show them they can fuck me, but I refuse to let them into my own personal headspace.

I lift my left leg and get up on the table and crawl to the center of it.

"Lie on your back."

I lay on my back.

"Bend your knees up, open those hot legs and let everyone see your sweet cunt, slave."

I do as he commands.

The three men from around the table stand and walk to the edge where I'm lying.

"Whoa, she's got a piercing. You're certainly right. She's got a sweet little pussy. I'll give you ten thousand for her."

My head snaps over to a bloodied and bruised Milina, and silently I pray for her not to say a word. Her eyes are tightly closed and she can't see how these beasts are reacting to me.

"Don't be ridiculous. She's not for sale."

"I'll give you twenty thousand for her," the Southern devil says.

"You're insulting me. Taste her, fuck her mouth, but don't come in it. Come all over her, but she's not to taste your cum."

Tears are rolling down my cheeks. My hair's lying around my shoulders collecting the majority of the moisture, keeping my tears from hitting the table.

Small cries are coming from Milina, and I'm doing all I can not to make a sound. To hopefully protect Milina, and as much of me as I can. But the careless words they're saying about my body, the fact that they're so lax in their attitude toward me, is enough to cause nightmares in any sane person.

I feel the first intrusion to my sex, two fingers go straight inside me and begin their exploration of something they don't have permission from me to do.

"Fuck, she's tight. I bet she can grip a cock and milk it with these tight muscles. I love this little piercing too," the scariest one says as he flicks my clit ring.

"Wait 'til you taste her, she's sensational," *he* says.

He pulls his fingers out of me, and I hear him slurping them clean. "Damn, she does taste good. I'll give you forty thousand for her."

"No, she's not for sale," *he* says again, with a certain finality in his voice.

"I may just have to steal her from you," the suave cool voice says.

"Ha! You can definitely try; I do like some competition. But she won't go anywhere, because, I have *her*." I imagine he's pointing to Milina.

"What's she like?" the Southern man asks.

"She loves a good ass-fucking, so I've been told. I've only fucked her mouth-not the best at head jobs-but my boys said she squirms and moans for a whip. As a matter of fact, they said she loves the cat best of all."

"Really?" two men say together. *His* disturbing and repulsive statement obviously piqued an interest in these perverted motherfuckers.

"Come up here, sweet lady," the Southern guy instructs Milina.

I tilt my head and my eyes fly to *him*, silently pleading with him about our arrangement.

"Up," *he* says to Milina.

Her damaged body struggles to stand from the carpeted floor, I can tell that she's aching and sore by just her jerky movements and small cries of pain.

"Please," I say to *him*. Trying to remind him of what we agreed.

He walks over to the side of the table, his groin close to my face. He leans down and looks into my tear-filled eyes. "What is it that you want, slave?"

"You promised that you'd let her go if I did everything you want me to. I'm your good slave, Master. Please don't let them hurt her."

He straightens his back, puffs out his chest and scrubs his hand over his chin, like he's considering my plea.

"Felix," he says without even turning to look at the big, beefy thug standing by the door.

In four large strides, Felix is beside him waiting for his next command.

With just a flick of *his* eyes, he tells Felix what to do...hold me down.

I start to scream and kick, yelling as loud as I can. Hoping against hope that someone might hear me and intervene.

I know, in my heart, my resistance is pointless. They've done this before, I'm sure, plenty of times. I'm nothing more than a toy to them.

I manage to kick the guy going down on me in my struggles, he bolts upright and I see a gun in a holster when his suit jacket flares back.

"Little cunt!" he yells at me and punches me in the stomach with what feels his entire body weight.

The punch itself is excruciating, Felix grabs my arms and pins them down, immobilizing the top half of my body.

I feel like I'm about to throw up. There's vomit rapidly rising up from my beaten stomach. My body's shaking, trying to regain just a bit of my former self. Someone's tugging at my hair, reeling my head back and putting my neck into an uncomfortable position.

"I told you what I would do. You've fucking embarrassed me; now you'll watch her die!" *he* screams at me, his face ashen with anger, his hands balled into fists.

"NO!" I yell as one of the animals grabs Milina, locking her elbows together behind her back.

He takes a running leap and kicks her in the stomach. Milina lets out a guttural, throaty cry as her body tries to bend forward, completely winded by the blow.

The animal holding her arms behind her back jerks her head up by her hair and *he* lands a punch to her nose.

There's an ear-deafening crack and blood pours out of it. Milina's crying, and the tears pouring down her cheeks are making me hurt more.

He backhands her across the face. The sheer force behind it causes her already-swollen lip to split.

The others in the room are chuckling and encourage him to keep going.

Everything inside me is dying, watching my best friend being maliciously attacked by the Devil.

The assault keeps going, his fists keep hitting, and I watch as Milina slumps against her human restraints.

Just as I close my eyes, and I finally reconcile myself to my own life of whoring, I hear a gunshot. A definite echo, the sharp and precise sound of a weapon.

Everything stops.

Even Milina's whimpering is silenced.

My eyes widen.

The intensity of my heart's pounding increases.

Everyone freezes for the longest second.

The door flies open and I'm met with a sight I never thought I'd see.

Sarge.

THIRTY-ONE

"Jaeger!" Sarge yells from down the other end of the whorehouse.

The Crowes have managed to take out six of Cain's men. The restaurant at the front is completely cleared, and now Hunters are inside the whorehouse looking for the girls.

We're in and have secured part of the pussy shop, but I can tell by Sarge's tone that he's found them.

I don't hesitate for a second. I bolt down the long hallway, with Hash, Wake, Dodge and Cruise behind me. The door's already open and the moment I'm inside the room I see her.

A huge guy has his arm around Phoenix's neck, holding her in a choke hold. Sarge's fist has just connected with the guy holding Milina, and Cain's looking over his shoulder at me, smiling.

There's a long meeting table in the center of the room. Some of the chairs are upturned and some are still in their rightful spots.

My eyes narrow in on Phoenix. I see she's totally exposed except for some stupid looking tassels on her tits. But her skin, it's covered with bruises and marks. Her eyes find mine, and for a split second I see a look of sheer terror and panic cross her face before it changes into relief. I've come to get my girl back, and I think she's glad to see me.

They're on the other side of the room, opposite end from me.

Cain steps away from the bedlam that's unfolding around the rest of the room. He rubs a hand to the back of his neck and eyes me with a look that's supposed to inspire terror from me.

First and foremost, I'm a street fighter. I've snapped the necks of men bigger than him, and never thought about them again.

Today, I'll take great satisfaction in knowing that Cain will be dead within the next few minutes.

"Jaeger," he says as he straightens his shoulders.

"I just want the girls." I take a step toward the table and Cain takes an opposing stride.

He shrugs off his suit jacket and puts it on the back of one of the chairs.

Looks like this is the way it's gonna have to be.

He carefully unbuttons his shirt, and takes it off. His chest is filled with scars and angry red lines cover his torso, from his neck all the way to where his trousers sit on his waist. Looks like he might know a thing or two about fighting.

"They aren't yours anymore."

"They'll always be mine," I say, beginning to circle the table, one careful step after another.

My legs slowly crossing over the other, my chin lowered, my shoulders back, hands in tight fists, ready to strike my opponent.

Cain knows what I'm doing. He's keeping up with me, circling the table, two alpha sharks in a stand-off. Both ready to exchange, both ready to battle, though neither ready to die.

I grab a chair and throw it at Cain. He ducks and it misses him. He jumps up on the table in one swift maneuver.

I step back and watch as Cain lands in a defensive stance. Left leg forward, hips rotated though his arms cross in front of his chest.

"You've made it personal," he says as he lifts his chin with superior confidence. "You've already lost this battle."

Cain lowers his arm, inviting me to join him in this duel. He's cocky and believes he can defeat me.

I jump up on the table, opposite end from Cain. My right arm is up near my chin in a fist and my left arm is hovering around my mid-section, left leg out in front, ready to take him on.

Cain straightens his stance, the arrogant motherfucker telling me by his position that he's not at all worried about me.

I charge for Cain, throwing a right cross with a tight fist to his face. Cain steps away from it into my blind side. I kick with my left leg to hit Cain's right thigh, but Cain lifts his leg in defense, and I only make glancing contact with his shin. I come in with a right elbow to smash his nose, but the ass brings both hands up to block.

Cain's right hand is still cupping my elbow, while his left hand comes around and pulls my head into his upper arm, squeezing me there, cutting off my line of sight.

I feel Cain take a long step forward; we're hip to hip now. I know that a throw is coming.

He pivots his body. My own gets washed away with the force of his rotation and he throws me to the edge of the table.

He drops his knee, intending to break my ribs, but I roll to the left off the table, jump straight up and back three feet into a defensive posture.

"You've become soft; you're no longer a fighter. She's made you into a pussy," Cain says as he moves to the edge of the table.

He uses the table's ledge, jumps off, rotates his hips and comes at me with a flying side kick. I step back; he misses. He lands and now I have the upper ground.

As he lands, I kick his left thigh. There's no time for him to defend. He buckles and I get a chance to strike a right punch to his temple. He falls to the left, and uses his body weight to roll and get straight back up.

Cain charges toward me. I throw a punch in anticipation of the exchange, but Cain fucking squats, back straight, wrapping his arms around my thighs as his head comes under my left arm and drives my back into the table.

My lower back hits the table's edge, and with a long, extended arm he covers my entire face with the palm of his hand. He lands a punch to my temple.

Shit, I gotta get out of this hold. A few more hits like that and I won't survive.

Another punch to the temple and it's time to make my move.

I grip the arm that's on my face and lock it into my body. My other arm protects the side of my head. When he goes to strike again, I cup the back of his head and roll him off me.

But Cain grabs onto my arm and rolls me over too. Now he's in prime position.

He sits on my chest, knees either side of me and he starts hammering into me.

I bring my hands up to defend my head. His fists are coming hard and fast.

He lands one, square on the chin. One more like that and he'll knock me out.

I hear a whistle and look in that direction.

There's still mayhem happening in the room, Phoenix is struggling to get out of her head lock, the boys are fighting the other two suits that were in here when I charged in. It looks like there's a few more of Cain's men fighting with mine.

One of the suits is down, one of Cain's thugs is down, Milina's in a tight ball with her knees up and her back against the wall. It's pure chaos.

Cain and I both look in the direction of the whistle, and he momentarily ceases his attack on me.

One of his thugs throws Cain a serrated hunting knife. Cain catches it by the handle, and we both know what's about to happen.

I bring my hands up in defense and his first stab is straight into my arm.

Immediately, I feel the blood pour out of the wound on my arm, and I hear a high-pitched scream.

"NO!!!!" Phoenix yells with such passion and intensity.

"You fought with your heart, and now it's gonna cost you your life," Cain says as he draws the knife back above his head for the death blow.

"Fuck you!" I say to Cain. My jaw's clenched in anger. I'm drawing on all my strength to roll him off me and to finally finish him.

A sound that I'm so familiar with brings everything to a halt.

It's deafening in a room like this; it echoes through the entire place. My ears are ringing and my entire body is humming with adrenaline.

I stand to my feet, staunching the bleeding from the cut in my left arm with my right hand.

Looking around the room, my men have guns on two, and the rest are down. Their chests aren't moving, their eyes are open, and there's a lot of spilled blood.

I turn around to see Phoenix's angry, vacant stare. She's holding a gun with steady hands, pointing it at an immobile Cain.

"Sugar," I say as I step up to her.

"He was going to kill you, then me and Milina. Fucker had to die," she says, her voice flat, devoid of any emotion.

"Give me the gun, sugar," I say, stepping up to her side as I put my hand on hers.

"He was going to kill you, then me and Milina. Fucker had to die," she whispers, repeating her words. Shock is starting to set in. I gotta get my girl away from here.

"Phoenix." I lower my tone and move my body in front of hers. "Give me the gun," I say again, trying to ease her with just my tone.

Her eyes are wild, and she's starting to shake.

I look to Sarge, who's wrapped a badly beaten Milina in his t-shirt and has her in his arms, walking her out of the room.

"Clean this shit up. Get rid of them," I say to Hash, Wake and the rest of my brothers.

They all nod, understanding my instructions.

"Nix, look at me." I pry the gun from her fingers, put the safety back on and tuck it into the back of my jeans. Phoenix's eyes are glued to Cain, who's lying on his back, arms out beside him, with a hole through his chest.

"I killed him," she whimpers as her big, blue eyes fill with tears.

I cloak her in my body, turning her and shielding her from what's just happened.

Jason comes into the room and looks around him, before his eyes settle on Phoenix. "She alright?" he asks me.

"Get the truck," I say, shaking my head. He bolts out of the room and goes to get the SUV. I take my bloodied and half ripped shirt off, "Lift your arms," I say to Nix.

Without hesitation she lifts them above her head and I slide the shirt over her.

"I'm sorry, Jaeger," she whispers as she begins to sob.

"You've got nothin' to be sorry for, sugar. You didn't do anything wrong."

"I'm sorry you had to come looking for me," she says as she leans into my body.

"I couldn't stay away even if I wanted to."

She's struggling to walk, her body is trembling and she's crying a fuckin' river. I hate seeing her so God damned broken.

"Jaeger?"

"Yeah, sugar."

We're taking it slow, one small step in front of the other. I'd carry her if my mother fuckin' arm wasn't ripped up by that fucker's knife.

"I..." She collapses.

What the hell?

THIRTY-TWO

"Hey," I say to Sarge as he walks into the kitchen, and grabs a cup to pour some coffee into.

"Hey," he replies.

"What did Doc say about Milina?"

"Doc's still in there with her. They fucked her up pretty good. Makes me wanna dig 'em all up and fuckin' kill 'em again." He drinks his black coffee as he sits at the table.

"Yeah." I nod, wishing I too could kill them all again. Slowly, and with a lot of painful torture.

"Phoenix?" he asks as he lifts his head from his coffee.

"She's passed out. Somethin' about her mind protecting itself from everythin' it's seen. I don't really know what shit Doc was saying, just that Nix needs the rest."

"Was she raped?"

"Doc said there wasn't any scarrin' or rips or anything in her pussy or ass, but I'll ask her when she wakes up."

"Lina's been beat up pretty bad, probably take her some time to recover."

We both go quiet. I'm not really sure what to say to him about his girl. All those fuckers are dead. Can't really kill 'em any more than they are, or I'd be first in line to fuck 'em up real good.

"Bank manager's supposed to be coming out so I can sign the papers for the farm, but seein' as there's a hole in the building, and FBI is due, I'll take Hash and we'll go in to the bank. You alright looking after the girls?"

Sarge shoots me a look, telling me that if I question him again, we'll settle it in the ring.

"How's the arm?" I ask, pointing to his gunshot wound.

"Just a scratch. Yours?"

"A few stitches, nothin' serious."

I finish my coffee, and walk down the hall toward my girl.

When I open the door, she's lying exactly how I left her. Her hands tucked up under her cheek, lying on her side.

Her wild red hair is all over the place, in complete disarray. She looks so peaceful lying in my bed.

I sit beside her and run the back of my hand over her face, just tucking the loose strands away behind her ear. Phoenix shifts in her sleep, moving closer to me.

This damned chick has seriously screwed me over. I've never felt anything like this for a woman before, never wanted to protect someone with every part of me.

Her little moans rip through my damned heart and I know that I need her close to me, to guard her and keep her safe.

·•✥•·

"Skinny," I greet him as Hash and I walk into the Crowes clubhouse.

"Jaeger, hope you brought the deeds," he says as he leans back in the seat while some chick gives him a blowjob.

He extends his arms to the back of the chair and nods to another club whore to get us a drink.

She scurries off and comes back with a bottle of tequila and three shot glasses.

"Drink?" he asks as Hash stands by the door and I sit on the single chair opposite him.

"All good," I say, declining his offer.

"She can make you come in about four minutes," he says pointing to the chick who brought over the tequila.

He motions for her to get on her knees in front of me, and immediately she does.

"Nah, I'm good there, too. Just dropping the deeds off."

He grabs the hair of the chick who's giving him a blow job and snaps her head back. Her mouth is all pouty and red, she must've been suckin' him off for a while.

"Take Trix and go to my room, when I come in there I wanna see you eatin' her pussy," he says to the chick on her knees in front of him.

"Sure thing, Mr. Prez." She giggles, gets up from her knees and walks over to the chick Skinny just offered me.

They start kissin', and damn, they're fine. My cock begins to strain against my jeans, and I adjust it as I watch the girls take their tank tops off and suck on each other's pert little nipples.

"Want 'em?" Skinny asks as I eye-fuck the girls.

"Usually I'm all for shit like that, but I gotta decline. My girl's waiting for me," I say without taking my eyes off the two girls.

Damn, one strips the other's tiny little shorts and starts fingering her in front of me.

I hear a deep guttural moan from behind me, and I know that Hash has gotta be having a hard time watching these two girls.

"Him?" Skinny offers as he flicks a look over at Hash.

"He'll be alright, too."

The girl takes her fingers out of the other one's pussy and starts sucking on them, then goes back to kissing the girl. Fuck, I'm holdin' on, only just, but I'm holdin' on.

I gotta look away before I get up and jump in there, one can sit on my face as I lick her cunt while the other lowers her ass onto my cock and I screw her hard.

"Um..." *Look away, Jaeger. Nix will kick your damned ass.* "The deeds," I say dragging my eyes away from the sexy exhibition the girls are putting on for us.

"You brought them?" He sounds surprised.

My eyes go back to the beautiful girls caressing each other, each slowly moving their mouths against the other, devouring with leisurely sensual long licks of their tongues.

"If you want them?" Skinny offers, making me drag my eyes away from them.

"Nah," I say, my voice slightly husky. I quickly glance at them and stand. I hand the deeds to the land over to Skinny and take a step to the back door.

Back door – HA! I crack myself up sometimes.

"As promised," I say and back away from a scene that has the potential to see my balls detached from my body if Nix ever finds out.

"Excalibur's happy with how you handled shit," Skinny says as he stands and takes the few steps over to me.

"Good. Don't wanna piss off the cartel."

"They know you're running for the Pace family, but they've offered an additional job opportunity for you."

"Not interested," I say as I shrug my shoulders.

"They knew that was gonna be your answer."

"And?"

Christ, don't tell me that Excalibur will end up wiping us out.

"And nothing," he pauses for a moment, silently telling me that Excalibur won't bother us... *for now.* "We're good," Skinny states.

"Yeah, we're good." I chance one small look at the two chicks enjoying each other and walk out that door.

"Damn," Hash says. Clearly those two club whores had the same, if not a worse effect on him.

"I know, brother." I get on my Harley and start her up.

"Damn," he says again. He takes a deep breath, looks over his shoulder, like he can see them through the brick wall. He starts his bike and takes off.

GRIT

⋯✦⋯

Walking into the clubhouse, the only thing I wanna do is have my girl curl her body around mine, as close as she can get.

Although the two club sluts were all into fuckin' each other over at the Crowes' place, and I was ready to be on the receiving end of a seriously great blow job, I'll hold off on getting Nix to suck me off 'til she's ready.

The clubhouse is quiet, and I know that Sarge will be in one of the rooms down the back lookin' after Milina.

Tough motherfucker, my ass.

He's seriously pussy-whipped, and they haven't even screwed yet.

I walk into my room and Nix hasn't moved a damned inch.

Doctor said when her brain calms down she'll wake on her own, or some shit like that. I really wasn't listening, only heard the key points.

I toe off my boots and lie down under the thin blanket covering her and drape my arm over her waist, pulling her in toward me.

Holding her.

Protecting her.

Claiming her.

Ahhh, shit.

As I lay behind Nix, with her warm, soft body pressed against mine, strands of her flaming red hair falling haphazardly across my face, I finally figure my shit out.

I fuckin' love her, just... *shit*.

When did that happen?

Why did that happen?

I don't do stupid, meaningless emotions. Who the hell wants to feel like crap when they're left holding the damned pieces of a screwed-up, dysfunctional relationship? I saw enough of that shit growing up.

Nothin' stays. *Ever.*

People that should have had my back and been loyal to me have turned out to be my biggest disappointments. Just look at Aaron.

But does that mean that Nix will follow in the path of the others? She put a bullet in Cain's chest...*for me.*

And there's no chance in hell that I'll ever let her go.

She belongs with me. Not just because I wanna keep her safe, but because I God damn love her.

I. AM. SO. SCREWED.

THIRTY-THREE

Phoenix

"I'LL NEVER LET ANYTHING HAPPEN TO YOU AGAIN. WAKE UP, SUGAR, MY cock needs sucking," Jaeger murmurs in my ear.

What?

I open my eyes and I'm lying in Jaeger's arms. My head is resting on his upper arm, his bicep is hard beneath me, but his warmth is so inviting.

"What did you say?" I mumble, my voice all gravelly. My throat's rough and dry.

"Phoenix!" Jaeger half-shouts, scaring the crap out of me.

"What's going on?"

Jaeger moves me from his embrace, laying me back on the pillow, and raising himself up on an elbow to look down at me.

"How are you feelin', sugar?"

"Not well enough to do what you want." I try and stretch, but my body is tight and sore. "What happened?" I ask, trying to think back to the last thing I remember.

"You killed Cain," Jaeger says in such a deadpan, emotionless voice.

It takes me a few seconds, and I focus on an invisible spot on the wall. I can feel myself frowning as I bring a hand up to rub the back of my neck.

It only takes those few seconds to have an instant replay of everything that happened in that room with those beasts.

"I... I..." I start to panic. My heart's beating so fast it feels like it's about to seize or beat straight out of my chest.

My palms are sweaty and my body begins to tremble.

"Shhh. It's alright," Jaeger says as he wraps his arms around me, pulling me to sit between his open legs.

I notice his arm is bandaged, "What happened to your arm? Did I do that?"

"Nah, it was Cain. He was just about to kill me, and you shot him."

"I remember that," I whisper as I snuggle closer into Jaeger. "Oh, God, I killed him."

"You have to know that this entire bullshit situation had nothin' to do with you."

"Milina?!" I shout, trying to push Jaeger's arms off me. His grip is like a tight vice; his subtle aroma of tobacco swirls around me, and he immediately becomes my safe place.

"She's alright. She's with Sarge. We got the doc to come out and check you both out."

"Will she be okay?" I ask, nuzzling into his frame further.

I feel so protected here, comfortable, *loved*.

"It'll be a while before she's back to normal, but Sarge will look after her, and so will the club."

I feel tears begin to fill my eyes and I want to let them go, but I've been such a *girl* lately – always crying.

"Why did he take us?" I ask, my voice starting to break.

"Because of your father."

"My dad?" I lift my head a little and look up at Jaeger, whose own eyes look so forlorn and sad.

"Yeah, I'm sorry to be the one to tell ya', sugar. But your old man, he was a bastard."

"Huh?" I don't get what he's trying to say.

"Your father. He sold you to Cain to clear his gambling debts. Milina was just an added bonus."

What? That doesn't make sense. My father was definitely not a good person by anyone's standards, but to *sell me*? Who does shit like that?

"I gotta start at the beginning, 'cause otherwise, none of this shit's gonna make sense to you," Jaeger says as he sits up against the head board, dragging me with him.

"Alright."

"Your dad owed us money. He put up the farm as collateral. Obviously, he died and didn't make his payment. But he also put the land up as collateral to the Crowes too. Remember the MC that shot up your house that night?"

I nod my head and try to keep up with what he's saying.

"Cain, who was associated with us, wanted us to start muling his drugs. But the club said no."

I feel myself staring at Jaeger. My mouth falls open and already the questions are mounting.

"Your father sold you to Cain, I think 'cause he owed him gambling debts too."

"Did you know?" I ask, becoming apprehensive.

"Nah. But anyway, Cain wanted to go ahead with the drugs and Aaron wanted part of it."

"Aaron?" I ask. "Your friend?"

"My VP. He was the closest thing to a brother I ever had."

"Had?" What?

"Yeah, *had*." He looks down and I see regret flash across his face, before he becomes the arrogant ass he usually is. "Cain and Aaron staged a few things, making it look like the Crowes were our enemy. They figured we'd wipe out the Crowes, the Crowes' bosses would wipe us out, leaving Cain and Aaron free to reign over this territory."

"What things did they stage?"

"Made it look like one of our members was a mole at the table. Aaron killed him to make it look suspicious. Told the Crowes Hunters' business, making it look like the guy who'd gone missin' was the mole."

What a tangled web of deceit that all happened right under Jaeger's nose.

"How do you know you don't have another traitor?" I ask him.

He shrugs his shoulders, kisses the top of my head and pulls me tighter into his embrace. "I don't," he says after a few seconds of intense silence passes.

"Can we just go to the farm, please? I want to live there," I plead, knowing my haven is only a few hours away.

"Yeah, about that..."

I feel Jaeger's arms slightly loosen around me, and he takes in a deep breath. His chest puffs out as he holds the breath, waiting.

"What?"

"I don't own it any more. I had to give it to the Crowes for helping us to get you and Milina away from Cain."

I move away from Jaeger, and sit on the side of the bed, turned away from him. Running my hand through my hair, I find knots at the ends. I look at my body and notice that I'm wearing Jaeger's ripped, bloody t-shirt, which comes down to the tops of my thighs.

My body is covered in bruises. My legs and arms have angry blue and purple splotches all over them, but the worst thing for me...is the damn memory of everything that's happened.

Feeling like I'm going to be sick, I try to run to the bathroom. But my legs feel like Jello, and I instantly fall to the floor.

The repeated punches Cain gave Milina.

The guy who had me in a choke hold while he was trying to slip his fingers inside my sex.

In a hopeless heap I lie on the floor, crying at what shit my life's turned out to be.

Jaeger leaps off the bed and completely envelops me with his body, protecting me from myself and everything around me.

"You should've left me there," I cry, hating that I've caused him any pain.

"No way. No way will I ever let you go. But how did you get out of the choke hold he had on you?" He smooths my hair as he cocoons me with his touch.

"He relaxed the hold for a split second while he was trying to finger me, and I saw my opportunity. I elbowed him in the ribs, then swung around and punched him." I look down at my hand and stretch out my fingers. "Then I grabbed his gun and killed that animal that was just about to kill you." I go quiet for a moment. "I'm so sorry for everything that happened."

"I'm proud of you, Nix. But there's no reason to be sorry, you were just a bystander."

Jaeger's words resonate deep within me. He's right. It's not my fault any of this shit happened. It's all because of my useless father.

He chose to get into gambling after Mom died. No one forced him. He could've gotten help way before this got to the point of me being kidnapped and beaten.

I'm not sure how long Jaeger and I sit on the floor of his bedroom before I make a silent promise not to hold myself, Jaeger, or his club responsible for this entire dark situation.

I stand from the floor and straighten my shoulders, hold my damn head high, because I know I've done nothing wrong. And neither has Jaeger.

"Where are you going?" Jaeger asks as he stands and runs his hands up and down my arms.

"I'm going to take a shower and then have something to eat."

"Okay, I'll be here when you get out," he says as I achingly lift my arms over my head to take off the t-shirt I'm wearing.

"Oh and, sugar?"

"Yeah?" I turn to look at Jaeger over my shoulder, still stepping toward the bathroom.

"You're moving in here with me," he commands.

"What?"

"Just thought you should know. Gonna go make my woman somethin' to eat," he says as he walks out of the room, leaving me to process what he's just said.

What the hell is wrong with him?

Is he delusional? Maybe he hit his head.

Why on earth is he so adamant that I move in here?

But then, I stop to really consider what he's said.

He could've just walked away with the farm and left me to Cain.

But he called in a rival club, actually asked for help from them, and promised them the farm, in order to get Milina and me back.

Well...

Tick.

Tock.

Tick.

Tock.

He loves me.

THIRTY-FOUR
eight weeks later

"Nix?" I call over to my woman, who's helping some of the other old ladies set the table. She's deep in conver-sation with one of them, and doesn't hear me. "Sugar," I call louder. She's still talking, not even paying attention to me. "Red," I say no louder than my normal voice.

"Excuse me?" She swings around and puts her hands on her hips.

"I was callin' you, Nix, and you didn't hear me."

"I heard you, but I was ignoring you," she says as she turns and walks into the clubhouse.

"Hey, don't walk away from me." I chase after her.

Damn it, wasn't that me just a while back saying that I don't chase chicks, and now what am I doin'? Like a damn lapdog, chasing after my girl.

"For Christ's sake, will you just stop?" I yell at Nix as she looks over her shoulder at me, shootin' a filthy 'piss off' look.

"Go away."

"Not 'til we talk about this."

"Nothing to talk about, go away."

"I asked you a question and you haven't given me an answer," I say as I block her path from leaving the kitchen.

"That's 'cause you're a dick."

"No more than normal. What's the damn issue? It's either a yes or a no."

"Are you kidding me?" She puts the bowl with some green leafy shit down and crosses her arms in front of her hot titties. Man, I love sucking on those, but with the way she's standing she's seriously pissed off and I doubt she'll let me run my tongue over her nipples.

She scowls at me. I'm screwed.

"You're an idiot." She throws her hands up, clearly frustrated. "A damned moron. How you've survived all these years is beyond me."

I shrug my shoulders, "I can fight; that's how I've survived."

"You may be able to fight but you're an arrogant, pompous ass."

"Well, yeah. But that's not really givin' me an answer, sugar." I lean up against the wall, cross my legs at the ankle and my arms over my chest. I ain't moving 'til she gives me a damn answer.

"Really?" she says, her tone low and damned furious.

I am seriously screwed.

Just let it go, Jaeger – let it go.

"You want a damn answer? How about this, NO and go fuck yourself." She shoulder barges past me, taking that salad shit and bread rolls out for the barbecue.

"Why the hell not?" I say, again following her.

She slams the stuff down on the table outside and abruptly turns on her heel to look at me.

Half my brothers are here startin' the barbecue and all the old ladies are outside. With the noise of Nix smashing the bowls down on the table, it gets quiet real quick.

"No, you conceited prick," she yells, taking a step closer to me.

I swear the members of the club just multiplied.

"But why?" I ask.

Why don't I just learn to shut the hell up?

"Because you don't ask me to marry you while I'm on my knees and your cock is in my mouth shooting it full of your cum. You don't say," She sticks her chest out and slouches, obviously tryin' to mimic me, "'Hey, sugar, you give great head. I think we best make it real and I put a ring on that finger'," she says in a deeper tone, but then continues in a higher, pissed-off voice, " You don't say shit like that before you even tell me you love me. You're an idiot, and you can shove that stupid proposal up your damned ass, Mr. Dalton," she screams at me.

I hear a few snickers and look around to see Sarge pissing himself laughing at me, but trying to hide behind Milina so I don't kick his butt.

Hash is holding a beer and tryin' to contain his laughter, but he can't hold it in. Wake and Lion have their backs to me, but their shoulders are shakin' quickly; they're laughing at me too.

Sarge walks over to me, and smacks me one on the back.

"Can't call you Sarge no more," I say as his chuckles echo loudly outside.

"Not calling me VP. You can screw that," he says of his new role. "Seriously, you asked her to marry you while you were gettin' head?"

"Fuckin' intimate act and all that shit. Thought she'd like it."

Sarge's booming laughter rings in my ears. I'll put him down if he doesn't watch himself. "You, brother, are the dumbest prick I've ever met. Even I know that chicks want hearts and flowers and crap like that."

What?

Chicks don't want shit like that. They just want us to not lie to them. C'mon, what better way for me to tell my girl I want her with me forever, than when she's on her knees and I'm fuckin' her mouth?

"Nah, man, they don't want that crap," I say, not believing a word coming from my VP's mouth.

"Yeah they do, trust me."

"Man, you're talkin' out of your ass. How do you know what chicks want?"

"Lina," Sarge calls his woman over. She's at the ice chest getting a drink, and when she looks at him, her face comes to life.

She's as screwed as he is.

"What's up?" she asks as she reaches up to kiss him on the cheek.

"Do you chicks want romance, chocolate, and flowers?"

She looks at him and tilts her head to the side.

The last eight weeks has seen her body go from completely bruised to small light yellow blemishes left on her skin. The scars are still pretty obvious, but over time they'll fade too. Sarge has pretty much assigned one of the prospects to be next to her when she's not here, and two will wait for her to finish work so they can escort her home, when she gets back to her job – not that Sarge wants her to work.

Nix wakes occasionally in tears, and all I can do is hold her and tell her everything will be alright.

"We like to know we're appreciated," she says as she slides her arm around his waist and he leans down to kiss her forehead.

"What if say, this asshole, proposed to Phoenix while she was giving him a blow job?"

"You did not!" she exclaims as her head rips around to look at me, her eyes wide and incredulous.

Great. Two women pissed off at me. All I need is Cindy or Sandy, whatever the hell her name is, to be pissed off at me too.

"Yeah, I love her givin' me head and I love her. What's the problem?" I say, shrugging my shoulders.

"Please tell me you're bullshitting us?!"

I look her dead in the eyes, essentially tellin' her I ain't bullshitting.

Seriously, I don't see the problem.

"Haven't you figured her out yet?" Milina asks as she points toward where Nix should be.

"What?"

"She's tough, she's headstrong, and she'll take you on any day of the week. But she needs a man strong enough to love her, not only with his mind but also his heart and sometimes with his words."

"Right," I say. I think I know what I did wrong. She does want flowers and shit, but not all the time, just sometimes.

Well that's shit too. How am I supposed to know when I have to do and say romance crap to her?

Christ, this relationship shit is damned hard. Maybe if she tells me the day before, then I can have time to go get her stuff she likes.

I head inside to find Nix and talk to her. Seriously, how people can do this shit every day is beyond me.

I walk into the kitchen and find her getting the meat out of the fridge. She looks pissed but also sad.

"Hey," I say as I come up behind her and put my hands on her hips, drawing her into my body. The moment my body touches hers, I start gettin' hard.

"Hey," she says. Her shoulders relax a bit, and she takes a small step back into me. Her ass rubs against my semi.

"Sorry, I probably should've waited to ask you to marry me."

Her right hand's holding a kitchen knife. She stills her movements and lays it on the counter before turning in my arms and putting her arms around my neck.

"Yeah, probably," she says, sarcastically.

"C'mon, sugar. Screw the cookout." I link our fingers together and start walkin' out of the kitchen.

"Where are we going?"

"I got something important to tell you, and I need to tell you in our room."

She tries to hold her smile in, but really, her beautiful face has brightened the whole room.

We walk into our room, and I close and lock the door behind me.

Leaning up against the door I notice she hasn't turned around to look at me. Nix shifts her flaming red mane over one shoulder, and exposes her wickedly tasty neck to me.

The perverted part of me wants to rip her clothes off and drive my cock into her pert little ass. But the 'romantic' part of me is arguing, telling me I need to tell her how much I love her first.

Devil on one shoulder, and a tarnished saint on the other.

"Sugar," I say as I step up to her, and lower my mouth to the exposed part of her throat.

"Hmmm," she replies as she moves to the side, giving me more access to her sweet skin.

"I really want my cock in your ass."

I can feel her smiling as she rotates her hips and pushes back into my groin.

"Do you?"

Nix reaches behind her and starts palming my wood through my jeans.

"Hell, yeah."

My hands go to the hem of her tank top and begin to lift it up over her head. Screw this, too much time.

I grab it between my fists and rip the thing off her body. She moans as my hands go straight to her bra and I unhook those two little clip things in the back.

"God, yes," she murmurs in a low sexy voice.

"Take these off, now," I say as I smack her butt, then quickly get undressed myself.

Within seconds, she's still standing with her back to me, completely exposed.

"Hmmm, what should I do to you?" I say, though it's more a rhetorical question.

"Whatever you want," she answers, a purr coming from deep inside her chest.

I push my fingers into her red curls and pull her head back. Her neck is nice and long; she's got her eyes closed and mouth open, panting.

"That's right, whatever I want. And now, I wanna fuck this hot little ass," I say as I spank her once, hard enough to leave a hand print on her alabaster skin.

She instantly drops down a small amount, spreading her legs, wanting me to touch her pussy. The pleasure I'm giving her with such a small caress is clearly intoxicating her body.

GRIT

My lips skim over her shoulder as I continue holding her head back, not allowing any other part of me to touch her flaming skin. Her body curves into mine, as she tries to take the warmth between us.

"No way," I snap at her, and smack her ass again. "Not until I want you to touch me."

"Please," she begs, her voice husky and hungry.

I've barely touched her, hardly let our naked bodies touch, yet she's greedy and wants more of me.

"Please what?" I say as I jerk her head back further. Her back is slightly arched and her neck is completely elongated, but the little vixen has her butt sticking out, wanting me touch it.

"Please, just touch me," she pleads.

My left hand has her hair in my grip, so I slide my right hand across her tits. Her nipples are long and begging for attention. I pull on the left one and twist it, just enough to give her a taste of pain.

"God yes, please keep going," she moans.

I let go of her nipple, and grab at her jaw, forcing her to turn and look at me. She snaps her eyes open, and her usual big blue orbs are completely dark, greedy with lust.

"You don't tell me what to do. I tell you what I want. And right now I want you wet and ready to take my cock in your mouth, your cunt and your ass. And if you don't like what I say, then get over it, sugar, 'cause I fuckin' love you and this is me."

"You love me?" she asks, damned tears ready and waitin' to spill as soon as I admit I love her.

"Not when you cry," I say as her lips twist, playfully. "But yeah, I love you. Now, get on your knees and start sucking me off."

She winds her body around, standing in front of me, completely exposed, and totally turned-on. "I'll suck you off, Mr. Prez," she leans in and purrs in my ear. "But only because I love you too." She licks the shell of my ear, and draws her tongue down my jaw to my chin, where she sucks the scarred point into her mouth.

Slowly she kisses and licks her way down my body. I close my eyes and enjoy the sensation of having her so close to me. But her words have caused a shudder to tear through my body.

She loves me too. Why wouldn't she?

I can feel a smile tugging at my lips, but I try to hold it in.

"Now that we've got that sorted, get on your knees and suck me with that beautiful mouth."

Her fingertips starts tracing over my abs, slowly moving down the ridges as she gracefully lowers herself to her knees. Her hot breath teases my cock; her eyes hold my gaze.

I weave my hands in her hair, and guide her mouth to take my cock as far as she can take it. I want her to deep throat me, but I know she struggles with it.

A raw desire hums between us, the heat radiating off our bodies is enough to add to the world's climate control issue.

Nix lowers her mouth and licks the head of my cock. All I want to do is grab her head and drive my cock hard between those pretty, pouty lips, hoping she starts gasping for air as spit drips out the side of her mouth.

"Wait, sugar," I say, suddenly wanting to taste her pussy.

"What's wrong?" she asks, concerned.

"Nothin'." I hold my hand out for her, to help her get off the floor. "Come sit on my face. I wanna lick your pussy."

A gleam of delight passes over her entire body. Yeah, my girl wants me feasting on her pussy as she takes me in her mouth.

I lie on my back on the bed, and motion for her to come to me. Ha! Hopefully she'll come on me too.

She lowers her sweet little pussy to my face, and instantly, I'm met with my favorite taste in the world–Phoenix's arousal. God, when her pussy is wet like this, it's damned torturous not being able to get my tongue deeper inside her.

I wrap my hands around the top of her thighs, and force her down on my waiting mouth. My tongue goes straight for her needy, empty hole, licking her clit ring as I pass it.

"Oh God," she moans as she grinds her pussy into my face. My hands pull her further open, baring her mouth-watering wet slit to me.

I trace my tongue around her hole, and she grinds down further onto me, trying to find the position that'll set her off.

"I'll stop if you don't start sucking me," I mumble against her pussy.

She lowers her head and her entire body warmth is laying on mine. Phoenix is propped up on one elbow and I feel her hand go around my cock as she squeezes; her breath is hot on my head and I feel the spit from the slight touch of her tongue.

She's teasing me, making me crave more of her mouth on me. I flex my hips up, while I flick her clit ring with my tongue.

Her breathing sounds ragged as her hips keep rotating in small circles. Nix's tongue slides the length of my cock, her hot breath connecting with my skin. She kisses my balls, then sucks them into her mouth. Nix grazes her teeth over my sac and my own pulse beats hard like a damn drum inside me.

I extend my tongue as far into her slit as I can get it, and really hold her down on my face.

"Ahhh, yeah," she says around my balls.

The vibration of her words send shock waves through my entire body, and I feel my balls begin to tighten as she keeps her mouth on them.

Screw this shit, I want to be inside her.

I lick her pussy once more and move her off my face.

"Bend over the bed, sugar, I wanna take your ass," I tell her as I roll off the bed and grab the lube from inside the second drawer.

I watch Nix squirm and close her legs, trying to rub her clit with just the way she's standing.

"You make yourself come, and I'll make your ass so red you won't be able to sit for a week," I say to her over my shoulder as I squirt some lube onto my hand and rub it over my dick.

Smiling, she stands with her legs wide apart and leans her top half over the bed. "I wish I brought my Lelo with me," she says, looking up at me with a dark, dangerous expression.

"What would you do with a lemon?" I ask her, while I watch Nix pinch her nipples and pull them out.

"Lelo," she corrects me, "is the best vibrator in the world," she says.

Fuck me!

My girl is hot.

I stride over to her, and push her head down onto the bed, immobilizing her so she can't do much but take what I'm just about to give her.

I line my cock up with her ass, just pressing the head inside. She's so tight, it's taken every spark of control inside me not to ram my cock deep inside her.

"Wait," she moans. "Let me get used to you."

I can feel her hole trying to push against me. She's taking deep breaths and trying to adjust around me. I push in a little more, and instantly she relaxes on my cock.

"That feels so good. Push in further," she says as she moves back toward me.

I can't help but let her head go, and spread her ass cheeks apart so I can plunge further into her.

Looking down at where we're both joined as one is the sexiest sight I've seen since looking up into Phoenix's pussy a few minutes ago.

"You're so beautiful," I eagerly say.

My hands hold her inviting little ass cheeks open and I begin to thrust in and out of her. Taking my cock to the very edge of her rim, before pushing in with force; going deep and hard.

"How do we look?" she asks as she grinds her hips back into my groin, taking me deeper into her ass.

"Fuckin' hot, I want my phone so I can record it."

"Get it," she says, surprising me.

My jeans are on the floor beside us. I lean over and grab my phone out of the pocket and turn the camera on, setting it to record.

"Hold your ass open, sugar, I wanna get in good and close," I instruct her.

Phoenix's hands come around the back and she spreads her ass, ready for me to fuck her hard.

I slide into her with ease and start pounding into her, my hips are met with hers and my thrusts are hard and fast.

The room has that hot aroma of sex coating us. My balls are making that wicked slapping sound against her pussy and she's moaning and telling me to ram into her harder.

Who knew she'd be so damn horny, needing my cock as much as I need her pussy? *As much as I need her.*

Nix tightens her hole as I slide out, and the feeling alone is nearly my undoing.

"Do it again," I say, trying to keep my eyes open so I can continue recording.

"Hmmm," she hums, clearly enjoying this.

My thrusts are getting harder and deeper, my body ravaging Nix's, taking what I want from her, but also giving her what she needs.

My heart starts to pound and my pulse quickens. Sweat beads and rolls down the back of my neck. I throw the phone onto the bed and hook my right arm under Nix's leg, lifting it so I can get further inside her.

"Oh God," she barely manages to say.

We smash our bodies together. My chest lets out a ferocious roar as I slam into her, attacking her ass with my cock.

"Oh God," she moans again. Her voice is fierce with greed.

Our movements are frenzied, intense, coated with a raw, impassioned heat.

We're both letting out our own raspy sounds as we gasp for air.

"Kiss me, sugar," I say between heaves for breath.

She straightens her back, as I hold her leg up, Nix clutches on to me, knowing I'll never let her fall. She turns her head and drowns me in the sexiest, most intoxicating kiss I've ever had.

She bites on my bottom lip, and tightens her ass – simultaneously.

"I'm gonna come," I say, continuing to pump into her.

She snakes a hand around the back of my neck and brings me in closer, my chest flush with her back.

My left hand goes straight for her clit ring, and I flick it.

"Ahhh," she cries into my mouth, as her hips move urgently with mine.

I flick her ring again, and slide two fingers into her pussy and make small circles with my thumb.

"It feels so good. Keep going, I'm so close," she declares.

I drive my cock into her while ravishing Nix's pouty lips.

I slam into her once, almost propelling her forward.

"Ahhh."

I smash our bodies together again.

"Yeah," she mumbles.

And on the third ram, I come so hard.

Her pussy sucks my fingers in, and her ass contracts around my cock. My mouth on hers suffocates the cries of pleasure coming from her. Her body trembles as I hold her, wet with a sheen of sweat.

I stay inside her, not wanting this feeling to end. Not wanting to leave the warmth my girl is givin' me.

Phoenix's lips stay on mine, until she moves and turns in my arms.

"I love you," she says as she runs her hands through my hair.

I step back, looking into her blazing blue eyes. "I'll never stop wanting you. I'd rather fight with you than fuck another chick. Marry me."

She smirks at me, rolls her eyes and shakes her head, "You're an idiot," she says and waltzes into the bathroom.

For God sakes, what's not romantic about *that* proposal?

EPILOGUE

six months later

"**WHERE ARE WE GOING?**" **PHOENIX ASKS AS SHE SWINGS** her leg over the Harley and hugs me around the waist. We've been traveling for a couple of days now, taking some time for ourselves.

"Somewhere," I say, starting the bike up. "Put your helmet on."

"Yes Mr. Bossy. What's your problem? You've been cranky lately."

"If you agreed to marry me then I wouldn't be so damned 'cranky'," I say, making a stupid face at her.

She chuckles and puts the helmet on.

We take off down the road. The ride to get where we're going takes about an hour.

Her arms don't leave my waist, and I like her being this close to me.

When we get down to the Strip, I park the bike and get off, holding my hand out to Nix.

"What are we doing in Vegas?" she asks. Her eyes go up the side of the Wynn as she takes in the sight. "More specifically, why are we at the Wynn?"

"Because we're spending the night here."

"Why?" She gets off the bike and holds my hand.

"Just because. Do I need a fucking reason to take my girl out?"

"Really? After all these months, you're still calling me 'your girl'?

I'm a damned woman, Jaeger."

I snicker at her, knowing how pissed off she gets when I say certain shit to her. "Whatever, Red. Just get your ass inside." I tug on her hand and lead her into the reception area.

The young chick behind the counter looks up at us approaching, and she does a quick double take, looking between Nix and me.

"Good afternoon. Welcome to the Wynn. Do you have a reservation?" she asks as she eye-fucks me and ignores Nix.

I roll my eyes at her, "Yeah under the name of Dalton," I say. Her shoulders drop and her eyes immediately leave mine as she starts tapping on her keyboard.

She looks up at me and smiles, "Very good, sir. Everything's set as you requested, here's your key card." She slides the room access card across the counter and smiles.

Before she can say anything else that may let Nix on to what's happening, I take the key and turn, starting to walk away.

"Your room is the one on the left," the chick calls from behind me. Good, she's keeping her mouth shut, not to give anything away.

"I know where I'm going."

Phoenix doesn't know, but I booked the entire top floor. I want it to be just us, no one listening to her screams and getting aroused from them, no one to know what the hell I have in store for my girl.

Tonight, it's just her and me and no one else.

I lead her through the alcove of greenery and brightly colored flowers to the lift that will take us up to our floor.

"This is beautiful," she says, taking in the sights around us. She stops at a flower, holds it gently between her hands and inhales deeply. Her eyes close and as she savors the aroma coming from the pink flower.

When we get to the top floor, I lead her to the room and slide my card in, waiting for the door to open.

The moment it opens, I step to the side and let Phoenix go inside first.

"Oh my God," she says as she's bombarded with hundreds of tiny flickering candles. They're everywhere. There are rose petals spread all over the floor and the bed and the drapes are closed so the room is dark. But the light of the candles gives off a perfect illumination.

She steps further into the room and stands perfectly still, looking around. She clasps a hand to her mouth as her eyes travel the room.

Chocolates are on the table, with a bottle of Bollinger Grande waiting for us, strawberries arranged in an appetizing way on a silver platter and vases of long stemmed red roses are placed on every flat surface in the room.

She swings around to look at me, and I'm on one knee holding a ring out to her, waiting for her eyes to find me.

"Oh," she says as her eyes leak tears. Though behind the hand that's clasped to her mouth, I can see her smiling.

She's happy, which makes me happy.

"I don't do romance, Phoenix. I can't give you this shit all the time, 'cause it don't make sense to me. What does make sense though, is us. You and me, we balance the other out. I love you, and I want you to marry me." I pause 'cause she's crying.

"We make sense?" she asks as she kneels down so we're looking in each other's eyes.

"You're the only thing that I know is real, and I need you with me. I need to know that you'll never leave and I need you to know that I'll fight for you until the day I stop breathing."

Phoenix smiles and leans in to kiss me. Her kiss is slow, careful and gentle. But she still hasn't given me an answer.

"Tell me, Nix. Tell me you want to be my wife."

She peppers kisses up my jaw, reaching my ear she stops kissing me, her hot breath tickling the side of my neck. "Yes," she whispers.

I jump up, grab her hand, and head toward the door.

"Where are we going now?" she asks as I'm tugging her behind me.

"The Little White Chapel is two miles down the road. Sarge and Milina are waiting for us."

She pulls on my hand to stop me, and for a fleeting second I think I'm in for a new argument from her.

"Milina's here?" she asks.

"Yeah, sugar, and they're waitin' for us."

She leaps into my arms and kisses me, intensely and furiously.

"I can't wait to say 'I do'," she whispers in my ear.

My body reacts to her words. My cock starts getting hard and suddenly I can't wait 'til she's my wife.

"We come straight back here and you drop to your knees," I say to her as I push the down button at the elevator.

The doors open and she steps inside, a huge, fuckin' cheeky smile on her face, and her eyes filled with lust.

"I mean it, Nix. I want my cock inside your mouth."

The doors close and she turns to me, leaning up against the elevator wall. Her eyes flicker to me and she bites on her lower lip.

"You're an idiot."

THE END

"I'm not gonna be known as Phoenix Dalton."

"Whatever, Red. Tonight. On your knees."

"You really are an idiot."

"On your knees...*please*?"

ACKNOWLEDGEMENTS

What a ball! I've really enjoyed writing this book, it was so much fun to write an arrogant man. Jaeger truly had me in stitches with some of the things that he thought.

Thank you: **Debi Orton** – my editor. **Kellie Dennis** – my cover chick. **Amy** – my PA. **Hetty** -my promo chick.

My lovely street team: **Melinda, Patricia, Trish, Alicia, Heather, Shona, Mandy, Hetty, Amy, Rachel, Tanya, Brittany, Jess, Shanda** and **Maureen**.

My proofreaders: **Al** and the ladies at **Perma Editing and Proofreading**.

And to my very good friends, for always supporting me: **Tina, Mel, Lindy** and **Sue**.

Thank you to the blogs who continue to support me, but a very special mention to: **Bestellers and Beststellars of Romance**, **Panty Dropping Book Blog**, **So Many Books- So Little Time**, **Novels In Heels** and **Escape Reality with Books**. I can't express how much I appreciate all your support.

thank you to all my friends and fans.

Like me on FaceBook at Margaret McHeyzer Author

Subscribe at: http://mackandmilo.wix.com/margaretmcheyzer

Email: hit_149@yahoo.com

ALSO BY MARGARET

**THIS NOVEL CONTAINS DISTRESSING CONTENT.
IT IS ONLY SUITED FOR READERS OVER 18.**

On a day like any other, Allyn Sommers went off to work, not knowing that her life was about to be irrevocably and horrifically altered.

Three years later, Allyn is still a prisoner in her own home held captive by harrowing fear. Broken and damaged, Allyn seeks help from someone that fate brought her.

Dr. Dominic Shriver is a psychiatrist who's drawn to difficult cases. He must push past his own personal battles to help Allyn fight her monsters and nightmares.

Is Dr. Shriver the answer to her healing?

Can Allyn overcome the broken?

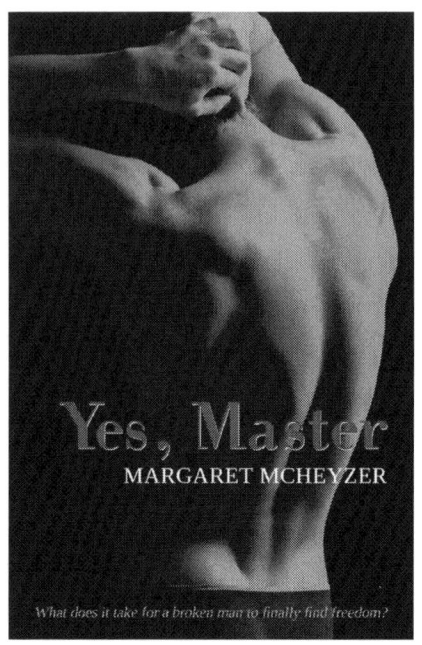

THIS NOVEL CONTAINS DISTRESSING CONTENT.
IT IS ONLY SUITED FOR READERS OVER 18.
ALSO CONTAINS M/M, M/M/F, M/F AND F/F SCENES.

My uncle abused me.

I was 10 years old when it started.

At 13 he told me I was no longer wanted because I had started to develop.

At 16 I was ready to kill him.

Today, I'm broken.

Today, I only breathe to survive.

My name's Sergeant Major Ryan Jenkins and today, I'm ready to tell you my story

HiT Series

Must be read in order

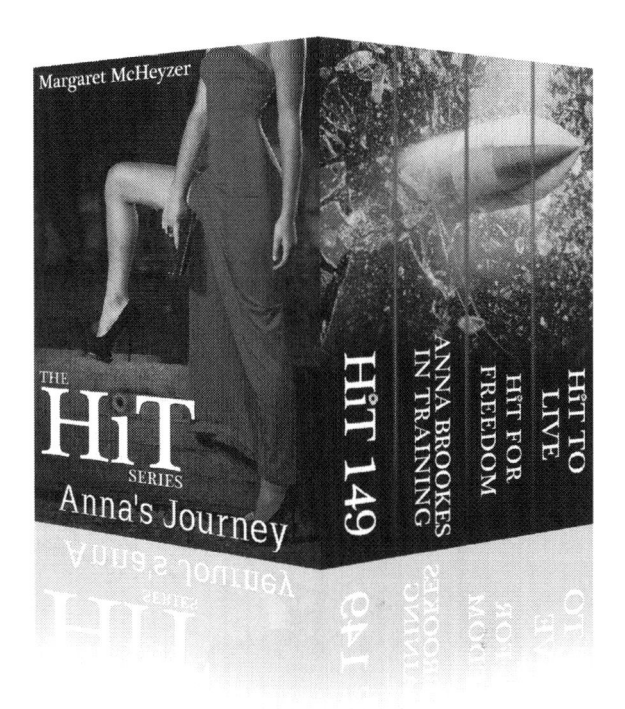

HiT 149

Anna Brookes is the most dangerous woman that you hope you will never know. Her life of danger started the day she turned 15.

The thirteen years that follow shapes her life to become the most deadly and lethal woman. HiT 149 becomes her most difficult target.

Does she pull the trigger or does she risk becoming the target herself?

Anna Brookes in Training
(HiT #1.5)

Imagine watching your Father die in front of you because two men were sent to take you. The two men were sent by Roman Murphy, the boss of Hunter Inc. The sole job of Hunter Inc. is to train and produce assassins.

Anna Brookes, a 15 year old girl with a love and panache for precision and handling of weapons was sought out by Hunter Inc.

One evening she encounters Lukas, a man she saves but a man who ultimately goes on to save her.

The months that follow sees Anna's intuition heightened and defined.

She is forced to deal with techniques that no ordinary 15 year old girl should ever encounter in their lives.

HiT for Freedom
(HiT #2)

Anna Brookes also known by her Professional name 15, did what she had never done before.

She didn't kill her target, HiT 149.

HiT 149 better known as Ben Pearson did something he had never done before.

He fell in love with Anna Brookes.

In Hit for Freedom, the sequel to HiT 149, a nemesis so powerful, terrifying and frightening is threatening the safety of Anna's love, Ben and his hometown, St Cloud.

15 must deal with a force that may be too dangerous even for her skilled ways. With limited information on her new HiT, she willingly infiltrates his trust to acquire the knowledge she needs to implode the operations of the deadly man.

HiT to Live
(HiT #3)

Anna Brookes, AKA 15, held the title of the girl with the golden aim. Through dedication and training she quickly rose to be the best assassin in the world.

But no amount of preparation could guard her heart against falling in love.

Anna's armor was severely crumpled when she met Ben Pearson, the one man that managed to get under her skin and stay there.

When Katsu Vang, a powerful player in the Yakuza, became a threat to Ben, Anna did the one thing she knew best–she went into assassin mode and fought the problem at the source.

Katsu Vang proved to be an admirable adversary that even Anna couldn't take down on her own. Because of her undercover intel work, Anna became a target for Katsu. She was sold into the sex trade and continuously injected with heroin until her body was hopelessly addicted.

Ben Pearson was hiding behind his own mask, which finally dropped as his true identity was revealed to Anna in HiT for Freedom.

Ophelia is Ben's right hand at the job he held as a front. Ophelia has her own vendetta and wants her mother's killer brought to justice.

Katsu has vanished but his power still poses an imminent threat to all concerned.

Anna Brookes is the common link between all the players...

The one woman that can put all the pieces together...

And the one woman that can tear everything down.

My Life for Yours

Margaret McHeyzer

He's lived a life of high society and privilege; he chose to follow in his father's footsteps and become a Senator.

She's lived a life surrounded with underworld activity; she had no choice but to follow in her father's footsteps and take on the role of Mob Boss.

He wants to stamp out organized crime and can't be bought off.

She's the ruthless and tough Mob Boss where in her world all lines are blurred.

Their lives are completely different, two walks of life on the opposite ends of the law.

Being together doesn't make sense.

But being apart isn't an option

Ellie Andrews has been receiving tutoring from Blake McCarthy for three years to help her improve her grades so she can get into one of the top universities to study law. And she's had a huge crush on him since she can remember.

Blake McCarthy is the geek at school that's had a crush on Ellie since the day he met her.

In their final tutoring session, Blake and Ellie finally become brave enough to take the leap of faith.

But, life has other plans and rips them apart.Six years later Blake and his best friends Ben and Billy have built a successful internet platform company 3BCubed, while Ellie is a successful and hardworking lawyer specializing in Corporate Law.

3BCubed is being threatened with a devastatingly large plagiarism case and when it lands on their lawyers desk, it's handed to the new Corporate Lawyer to handle and win.

Coincidence or perhaps fate will see Blake and Ellie pushed back together.

Binary Law will have Blake and Ellie propelled into a life that's a whirl wind of catastrophic events and situations where every emotion will be touched. Hurt will be experienced, happiness will be presented and love will be evident. But is that enough for Blake and Ellie be able to live out their own happily ever after?

Printed in Great Britain
by Amazon